Charlotte Leonard lives with her husband and three sons in London. She loves cold water. *Afterwards* is her first novel.

Afterwards

Charlotte Leonard

SIMON &
SCHUSTER

London · New York · Sydney · Toronto · New Delhi

First published in Great Britain by Simon & Schuster UK Ltd, 2022

This paperback edition published in 2023.

Copyright © Charlotte Leonard, 2022

The right of Charlotte Leonard to be identified as
author of this work has been asserted in accordance
with the Copyright, Designs and Patents Act, 1988.

1 3 5 7 9 10 8 6 4 2

Simon & Schuster UK Ltd
1st Floor
222 Gray's Inn Road
London WC1X 8HB

Simon & Schuster Australia, Sydney
Simon & Schuster India, New Delhi

www.simonandschuster.co.uk
www.simonandschuster.com.au
www.simonandschuster.co.in

A CIP catalogue record for this book
is available from the British Library

Paperback ISBN: 978-1-3985-0915-3
eBook ISBN: 978-1-3985-0914-6
Audio ISBN: 978-1-3985-1320-4

Typeset by Palimpsest Book Production Ltd, Falkirk, Stirlingshire
Printed and Bound in the UK using 100% Renewable
Electricity at CPI Group (UK) Ltd

For Nils, Jack, Finn and Noah

Two years afterwards

I am floating in the tranquil blue. It is summer and the tide is high. Lying back, I lift my toes until they break the surface of the sea. Bright orange painted toenails appear like tiny suns tracking their course in a small arc across a perfect sky. I drop my head and let the ocean hold me.

Sounds reach out over the water from the beach. There are the crests of conversations, people laughing and shrill yelps from children splashing in the shallows. A gannet sweeps across the mirrored sky above my head.

A buoy is tethered, close to me. I rotate onto my front and swim with confident and sweeping strokes until I have it in my grasp. Holding on, I tread my legs under the water and survey the land. People cluster on the beach, their territories marked out with towels and sun umbrellas and a plethora of coloured bags. A seagull lands on a large blanket. I smile as a tourist flaps her arms around and the bird begins to flap its wings as if mimicking her movements before it rises up and flies away.

A little to the left, I spot them waiting at the water's edge. They wave and I wave back and grin. The sunlight catches in the gentle ripples that I make until everything surrounding me is shimmering and bright. I take a breath of fresh sea air that smells of shining metal, minerals and clean laundry drying on a line. And then I start to swim. I propel myself towards them all and towards her.

This is real happiness, I think. *This is not what I imagined would come afterwards.*

What came before

December

The End

The dahlias are in the vegetable drawer of the fridge. They are bright pink, tightly bound in a cone of brown paper and cellophane. The petals shock, violent, against the plastic-wrapped sprouts and bags of potatoes.

The food shopping is packed away. There is enough food to last the two of us at least a week. Jay has bought all of the ingredients for the festive meals that he's planned. He has even remembered to buy more peppercorns. He's filled the grinder up, spilt just a few. They lie like excised crows' eyes on the granite worktop.

Everything else is neat, just how he likes it. Neat and normal.

'I'm home,' I call. But the sing-song clatter of my voice dissolves into the silence of the house. I run my fingers along the cool dark granite and wait.

The dahlias are in the fridge. He must have bought them at the supermarket today. A split-second decision or a planned and sweet intention. I don't know. And then he

5

must have packed them away with all the food. With the pale turkey and winter vegetables scrubbed clean of earth. The flowers are a stark slash of colour. Chilled and forgotten.

Misplaced. His mind elsewhere.

I find the cold dahlias in the kitchen.

Then I go upstairs to the bedroom and find Jay.

Shock

'I know how awful it is to find a body,' the policewoman says. Her voice is low. She has been here before, sitting with loss. I perch on the sofa cradling a cup of tea that I don't remember asking for or taking.

The mug is a favourite, Le Creuset from a set of two with handles curved like half-wedding rings.

I don't like tea, I think.

My hands won't still, as if my body is being disturbed by an unseen force from far away. The rotation of the earth, the deep shift of continental plates, some tsunami somewhere.

'Drink your tea. It's got sugar in.' She moves her body slightly on the sofa, turns a page in her notebook, tucks her hair behind her ear. 'It will help you with the shock.'

Shock.

The word hangs there in my mind, attaching meaning to itself. I sit still. Drink down the tea for shock.

I'm sure I'm drifting in and out of consciousness but I

must be wide awake because the police lady keeps on talking at me. She tells me she is a 'liaison officer' but her name has filtered from my mind. She must have mentioned it.

I stay on the sofa, staring at the Christmas tree lights, silent as time slurs and blurs.

'I'm sorry, love. We've got to ask some questions.'

She carries on talking as my mind begins to drift.

We were in Dubai and the hotel pool was piping music underwater. It was night. The city filled the sky with almost-light. Jay and I were diving to the bottom of the pool, breathing out bubbles of air and holding hands. There were lights that changed colour beneath the surface. Jay swam over and held his face close to pinks and purples, blues and greens. Down deep it was the two of us, no interruptions, only us.

I am underwater now.

This is the very bottom.

A few words filter through. Inquest. Coroner.

'We'll need to take some of his things away with us. I'm sorry. They'll be returned as soon as possible and we'll take good care of them.'

A low moan escapes my mouth. It comes from somewhere deep that I did not know existed. They cannot take his stuff. I grip the mug. I grip it like it's his warm hand or beating heart.

Please don't take his things, I think.

They take his laptop, his mobile phone, the belongings on his desk. Some migraine tablets and the paper diary that he keeps.

Kept. The diary that he kept.

'You need to tell us when you saw him last.' Her voice is louder now. More solid.

My sister has appeared. I don't remember Jude arriving. The doorbell didn't ring. The house is full of people now, shapes that circle the periphery like planets round a burnt-out sun. I can smell the cloying scent of the felled tree that sits in the far corner of the room, weighed down with festive baubles and bright lights. It makes me think of decimated forests and Nordic nights that never end.

I stare into the mug of tea as sounds focus and fade, fade and focus. Jude pulls the blue woollen blanket over my shoulders and squeezes my thigh. She rubs my back in a circular motion, round and round, like I am one of her boys.

'Tell her what happened,' says Jude. 'You need to tell her.'

But I don't know what happened. I came home and now I'm here.

'Mum and Dad are at the airport now. They'll be here tomorrow,' she says.

Tomorrow cannot come. I only want yesterday.

I grapple with sentences. I know I have the words in me but I'm struggling to locate them. Linking words together is exhausting. I take a breath.

'We left to go to work together. I got off first. He smiled.'

The words escape my mouth staccato. They do not sound like mine.

I'm stuck. Stranded on the platform, on this sofa, left here without words.

We were standing on the tube carriage, pressed close into each other. I leant my head against Jay's jumper and breathed in deep, his aftershave and him. At my stop he grinned, kissed me goodbye and I reminded him to buy the pepper- corns. I walked up the stairs passing a line of people on the escalator, out into the square of light, towards the waiting day.

My last words spiral round my head on a tight loop, mocking me.

'Don't forget the peppercorns.' 'Don't forget the pepper- corns.' 'Don't forget the peppercorns.'

He didn't. He remembered to buy peppercorns.

He forgot to stay alive.

Denial

The dahlias are in the vegetable drawer of the fridge. They are brilliant pink, carefully bound in a Cornetto-cone of parcel paper. The petals sing, bright, against the green of sprouts and the bags of white potatoes.

The food shopping is packed away. There is food to last the two of us a week or so. Jay has bought all of the ingredients for the festive meals that we've planned. He has even remembered to buy more peppercorns. He's filled the grinder up, spilt just a few. They lie like tiny jewels on the kitchen worktop. Everything else is neat. Just how we like it.

'I'm home,' I call. And the sing-song chatter of my voice fills the hallway of our home.

'Hey, love,' calls Jay from our bedroom up the stairs. 'How was your day?'

Anger

I want to throw the tea across the room. Break plates. Smash time.

The stupid policewoman knows nothing at all. 'I know how awful it is to find a body,' she said. But I didn't find a body. I found my husband, I found Jay, hanging in the bedroom from a rope.

The stupid fucking woman.

Finding a body would have been bearable.

Terror

'Take these now, Em.' Jude presses two small tablets into my hand. 'They'll help you sleep.'

I swallow down, obedient.

My body is a strange vessel now, something other. I can hear the teeth inside my head, a jilted sort of tapping, and the noise of my pulse, loud as breaking waves. I wonder if my heart is attempting to leave me, swimming up from my chest cavity and out of my ears.

Jude pulls the duvet up over the two of us and curls her warm body around mine. The bedding smells of my little sister's life, not mine. She strokes my hair from my forehead, slowly, rhythmically, easing me into the warm arms of a drugged oblivion.

We were at Jude and Rob's, the adults drinking in the kitchen and laughing far too loudly at old songs. One of the boys woke up. I headed to the toilet, stopped and watched them for a while. Jude was wrapped around my nephew, stroking his forehead and humming a quiet lullaby. I wondered if one day I'd ever want a baby of my own, if I'd feel a desperate need to soothe a little body into sleep like that.

Screaming wakes me. I cannot breathe. The weight of the duvet is suffocating and I can smell Christmas trees. I have dreamt that Jay is dead, that I have found him hanging by his belt and that everything is broken now. I can see his face contorted, smell shit and death, and hear a woman somewhere screaming something.

'I've got you. You're okay,' tries Jude.

I was walking from the station. I texted Jay to tell him I was almost home but I didn't hear from him. I imagined him still on the underground or sat at his computer, deep in concentration, happily lost inside minute adjustments of light levels and contrasts.

In the room next door a wailing starts. Small frightened boys startled from sleep. Together we scream and wail, scream and wail, a cacophony of terror in the darkness.

In the kitchen I found dahlias inside the fridge.
In our bedroom I found Jay.

'You're okay,' says Jude.

But I'm not okay. I am the furthest from okay that I have ever, ever been.

14

Everything

The smell is acrid. Acid and insides. Jude leans over the bathtub and turns on the taps. She stands there stooped, making figures of eight with outstretched arms. She whirls in bubble bath, mixes hot with cold. She is a wonderful mother, a warm witch. Crouching and swirling, checking the temperature, making things good.

The edges of the bath are strewn with life. A pink plastic duck with a gold crown. A tube of children's toothpaste, spiralled tight by tiny hands. The lid is missing and the paste has congealed at the opening; a small hard orb, like discarded bubble gum. A wind-up deep-sea diver waits patiently to swim.

I lie down on the bathroom floor and stretch my hands across the tiles, splay fingers wide, press my cheek against cool porcelain. Down low the spinning slows. I breathe in the smell of cleaner used to wash the floor and the slight musk of the damp bathmat. A small stripy sock has missed the washing basket and lies forgotten, turned inside out, beneath the sink. I think about the things we share. We are both down here. Both inside out.

Jude pulls away the layers of my clothes. Sweat- and vomit-drenched pyjamas stuck fast to clammy skin.

'Arms up,' she says softly, as if I am her child.

She pulls my top up and off, forcing my head out through the grip of damp, inverted clothes. It is a strange and silent birth.

I can hardly stand it; feeling everything at once, all of it unfiltered. I am skinless, raw and inside out.

Remembering

I am curled like a comma, resting deep among the pillows and the duvet of our bed. The lamps glow butter low and the old fireplace is strung with battery-powered golden stars. A patchwork quilt wraps warm around the bed. The house smells festive; of enchanted pine trees and child-like anticipation.

I am lost in words, cradled inside a book. I make my nest among the pages and the lines of ink. The letters sweep across the page like swallows' tails.

Jay lies next to me, scrolling through Instagram, his face luminous in the glow of the screen. He nudges me with his toes under the warmth of the duvet and shows me a photo that he's found.

A new Nick Knight photograph. A pile of pastel-pink roses entitled 'Roses from my garden'. They are paler than ballet shoes, all petals and stamens, dying slowly into the grey and white foreground. The roses are collapsing, caught on the cusp between beauty and decay.

I glance up from my book. I find the photo sad but he tells me that it's beautiful and talks of lighting, shadows and the complexity of contrasts. He studies the picture like a puzzle. I can almost hear the static of his thoughts. Tomorrow he'll be in his studio, playing with light, adjusting filters and levels, trying to recreate the subtlety of the glow.

Jay asks what I'm reading, pulls the book of Japanese myths from out my hand and laughs. He wonders if there's anything I will not read. I tell him he should read it too and he replies he doesn't have to, that I read enough stories for the both of us. He reaches over slowly, catches a strand of hair with the tops of his fingers and hooks it behind my ear.

Next to him his bedside table is empty except for a small brass lamp and a glass of water on a coaster. The drawer is neat; a pair of cufflinks that I've never seen him wear and some moisturizer. We lie, our faces so close that he is breathing in my breath. I slowly rub my thumb over the silver scar that runs beneath his eyebrow, a pale indentation in the softness of the flesh. He looks at me so deeply that I wonder what he sees.

Photos are still stories, he insists. He tells me of the stories he creates every day for different clients with his camera. Stories about aftershave, designer shoes and lipsticks that can transform a person to be better than before. He says he mostly hates the stories that he has to tell.

And then he grins at me. That grin. That grin that makes the world wait.

And his eyes burn constellation bright with want and love and lust.

But that was all before.

Snow

The police liaison officer is now a presence in my life. She makes a point of telling me her name again and this time I know I won't forget: Amelia. Jay is gone and now Amelia is here.

'We've found no note,' she says. 'It's not unusual. Less than a third of them leave notes.'

Them, I think.

The air escapes my lungs and I start to feel sick but she doesn't seem to notice. She actually looks quite pleased that she knows this neat statistic, can offer up the fact to me. As if the telling of it somehow helps, as if there's solace hidden in the undeniability of numbers.

Amelia sits across from me at Jude's familiar kitchen table, with papers and a pen held poised. Her hair is not how I remember it. It's tied up in a ponytail, drawn much tighter back from off her face than yesterday, a little more austere in the harshness of the morning light. I pull my jumper down over my hands, hide my fingers inside folds of wool. Rob is playing with the boys behind the closed door of the living room and I can hear him roaring like a lion and the boys respond in high-pitched squeals as they find a deep delight inside the pretence of their fear.

'Emma, can you think of any reasons why Jay might have taken his own life? We tend to see more of these deaths in spring, not over Christmas. Is there anything specific you can think of?'

I bite the nail off my left thumb, sift through the mess of swirling thoughts. I do not know. How on earth can I not know? I am his wife. There are crudely cut-out snowflakes that are stuck in random patterns on the kitchen window-panes behind Amelia's head. When I squint her face becomes a hazy silhouette against a scraggy paper storm.

'His work, I guess. It's stressful in the run up to the holidays. And he's always hated winter.'

I grasp at random reasons like a child attempting to catch snowflakes, flailing and failing to capture something solid. There is a paper snowflake that I focus on while speaking. It is asymmetrical and messy; an almost-circle filled with jagged little scissor slits. I cannot get my mind to place Jay in the past, to anchor him in time. He keeps on swimming up into the present tense of sentences.

'Any other reasons? Can you think of absolutely anything at all?'

'He wanted to move house,' I say. 'And have a baby. He always wanted us to have a baby.' I swallow hard, the words sticking inside my throat.

A young boy barrels fast into the room, too fast for his own feet, as if the weight of his small head is giving him momentum. I worry that he'll topple. Fall.

'Mummy. I want juice,' Max says.

Rob follows swift behind with Oscar lodged neatly underneath one arm and mumbles an apology.

'It's fine,' Amelia says, Jude and Rob's home not quite their own in her official presence.

'Are you being a good boy for Father Christmas? What's the magic word?' says Jude to Max.

We watch Jude fill a bright and plastic drip-proof cup with apple juice from the fridge and dilute it with water from the tap. Oscar follows with his own demands.

'Me too. Me too.'

'Please!' Max proudly yells, so obviously delighted to know the word the adults want to hear. Amelia smiles, ruffles the soft hair of the small boy as he takes his plastic cup and, grinning, goes to climb onto his mother's lap. Jude mouths a silent sentence to her husband.

'The lion's getting hungry, boys,' Rob coaxingly responds. 'I wonder what he'll find to eat?'

'Meeeee,' yells Max and slides himself off Jude's high lap and down onto the floor, before careering out the room.

'No, me,' calls Oscar, chasing fast after his brother with slightly wobbly toddler strides as Rob begins to growl again.

I focus on the snowflake, on the paper cuts that let the light shine through. I cannot tell Amelia that I wonder if the real reason Jay has gone is simply me.

Jude is quick to catch my eye. A glint, a spark, we nearly smile.

Despite no note, there is a life insurance policy and an online will. Dad and Jude discover them while trawling through Jay's emails. The will was made the previous October and logged with an online company that someone thought a good idea to actually call 'Farewill'. It makes me think of people leaving for a voyage on a boat, a cheerful cruise to somewhere nice, departing from a dock with heavy luggage, happy waves. Dad reads the document aloud. The witnesses are people whose names I do not recognize and the contents of the will are brief, leaving everything to me, with the singular request that Ben receives a number of Jay's photographs that are currently all hanging on the walls inside our home and when taken down will leave large spaces. More emptiness I didn't choose.

The will just makes my mother cry again and I sit there at the table holding tight onto her suntanned hand, not exactly sure which one of us is looking after whom. Dad and Jude have both got out their laptops, paper and some pens, and are making lists, both of them attempting to chisel out some order from the chaos that surrounds me now. They write down all the things we need to do, the people that we need to tell. Dad writes FUNERAL in capitals and underlines it twice as if it's something that we might forget. He draws a little arrow and underneath writes down the names Martin and Anne. I close my eyes. Wish everything and everyone away.

Jay was standing by the open fridge, the light casting a halo round his solid frame. 'It's our wedding, Em. I don't want Anne and Martin there. It's been forever since we last spoke and you deserve a perfect day.' I stood up and wrapped my arms around his chest, kissed the back of his soft neck and ran my fingers through his thick, dark hair. 'But they're your parents, Jay. Whatever happened, can it really be that bad?'

My mobile phone begins to ring again. It never seems to stop. I do not recognize the number and push the phone across the table towards Jude. She answers it for me.

'Em, they need to speak to you,' she finally says.

The coroner sounds formal and sincere. He sends his deep condolences and talks of issuing an 'Interim' certificate of death. I do not understand quite why. Death does not exist within the space that is an interim. It is definite and done. He keeps on talking, telling me that a post-mortem will need to be performed, that an inquest will follow in a few more months.

'But why?' I ask.

'Any violent death must be investigated. We need to know for certain how Jay died.'

He hung himself, I think. *It's fucking obvious.*

He talks about the estimated timings of 'these things' and mentions the 'releasing' of Jay's body back into my care, despite the fact that both of us know that my care can't make the slightest bit of difference to things now.

Throughout the conversation Dad has carried on writing his list. The words stretch out onto a second page. A litany of death to-dos. He puts a small black biro star beside a line, checks something on the laptop and waits for me to finish on the phone.

'Are you okay for money, Em? The life insurance policy contained a suicide clause but that lasted for two years and it ran out on the fifth. It's a few weeks over that so you'll still receive the full amount but it may take a little while. The mortgage and the funeral . . . you know that we can help you, love.'

Did he wait the two years out? I think.

I hadn't thought about the money, the practicalities of bills and the funeral expense. I wonder for the first time in my life just how much it costs to say goodbye.

'My salary can just about cover the payments on the house. It's only Jay's account that I can't access. But I never could before. I don't know anything at all about his finances.'

'Really?' asks Jude. She sounds surprised. 'You didn't have a joint account? Do you know how much he earned? Not even after all these years?'

'No. That's normal, though.' A long look passes round the room between my mother, dad and sister, a look that tells me that it's not. 'Well, isn't it?' I ask them all, the family I have left.

Solitude

'It's for the best,' somebody said, 'especially with the boys around and Christmas Day tomorrow.' I should go stay with my parents for a while. Amelia approved and took my dad's phone number too. There's a funeral to organize and Jay's mother keeps on calling me. I switch the phone off, bury myself beneath the blankets of my childhood bed. I only want the walls for company and the plastic stars of my newly shrunken universe. Andromeda, Draco, Virgo and Orion, flat and dull above my head.

The room is both familiar and strange. The posters and the postcards of my youth have gone, the Blu-Tack grease stains that my mother hated have long been painted out. I imagine her choosing the colours, expressing herself in Farrow & Ball, and my dad, busy with dust sheets, covering my childhood but leaving stars. A guest room full of sky.

I'm a visitor here now. All grown up and out of place. At thirty-four, too old to be looked after, too young to be looked after.

I stare at the small crack that has been missed. It runs above the dressing table with its antique mirror and cut-glass vase just small enough for snowdrops. I stay in bed for ceaseless time just staring at the crack that spans out wide like gently broken veins.

'Here's some tea, sweetheart,' my mother says, excusing herself into the silence, and I close my eyes to block her out. 'It's got sugar in. It's good for shock.' I can smell the tea, its overpowering scent of bitter earth and candy canes, and I'm reminded of the policewoman sitting on my sofa, saying the same words. 'You have to drink, sweetheart. And eat something. You need to eat. It's been five days.'

I scrunch my eyes up tighter like a child.

I don't, I think. *I won't.*

'Please drink,' she says and something filters through. My mother saying please. I reach across and drink some water from last night's glass beside the bed. It's tepid now and dust has settled lightly on the tension of the surface. A feathering of fibres, chalk, discarded human cells. I don't want this water. There is nothing she can give me that I want, but my mother stands and waits so I swallow down a mouthful to appease her.

January

Adrift

A book arrives in the post with the title *Dead People Suck*. I almost laugh. It is wrapped up in brown paper and tied with trendy garden twine. Inside the cover my boss has written in her familiar pencil whorls: 'You've lost enough. Don't lose yourself,' and underneath: 'Facebook – Survivors of Suicide.'

Facebook feels like a sharp slap with its stream of fireworks and New Year's celebrations, the images as bright as lollipops. I scroll past endless parties and wide Bacardi grins and stop at a dead grandmother. Corrugated skin and rumpled limbs hang loose around a lipstick smile. Seventy-four people have added a crying emoji. Twenty-two have opted for a love heart. The comments fill with familiar platitudes: 'So sad but time', 'a life well lived', 'a spark until the end'. There's a language written in our lineage for this ancient kind of loss.

And then I find him. Jay. Offered up to the internet by his assistant Ben. The image jolts my heartbeat out of time and the oxygen escapes my lungs. This was not Ben's news to share. This loss is mine.

In the photograph Jay stands before an urban, bright, graffitied wall, a place I do not recognize, his camera slung across his chest. A smile rendered meaningless rides easy on his lips. Beneath the picture Ben has written: 'Sleep deep. My world will never be the same,' and added a web-link to the Samaritans.

People spew their confusion all over the comments and send Ben their love. Questions of what happened and exclamations of disbelief are interspersed with black emoji hearts and pinprick sorries. 'Oh no, not another one,' somebody actually writes.

Fuck them, I think.

But I thought that too. This is an awkward kind of death.

The Facebook group has 11,732 members. Another group has thousands more. So many of us all adrift in the digital clutter, attempting to tether ourselves to solace. 'The full name of your loved one, your relationship to them and when they passed,' the algorithm asks and I type slowly, tapping out each letter. My loss is now the password to a club I want no part of.

'Jay Anthony Bell. My everything. Fifteen days ago.'

My finger presses firmly on delete and I watch the words undo themselves and disappear one letter at a time. I will life to unravel backwards with the words, for time to rewind minute by minute until we reach before. I cannot do it, I will not do it, I refuse to type his death.

Fight

'Have you spoken to a vicar yet?' Jay's mother Anne demands of me.

There's an anger in her voice which clips the edges of her sentences and sheers the niceties away. I fiddle with the corner of the bedding, rub the fabric with my fingers. There are seventeen missed calls from Anne logged on my phone. I can't avoid her anymore. I do not want to speak to her but I know that she won't go away. Jay's life tied all our lives together loosely, our only unifying feature, him. Now Jay's removed himself, absconded suddenly to leave us women side by side, pulled far closer than is comfortable.

'No,' I utter down the phone.

'We need a date.' Her words sound cold. 'People are asking when and where. I've found a photograph from off your Instagram account and someone good to print the order of the service. And there's a prayer I want his dad to read.'

'I don't think Jay would want a service in a church,' I say.

'He was christened and he boarded at a Church of England school. He's a Christian, Emma.' Her voice is resolute and firm, an almost shout.

'But he hasn't been to church since school.'

I sit up in bed and wipe the sweat that's building on my forehead, crunch my fingers up into a fist.

'My son, Emma, my only son, he's dead. He deserves a proper Christian burial.'

She sounds hysterical and angry now.

'I know he's dead. But a church is not what he'd have wanted,' I try again and watch my fingers bleach of colour as my nails dig into my palm.

'Don't tell me what he would or wouldn't want. You clearly didn't know my son. You couldn't even keep him here, alive. You claim you don't know anything but you surely must know why he died? You lived with him, for heaven's sake. You married him! So tell me why my son is dead. Tell me, Emma. Why has he done this awful thing? The answer has to lie with you.'

There is silence on the line as her words kill off the conversation. I wait until my breathing calms enough to speak.

'I'm sorry. I don't know,' I say, my voice compressed and tight.

There is another pause. A long and awful silence as we wait for this to end.

'I don't know how you sleep at night,' she finally says and cuts me off.

36

Lost

I do not sleep. I stay in bed, ignore my phone and wait for time to pass me by. Outside I hear the familiar crunch of shale and shattered flint as a car pulls up across the gravel drive. There are voices in the kitchen now. The murmurings of family. I can make out Dad and the sound of Jude, the top notes of a conversation.

My sister creeps into the stillness of my room. There's a shallow indentation in the bedding; a soft hollow by my right hip that's been left behind from when my parents sit with me and try. I have named the place 'The Visiting Space'.

Jude finds the hollow, settles in. Her cheeks are winter pink, all blaze and burn and she smells of hair conditioner and cold. I stare at the different coloured smudges on her fingertips as she cups my hand in hers. Bright purple, pink and orange felt-tip stains.

'Em, oh Em.' She gathers up my torso in her arms. 'How are you doing? God, I'm sorry. No. That's such a stupid thing to ask. You're shit. Of course you're shit. I mean, for starters you're back home with Mum and Dad.' She winks at me and gently smiles.

'It's okay,' I say, biting my lip.

She squeezes tight, then makes some space to take me in.

'You look awful. Are you eating? When did you last eat? Is Mum not feeding you?'

'I don't know,' I say. And I really don't. I can't remember when I ate, and then, 'He's dead,' I add. 'He didn't leave a note.'

'I know,' she says. 'I'm so incredibly sorry, Em.'

Jude hands me a card that has arrived by post from everyone at work. A flock of pale grey birds and the curling calligraphy of 'Thinking of You' embossed in silver over fluffy Pixar clouds. Inside, blue and black names of colleagues spread like bruises over pale skin. Only a few people have braved language. They stick with 'sorry' and 'so sorry for your loss'. So many biro sorries scrawled across a page.

A murder of crows.

A cloud of bats.

An abandonment of sorries?

My life is full of these apologies now. People leave them with me, attached to large bouquets of flowers and delivered to my parents' door. Sorries arrive daily in the post, in my in-box, on my phone from people I hardly know. They are served up in Tupperware containers of home-made soup and cold, congealed lasagnes. I have more apologies than I could ever need except the only one I want. The 'sorry but I love you' note. The 'sorry but here's why'.

My little sister shifts her body slightly in The Visiting Space, deepening the indentation.

'I've spoken to his mother, Em. Are you absolutely sure that you don't want to be involved?'

'She blames me, Jude. She says I didn't know him.' My voice is quiet, sullen.

'That's just not true.'

'I didn't know he wanted death and I don't know what he would have wanted from a funeral. She can have her Christian burial. Nothing matters anymore.'

Jude looks down and rubs the crosshatch denim of her jeans, kneading thigh muscles with the firm edge of her palm. Downstairs my mother drops a baking tray or frying pan, something large and metal on the kitchen floor. The crash rips through the house breaking nothing at all.

'Emma. Are you sure that you're okay?' asks Jude.

A teardrop forms in the corner of my eye, growing until it can no longer be contained and it spills up and over the lip of lashes. I feel it rolling slowly down my cheek. And then another, and another until I'm sobbing hard, tears flooding outwards faster than the feelings. I gasp for breath, like a woman drowning in the saltwater of her own sadness.

Am I okay?

It's the question I need most. But I don't know what the

answer is. I am breathing still. I am waiting here in bed for time to undo itself and for Jay to come back to me.

I am everything that is obvious.

Brave

Raindrops race each other down the glass as I lie across the back seat of the new Audi. I pick two drops and will the left-hand one to win. It is strange being driven like a child. Dad drives and my mother rests her arm across his smartly suited shoulders. She touches him more often now, I've noticed. No one speaks as the car swallows up vast sections of the motorway and spits them out behind.

My mother turns on Radio 4 and *Woman's Hour* fills the car. Five culturally diverse grandmothers unite in their criticism of modern-day parenting and a shared distrust of iPads. The raindrops start to slow and the sky shifts itself towards the west threatening sun. I close my eyes and breathe in chemicals and something like leather as the belt clasp digs into my ribs. It hurts so I stay there, pressing myself into the pain.

Just outside London we stop at the services and I spend too long in a toilet cubicle, grateful for the privacy of plastic walls. It is easier alone.

'Em. Emma. Are you in there?'

My mother sounds desperate. She has read somewhere that losing Jay to suicide puts me at risk too, as if the violence of his death is contagious, catching, and any moment on my own may be my last. I look around at the safe square box with its sealed sanitary bin and rounded toilet roll dispenser. 'No, I'm dead, Mother,' I want to say. 'I have drowned myself in the toilet bowl. I have managed to suffocate myself with a stranger's sodden tampon.'

'Yes,' I say instead, 'of course I'm here.'

Outside Burger King I sit with Dad. He leans forward, far across the table, and takes a bite of Flame-Grilled Whopper, being careful of his shirt. People stare just a little too long; Dad in a fitted suit and me in my Karen Millen death dress, the one I wore last year to Grannie's funeral. It is large on me, falling in unnecessary folds around my frame. I am less now, the soft edges of myself have disappeared, leaving angles. A far sharper cut of flesh.

Dad wipes his fingers on a deep wad of paper napkins and hands me a clean white handkerchief from his suit pocket. I look up at him.

'Just in case you need it later,' he says.

I take the soft square of fabric, rubbing the raised letter of the embroidered S over and over between my finger and thumb.

Dad, who was hardly ever home, was home. It was summer, warm and dry. The light was the golden light of childhood

and Jude and I were swinging high up in the clouds. I
jumped mid-air and tripped, toes over sandal tips. The
concrete scraped my knees and blood trailed slowly down
my shins like racing raindrops. Dad took his handkerchief
and gently dabbed my skin. 'Let's get you home to Mum,'
he said. 'She can magic this all better.'

'You need to eat,' my mother says, passing me an M&S
cheese sandwich made with soft white bread and bland
butter. The food of childhood and illness. I take a bite and
try to chew, but there is not enough liquid in me to swallow
down the clot of bread that sticks there in my throat. I push
away the sandwich as my stomach twists and bile rises and
I see my mother glance at Dad. The language of a marriage.
The speech that I have lost.

Wrong

'The Lord will keep you from all harm.

'He will watch over your life;

'The Lord will watch over your coming and going

'Both now and forever more.'

Who the fuck chose that? His mother? *'The Lord will keep you from all harm.'* Is she serious? We have failed quite spectacularly at that.

Both 'The Lord' and I.

Dad is sweating more than usual and my mother looks panicked, slightly manic, as if she is burning calories with her brain alone. I suppose they're both worried that I'll crack or cry but I'm barely even here. People are watching, all eyes on me and the wooden box, like a backwards kind of wedding. All of the attention and none of the joy.

The vicar, or possibly a priest, continues speaking. We stand packed close to sing a hymn that no one actually knows. Someone to my left is singing louder than the others, her voice rising up as the notes drop down. A cousin of

Jay's who I only recognize from Facebook reads a poem that she wrote full of not-quite rhymes and lines I swear I know from somewhere else. This funeral is not for Jay. While I hid in bed his parents picked out random hymns and wrong readings. They even chose a God.

I stare at them across the aisle. His mother held up by the right angles of the wooden pew. She is smaller in the flesh than I remember her, slightly drawn in and puckered up as if collapsing inwards on herself. His father sits further along, the space between the two of them the width of Jay. He stares ahead. Ironically this is the most time they have spent with Jay in years.

The burial is all wrong too. There are roses for Jay's coffin. There should be daffodils instead.

We were walking through the park on our first date. It was spring and all around the daffodils had sprung; an orchestra of yellow playing out across the grass. Jay knelt down and gathered up a clutch of bright into his hand. He beamed at me as he offered up the stolen flowers and a kiss, a tract of damp across each knee. I took the flowers and the kiss and I let myself imagine what a life would look like with this man.

Around me people cry. The air smells of winter; desolation reeking from the skeleton trees, crisp cold and damp soil. I look across the cemetery with its chequerboard of death. The rows and rows of love and loss.

I want to leave. Jay isn't here.

The man from God delivers words as we stand around and watch him work at this strange midwifery of mourning. Someone hands out roses to the crowd like glow sticks at a festival. Jude reaches over, squeezes me.

I am at Jay's funeral. My husband's dead.

And the trees press down and the sky falls down and everything that broke before is broken still and breaks again.

His shredded neck.

His fractured kneecaps.

Shattered joy.

The sounds fade out. Time slurs and blurs.

The air is pressing on my lungs, too dense to breathe. I cannot speak or walk or be. This cannot be. I'm supposed to drop the rose onto the coffin but I can't let go. I grip it tighter waiting for the thorns to hurt but the stem has been curated smooth, each leaf, each thorn, removed.

And the sky falls down and the trees press down and time fades out and all around sounds slur and blur.

Inside the pocket of my coat is a large beach pebble, round and cold from a summer trip to Brighton beach. It is ringed with quartz, a perfect looping band which according to my mother means that it will bring good luck. I have a sudden overwhelming urge to pop the pebble in my mouth and swallow it.

I imagine it sinking in my oil-slick stomach, making me heavy, holding me here. Or catching in my throat and blocking out the air. I read a novel where someone killed themselves by swallowing a pack of butter wrapped in foil. The kind you find in B&Bs alongside dainty pots of strawberry jam and apricot preserve. I think of him, the fictional man desperately choking on a rectangle of dairy; such a British way to die.

Jay died.

I don't believe in God.

God, help me please.

Rising

My fingers grip tight and pale around the unfamiliar toilet rim as I heave into the bowl. The bile floats there, fluorescent, like coagulated Lucozade on the surface of the water. I breathe in the sickening spice of strangers' urine and the scratch of cheaply scented bleach and begin to retch some more. I am stuck here on my knees, bent down without a prayer. I am flailing, ailing, out at sea.

As the swell of nausea retreats sounds start to slowly reassemble in my ears. I can hear the gentle roll of conversation from the bar, like the deep drag of pebbles pulling backwards with the tide. There is the clink of glass and a high-pitched seagull cry of laughter. I am crouched, my back against the brickwork now, still waiting for the looming walls to shrink to normal size. Hung above the cistern is a photograph of 1920s swimmers screwed tight into the bricks. The women stand together, strong and ready for the waves. Solid smiles. Woollen hats. Loosely knitted bathing suits.

'Em, Emma, is that you?' says Jude.

'In here.' I swallow down an acrid trace of sick, lean up and flick the lock to let her in.

She looks at me in silence. I watch her eyes crunch tight and her forehead knit into a frown of sisterly concern.

'Come on,' she says. 'Let's get this done and get you home.'

'I need to speak to Ben,' I say.

Jude takes my arm, threads it through the tight loop of her own and leads me from the toilets and back into the pub. The 'Karen Millen Death Dress' is stuck to me in sweat-drenched swathes. I pick at it, pulling sections of material from sodden limbs, but it contracts back and sticks again like bandages on skin.

Relatives and friends have spread like spilt molasses into different rooms and out around the bar. There are people, people everywhere. Some I only recognize from Facebook and from Instagram. They quickly pool together into tighter groups: his family and his football team, some friends from his old boarding school, the clients that he worked with and the people that are here for me. All drinking, laughing, raising toasts and dabbing at themselves with clasps of Kleenex.

The sounds collate into a solid mass of noise, people louder than their usual selves as if compensating for the silence of the funeral. Everyone seems larger, drunker, hornier, just a little more alive. Death working on the living.

Strands of conversations catch inside my ears as Jude steers me through the undulating mass of mourners.

'. . . just can't believe he's gone . . .'

'. . . someone said he didn't leave a note. It's just so . . .'

'. . . well, at least there are no kids . . .'

'. . . I heard she had to cut him down . . .'

'. . . yeah, next Thursday. They're playing the O2. It sold out months ago . . .'

She moves me to the left, takes a turn towards our parents, when Ben stumbles into us almost yelling out my name and pulling at my arm.

I was sitting in the corner of Jay's studio, silent so as not to break the sanctity of work. Ben was measuring the light and laying out the lenses Jay would want. I watched the pair perform their gentle dance, a choreography embedded into years. The men rotated slowly round each other, anticipating moves, Ben knowing what Jay needed without any need for words.

I throw my arms around Ben's body and squeeze him hard. He doesn't hug me back. His limbs hang loose and limp inside the clutch of my embrace.

'Emma, I don't know what to say.' His words catch in a net of sobs, then fall in torrents from his mouth. 'I don't know how to live without him. I don't know how to work. Or breathe. I'm dying, Em.' His eyes are red and bloodshot and barnacles of sweat are tethered to his forehead. He holds a pint of beer that slops and swills around the glass. There is terror in his eyes. He reminds me of the whale in the Thames, the one that became caught just where the river curves, a creature lost and swimming fast towards the sand-banks of his own demise. Behind him I see Anne, Jay's mother, watching us from the far corner of the room. 'I've let all the clients know, Em. But some of them, some want to know if the studio can still fulfil the briefs we had. Em, I'd be doing all his work, Jay's work. And I'm not Jay. I need him, Em. I really, really need him. I can never fill his shoes . . . Oh God . . . His shoes . . .' Ben starts to sob more loudly now. Two trails of snot begin to run from out his nostrils and his lanky frame sways left to right like the towering mast of a quickly sinking ship. I bite my lip. I bite it hard.

'I miss him too,' I say, my jaw clenching my teeth together, tight. The words don't permeate his drunkenness.

'I took this. I thought you might want this.' He reaches down into a leather bag and tips a slug of beer over the floor, over his clothes. 'Oh shit,' he says, through snot and tears. 'It's from that trip you took . . . with Jay . . . the Cornwall trip.'

'What trip?' I ask. 'We didn't go to Cornwall. I've never even been.'

Ben doesn't hear the words I say. He is crying hard and patting at his beer-soaked clothes with arms that are not helping. 'What trip?' I say again with force.

'The Cornwall trip. I haven't looked. But I thought you'd want the photos. For the memories,' he slurs.

My legs are suddenly unstable, my body far too heavy

to hold up as if the whole of me has taken on the weight of water. Jude puts her arm around my waist to steady me. I take the camera from Ben's grasp before it falls and suddenly the floor tiles begin to spin and move, making geometric patterns at my feet. And a ringing starts to fill my ears, shrill and loud as the walls begin to grow again. Deep down low the bile in my stomach pit is pulling up, unanchored from acidic depths as a grim swell inside me rises up and I vomit bile. A pathetic glop of orange on Ben's shiny funeral shoes that he doesn't even notice.

Camera

I lie in bed staring at the Canon camera. It sits there, dense and bulky on the duvet, taunting me. It is the colour of ashes, curved at the edge for the grip of a hand. Jay's favourite. Not his best or his newest and smaller than his studio camera. His old 5D, outdated now, replaced by newer models with fancy Wi-Fi and built-in tricks. I stare at the camera and listen to the beating of my heart, the sound pulsating in my ears.

Here I will find Jay. I count to ten, my breath held in my lungs, then reach to pick it up. The camera is heavier than I remember. The solid weight of captured souls.

We were walking to a restaurant, Jay holding my left hand. He slowed his stride so that we almost walked in time. His camera was swung across his torso. It bumped and knocked, heavy and hard against the soft shell of my ribs. 'Do you have to take that everywhere?' I asked and he just laughed.

His deep warm laugh. 'It's what I do, Em. If I didn't bring it, I might miss something. I might miss a perfect moment. I might forget something I love.'

Images

I start at the beginning and scroll through all the photos, spinning the ridged dial frantically with the soft edge of my thumb. The first twenty-seven are his usual work. All bold still lifes. The images are sharp and clear, plain objects seen as more distinct through his unique perspective. Bright colours, neon blocks, thick cubes suspended magically in air. They are familiar. Jay's particular visual signature.

I scan the solid shapes and the dense slices that the shadows make. There are designer glasses, aftershave, bright nail polish spilling from a bottle on the whiteness of a floor. I stop and scrutinize the photo of the pink polish. The colours seem somehow condensed, the polish even less liquid. My husband's magic gift: to turn the things he photographed into something almost tangible so that you felt that you could reach your hands into the paper print and cut your fingers on the edges of a thing.

And then.

And then.

And then there is a shot of Ben that is nothing like the others. The backdrop is the studio. Ben's nakedness is partially obscured by the angle of his body and his face is turned towards the camera. Light falls on him through the large window to the left and seems to casually cascade in gentle waves and catch upon the contours of his dark brown flesh. There is a softness to the image. A subtlety. An almost glow.

'Come join us, Ben?' I turned to ask. Jay was picking up his things, busy packing up his day. 'He can't,' Jay said without looking, without a pause. 'I can't. I'm sorry, Em, but thanks. I've got a second date with this new guy,' said Ben. Jay grabbed his heavy bag, wrapped a scarf around his neck. I said goodbye for both of us.

I press delete. Erase the shot. Let the camera fall from out my hands. I do not understand what I am seeing here. I do not want to see at all. First a trip I didn't know about or go on and now this. I throw a pillow at the camera. Stupid fucking camera. I attempt to bury it from view. My brain feels swollen, as if it's pressing up against the confines of my skull and might explode at any moment. Inside the feelings froth and rage like cloudy, brown, polluted seas. Nothing makes sense. Nothing at all.

I wait and hope that calm will come. The digital display warns me there are four more photographs to see but my body won't stop trembling long enough to look at them. I remind myself to breathe. Just breathe. I close my eyes but all I see is naked Ben, lit up in gold.

I want to press delete in my own mind. But the image of Ben's body will not leave me.

Sound

I cross the hallway in the dark past my parents' room and the room where Jude once slept that my mother claims she uses for Pilates now. My pointed toes search out the silent spaces on the floorboards in a slow and delicate dance recalled from distant teenage memory. From the drinks cabinet I take a new bottle of vodka. I mix it with no-sugar orange squash from the kitchen cupboard in the dark. Once I would have tried to hide my tracks, marking the measures with my mind, replacing alcohol with water.

Back in bed I Google all the songs that are deeply inappropriate for death and gulp the sickly-smelling drink. I put my headphones on and turn the volume up as high as my iPhone will allow. Little warning bars of too loud sound flicker red as I listen to the irony and try to drown my thoughts in noise.

1. Live and Let Die by Guns N' Roses
2. Another One Bites the Dust by Queen

3. Fame – I'm Gonna Live Forever by Irene Cara
4. Waiting for the Worms by Pink Floyd

FUCK YOU DEATH AND FUCK YOU JAY.

Suspense

'You look,' I say. 'I can't.'

I thrust the camera towards Jude. I am huddled in the corner of Dad's office, my arms wrapped tight around my knees.

'Is this about the Cornwall trip?' she asks. 'Did you even know he'd been?'

I scrunch my eyes but naked Ben still flickers through the semi-darkness of the inside of my eyelids.

'He's away for work quite often. But the last few trips I thought he was in Birmingham. He never mentioned Cornwall and he wasn't anywhere with me.'

I stick a fingertip into my mouth, tear off the nail down to the quick, suck at the painful exposed pink.

'Give it here,' Jude says. She kneels on the carpet next to me and takes the camera from my hands. I bite into another nail as she switches the thing on. 'I don't know how you managed to not look last night.' She turns the camera over while I hug my knees into my chest, compress my ribcage tight. 'I'm sorry that I couldn't stay with you. Rob was struggling with the boys. They found the funeral confusing. They don't understand.'

I think about how they're not the only ones while Jude fiddles with a dial and tries to switch the camera on.

'I didn't.'

'Didn't what?' she asks.

'I didn't manage not to look at them.'

'So, you've seen all these already . . . And . . . ?'

Jude looks up at me and waits for me to say something.

'No, not all of them. I've just seen one. It's why I can't look at the rest.'

'Why not?'

'It was of Ben,' I say and hold myself a little tighter. I press my back against the radiator that emits a heat that almost burns and feels good.

'Of Ben?' she says, repeating me, looking perplexed.

'Promise? Promise you won't tell our parents?' My fingertips fill up my mouth and muffle all my words.

'Of course,' she says.

'Because they know Ben's gay and I can't cope with more questions or concern.'

'Questions about what? Why would they be concerned?' Jude asks.

'Because,' I pause and say the words out loud that I do not want to hear. 'In the photo he was naked.'

'What?' she says, her face scrunching and crunching in confusion. 'Ben was definitely naked? But Jay never

61

photographs people for work. That isn't what he's known for. Are you sure that Ben was naked?'

I nod, Ben's exposed form embedded clearly in my mind. Jude turns the camera over slowly in her hands and shrugs.

'Well, maybe Jay was trying something new?' she says, her tone less reassuring than her words.

I raise my eyebrows high.

'That's exactly what I'm scared of, Jude.'

Questions

I focus on my sister's face. I study the furrowed frown-lines that run across her forehead as she looks through the last images. I wonder if they're all of Ben, or Ben and Jay. She bites her lip while staring at the camera's monitor and I clamp my eyes tight shut against the things she might be seeing now.

'They're really not exciting, Em.'

Her voice infiltrates my self-inflicted darkness.

'Are they of Ben?' I ask, my breathing shallow, fast and barely there.

I hear Jude spin the camera dial and I open my eyes a little to let a streak of light inside.

'No.' She shakes her head. 'There's just a blue front door. Perhaps a cottage by the sea? I'm assuming it's in Cornwall, based on what Ben said. It has a porthole window and a metal fish door knocker. Although maybe it's a mermaid's tail . . .'

I open my eyes to see her turn the camera upside down as if a change of angle will somehow make things clear.

'And?' I say, impatiently.

She spins the dial to the right on my command.

'Then there's a picture of a sunset or a sunrise taken from a beach. But the last two aren't so obvious. Or actually any good in fact. Em, these two are shit. Perhaps Jay didn't mean to take these ones.'

'What do you mean?' I ask, grabbing the camera back from out her hands.

I scroll through the last images to see them for myself. There's a close up of a slate and granite wall, the type that I imagine can be found absolutely everywhere in Cornwall. The wall is unremarkable except for a small indent and a single rock that sticks out further than the rest. Why photograph a wall?

And then there is an image that's unclear. A sort of blur, a pale smear. A sweep of something soft perhaps. And in the corner of the blur, a pale smudge, a brownish dot. I don't know what I'm looking at and I'm not sure that I want to know.

I have to know.

Ink

Jude has left and I'm sat back in my favourite spot, leaning up against the radiator in the corner of Dad's office. I check my phone again. There are twelve new text messages but none from Ben. I don't read a single one but send my standardized response of a red emoji heart to everyone. Someone replies with, 'Was that actually meant for me?' and a smiling, yellow, winking face. I read the text and realize that I've sent a love heart to a plumber who is trying to chase a bill he sent for servicing the boiler in the house. 'No,' I type and set a timer for an hour. In an hour I can check again to see if Ben has been in touch. He hasn't called me back despite my endless messages and calls.

In the room the printer moans and shudders. I hold my breath as the grey bulk of machine delivers lines of ink. It pushes out the images a little at a time. A complicated mix of pixels; Magenta, Cyan, Yellow, Black. Small coloured dots combined to make a whole. I wait and watch, expectant. I stare into the dark opening and breathe the tang of chemicals and ink as the printer heaves and shivers and then stops. Four sheets of paper wrinkled in the tray. They lie there warm, the furrowed pages colour-drenched, all newly soft and limp.

I take Blu-Tack from the oak desk drawer and roll it into tiny balls. It feels like flesh. I squeeze each piece onto my thumb and pinch it hard. Compressed blue ovals peel off revealing perfect fingerprints. I bring the images upstairs and tack them to my bedroom wall, pressing the printouts onto 'Skimming Stone' grey. The pictures span out like a disconnected web across my mother's precious paintwork. I think of TV serial-killers and superheroes all plotting out their plans on large white walls. Bright red string linking granulated images, marking out the meanings that appear.

But the meanings don't appear. I sit and wait and fold my knees up tight, pull Jay's jumper out and down towards my feet. I tuck the wool under my toes and pin it there, a dark grey knitted tent. It smells of Jay. Of ancient oaks and thunderstorms and something that I once mistook for safety. I stay there in my tent of scent and wait and wait. They don't make sense. Nothing makes sense. My stomach sways, seasick on land.

'It's coffee,' says my mother, walking in and handing me a mug. 'I know you don't want tea.' A thought invades: why is she wearing leggings now? She is dressed up for Pilates or some exercise that I've never actually seen her do. My hair is twisted tight upon my head, a greasy cork-screw loop constrained within a thin black band wrapped round and round until it stays. I sniff the coffee, hand it back. I huddle in my jumper tent.

She spots the A4 pages that are tacked onto the wall. I know she's thinking of the Blu-Tack grease graffitied on her precious paint. 'It's Farrow & Ball,' she'll want to say. Instead she gently bites the inside of her lipsticked lip, pressing down the points of teeth into the hidden pink parts of the flesh.

'The paintwork doesn't matter, love.'

I know, I want to yell but don't.

We stay there silent in the room, both staring at the images. She holds the coffee with one hand and takes a mouthful, swallows down. The paper prints are drying now and curling at the edges.

'So, what exactly are those?' she finally brings herself to ask.

'If I knew the answer do you think that I'd be sat here now?'

'There's no need to take that tone, Emma.'

'I'm not,' I say, taking 'that tone'.

I want to fight my husband now. I want to slap him really hard. But there's no one but my mother here.

'I just don't get it, love,' my mother calmly says and takes another coffee sip. Her lipstick leaves a grease stain kiss on the outside of the mug. I shake my head from side to side. I do not get it either. I clearly did not know this man who left me here with only these.

The alarm rings on my iPhone to tell me that an hour

has passed. There are no new messages from Ben, just more condolences from friends and another from the plumber saying, 'That's a shame!' I delete the text and dial Ben, already knowing he won't answer.

String

They have to be of Cornwall but I don't know where. I do
not have a spider's web. There's no red string connecting
dots. Just pixels pinned up on the grey perfection of a wall.

I type 'red string' into my phone and there it is for eighty
pence on Amazon. It says that if I order now it will be here
by tomorrow and the postage will be free. Fifty metres of
'wrap-gift-hemp-rope-ribbon-twine-rope-cord-string-ball
red'. I read the many words for string all optimized for ease
of search and come untied.

I was hacking at the cord around his neck. I sawed the rope
with kitchen scissors blunt from cutting Friday pizza into
slices to be shared. Jay fell onto the bedroom floor. I thought
I heard his kneecaps break. I thought I heard the cartilage
connect with earth and shatter hard. I thought only of his
broken knees.

I broke his perfect perfect knees.

Inappropriate

'Jesus, tell me you've not started knitting.'

Dad stops typing, looks at me. He is sitting on the sofa, his laptop balanced on his lap, pretending he's not working. I am pulling endless strips of parcel tape off the sides of an over-sized brown cardboard box.

'It's string,' I say.

'Because your grandmother knitted all the God damn time. I don't think I could take it, love.' He starts to type again while talking still. 'We had to keep the TV volume up high just to hear the bloody thing. The clicking noise! It's a wonder I stayed sane.'

I smile to myself, the incessant tapping of the laptop keys so similar a sound to knitting.

'It's not wool, Dad.'

'Why order string? We have string here.' My mother picks a cushion off the sofa and shakes it violently until it finally relents and re-forms into a plump and perfect square. She

70

looks at the tight red ball, the size of a Christmas bauble or a clementine, and then back at me suspiciously.

'I thought I'd hang myself with it.'

She frowns and stares at me. Outside a car tears fast and loud along the lane. She holds the cushion to her stomach as if trying to stanch some sudden flow of blood that's magically appeared and is pouring from an open wound.

'That's not funny, Emma.'

Her voice is quiet, very low.

'It's not supposed to be,' I say.

'Now don't upset your mother, Em.'

Dad throws a glance and says the words he's said a million times before and then continues with his work, the pearl and stitch of sentences tapping out across the screen. I spin around and face my mother and take a breath.

'You know, when you order food online, things like crème fraîche or fromage frais, and you think you're getting tons and then a tiny pot turns up and dinner is destroyed? Well, it's just like that. I ordered rope and this arrived.'

I sit down on the sofa making sure to squash some cushions as I do. I rip more tape from off the box. The tape is stuck to yet more tape and the separation makes a screaming sound that hurts the insides of my teeth. My mother hugs the cushion tighter to herself as I crush the thick cardboard, force it flat between my hands.

'Red rope?' My mother finally sighs, the exasperation escaping from her mouth.

We stare defiant at each other, our eyes locked tight. The

rhythmic click and tap of laptop keys continues and then stops.

'Well, at least you won't be knitting then,' says Dad, catching my eye.

And Dad and I just laugh and laugh. The kind of laugh that spreads beyond the contours of a face. A laugh with roots as deep as veins that travels from your navel pit, that rises up and shakes your whole. Uncivilized and visceral. We laugh until our muscles hurt and the aching bones across my jaw from grinding teeth ache even more. My mother puts the cushion on the sofa, adjusts the angle slightly to the left and turns her back to leave the room.

Overheard

I hear them talking in the night. Low mutterings between them both about what to do and what to say and what they think and what it is I should be doing, saying, thinking now that everyone has taken Jay and boxed him up all neat and nice and tucked him deep into the ground and swept the dust under the carpet of his death.

'She hasn't seen a single friend,' my mother says.

Jay was standing in the doorway of our kitchen, which was crammed with empty glasses, bowls of crisps and people drinking wine. A group had gathered near the bread bin and were passing round a rolled-up note. He tried to yell 'hello' above the noise. I followed him into the hall. 'Really, Em? Again?' he said. 'It's only Wednesday night.' I said that I was sorry, that it wasn't planned. He turned his back and walked upstairs.

The mumblings of their conversation travel thick and fast along the corridor and down towards my room like a rumbling riptide of concern.

'But she spends hours sitting there.' My mother is still whining on about the photographs and bits of string. 'Shouldn't we be doing something, call someone? The doctor maybe?'

'I'm sure she'll get there, love. Just give her time.'

Dad's voice is calmer than my mother's but I can hear the worry lurking in the loops and ligatures that form his words.

'But this obsession with the photographs. She's been staring at that wall for days. She needs to find a way to live now without Jay.'

But I don't. The only thing I need to do is work out what those photos mean.

Normal

Dad drops me at Jude's flat before heading to his London office with promises that he'll be back by six and will keep his mobile on him 'just in case', as if my sister is incapable of looking after me alone.

'I don't know what they think is going to happen. I feel like I'm ten again. They get nervous if I'm out of sight.'

I sit there at the kitchen table, my mobile clasped inside my hand in case Ben rings. The wooden tabletop is a universe of tiny indented stars from when small nephews have battered out frustrations with their dinner forks. The adults have left their marks here too. A scattering of little moons, crescent stains of whisky and of wine.

'They just love you, Em. We all love you.'

A vat of Bolognese is on the stove that smells just like our mother used to make it. Jude stirs it with a wooden-handled spoon, while chewing on some gum.

'They're our parents. It's their job, Em. They're supposed to worry about you.'

The kitchen smells of bay leaves, warmth and velvet-coloured wine and the cooking steam is fogging up the windows, creating a cocoon. She chops and stirs some more as we half-listen to the comfort of the radio and the drone of London traffic, a sound I didn't used to hear when it sounded of my home. 'I worry too. Those photographs . . .'

'Oh, don't start too.'

'I'm not. I promise that I'm not. I'm not our mother, Em. I just don't see how anything that's good can come of chasing answers now. Perhaps some things are better left?'

'How are they better left?' I ask, my voice rising like a building wave. 'They're already fucking awful. And it couldn't possibly get worse. Could you leave things alone if Rob had died and left you with some photos of a naked man and a place you didn't even know he'd visited? Wouldn't you go seeking answers?'

I suddenly run out of words.

'Yes.' Jude sighs and takes the spoon from out the sauce. She lays it down carefully on an empty plate beside the pot. 'I didn't mean to make you mad. You're right. Of course, of course I'd want to know.'

'You really would. And so do I.'

She offers me some chewing gum, a habit that our mother hates. A sisterly apology.

'But the one of Ben is probably just nothing. You might be reading something into it that isn't even there. Maybe Jay was moving into portraits. Or trying something more artistic? Something less commercial?'

'I guess that an affair with Ben could be classified as art. I mean, he's beautiful. That's obvious.'

'I really doubt it's that. Jay never mentioned liking men. Or anyone who wasn't you.'

'Then why won't Ben just talk to me?'

'I honestly don't know,' she says.

I close my eyes and rub my hands over my face. We settle back into an easy silence that only siblings are capable of resurrecting with such ease.

'Do you miss work?' she finally asks.

I have to think before I answer.

'I'm not sure,' I say. 'That feels like a different life.'

I was standing in Manolo heels and a vintage gold crepe skirt. Someone had printed me a party hat embellished with a picture of my face and new title of 'Executive Creative Director'. I looked around at the large advertising agency and everybody drinking good champagne from paper cups. I'm making it, I thought.

'I guess I do,' I add. 'I just want to feel normal. I miss being so engrossed in work that time flies by. And clothes shopping at lunchtime, and buying lunch at Pret. You know, the normal things.'

'Not really, no! Being a mum at home doesn't come with breaks or lunch at Pret.' A smile slips onto her lips. 'And anyway, you've never been that normal. And you could always go back?'

'You mean right now? Like this?'

I gesture vaguely at my greasy hair and Jay's woollen baggy jumper pulled down loose over my wrists.

'Yeah, well, maybe not just yet.' Her smile widens to a grin. 'You'd frighten off the youngsters in the office even more than usual. If they weren't afraid of you before, can you just imagine now?'

Now that Jay is gone. Now that normal is not normal and can never be again.

'I don't think I could concentrate,' I say. 'And how on earth am I supposed to ever care about an ad campaign again?'

There's the drumming of a digger somewhere and the gentle clinking ring of scaffolding unfolding upwards far away. The rhythmic bleeping of a lorry reverses loud into the sound like a backwards-beating heartbeat.

Jude rips a piece of kitchen towel off the roll, spits her chewing gum inside and throws the crumpled mess away. She pulls out a mismatched wooden chair and joins me at the table, drinks some water from my glass and hands it back to me.

'But you love your job. I've never found that in a job. It's rare, you know. You're lucky, Em.'

'I don't exactly feel lucky at the moment.'

'With your work, I meant. Some days I wonder if I got knocked up just to avoid the office politics. It was drastic but it worked,' she says and laughs out loud.

'Where *are* the boys?' I ask.

'They're doing extra sessions now at nursery. It's really good for them to socialize.' Jude gets up again and turns towards the stove, adjusts the flame down low so that the blue is barely visible. 'Actually, that's a lie. I mean, it probably *is* good, but they're mainly there so I don't have to take them to a music group or a swimming class or any other class that makes me want to blow my brains out . . . fuck. I'm sorry, Em.'

'It's fine,' I say.

'It's not. I didn't mean to say . . .'

'I know. It's really fine.'

'And I wanted to see you. And maybe even get my hair cut.'

I stare at Jude's long mass of hair that looks uncut no matter what. Crazed curls escape in wild tangled waves around her face. Dark, unruly witch's hair. How strange that the world keeps on spinning and that Jude's hair, my hair, keeps growing even though Jay's gone.

On the tabletop my mobile screen comes suddenly alive with light and makes me jump. A text from Dad: 'You still okay?'

'That Ben?' Jude asks.

I shake my head.

'I keep on ringing him and I've left more messages than anybody sane would ever contemplate. But nothing. It's like he's simply vanished.'

'He can't just vanish.' She is quiet for a minute. 'But he's not answering the door.'

79

'What?' I ask. 'What do you mean?'

'I went to try and talk to him. Of course I did. I'm your sister, Em. I've been over to his flat a few times now but the lights are always off. If he's home he isn't answering. And he isn't at the studio.'

'So, you couldn't leave it either?'

She simply shrugs and says nothing but pulls a smile full of pity before dishing up a bowl of food I have no hunger for.

'So how is being home again? You and Mum about to kill each other yet?' Jude asks.

'Not quite. I'm getting close. She keeps on making me hot drinks. I think she thinks that life's problems can all be solved with sugar and organic milk.'

'Oh God, I'm sorry, Em,' Jude says and grimaces. 'That's truly awful . . . Milk?! What's wrong with her? It's vodka, ice and lime. We both know that!'

Drunk

'Fuck off. FUCK OFF.' I slur the words towards my mother. 'They're staying there!'

I'm feral and I'm yelling. It seems that Jude and I were wrong. Vodka isn't a solution.

'What's going on?' Dad rushes to the bedroom, bringing half the bath in with him. He is dripping water on the carpet from the inside of his dressing gown. It trails down his hairy legs. It pools around his giant feet.

'She's lost it, Steve. I think she's drunk.'

'JUST GO AWAY.'

'She needs to take them down,' my mother says to Dad. 'Just look at what she's done!'

I'm sat cross-legged on the floor. The photographs are mounted on the wall and I'm surrounded by four empty packs of Blu-Tack, some scissors and a tiny pile of short red threads that look a bit like tampon strings.

'She's mad,' she says.

'You're mad,' I yell.

But she may just have a point. I've chopped the string into small lengths and, lacking anywhere to put them that makes sense, I've tied four into nooses and hung them with more Blu-Tack from the bottom of each photograph, each blurred and slurred confusing shot.

'Let's all just take a breath,' says Dad.

'I can't put up with it!' my mother says. 'Just look at all the Blu-Tack on my walls.'

She's spotted all the small blue dots. Four sheets of Blu-Tack rolled up tight into a hundred tiny balls and pressed flat onto precious walls. I've squished and squashed them everywhere. The room looks like it's snowing blue, around each print, around the room. A blizzard that is beautiful.

'FUCK OFF!' I say and take another swig of cold, transparent vodka sludge as dense as frozen sea.

They both retreat. Dad walks out backwards, leaving forward-facing damp footprints that make it seem as if he walked into the middle of the room and simply vanished.

Conciliation

My mother wakes me gently in the morning. My head is throbbing with my heartbeat and my mouth is dry but I can feel her warm fingers stroking down across my forehead to the arched bridge of my nose. I am briefly taken to a time when my mother's stroke could mend. She perches in The Visiting Space and I open my eyes to see her holding a gold notebook. It's the same size as a child's hand.

'For you,' she says. 'I ordered this for you. I thought that it might help.'

The daylight is too bright and I squint to shut some of it out. I stay silent as my mother smooths the non-existent creases from her Sweaty Betty leggings. She crosses her slim legs and then uncrosses them again. 'It's a gratitude journal. You write down one thing every day you're grateful for. One website said that it might help.'

I do not speak.

'I'll just leave it here.' She places the gold journal and a pen beside my bed, leans down to kiss my forehead. 'I'm sorry, love . . . that I got cross.' She leaves herself a thoughtful pause, gets up and moves towards the door. 'This is hard on everyone, you know,' she adds, escaping quickly out the room.

I check my phone. Nothing from Ben. The notebook shines beside the piles of crumpled Kleenex and the unread books. Alone now I sit up in bed. I take the cap off the pen and open the notebook. The spine breaks loud, a glorious crack, and large across the empty page I scrawl in felt-tip pen the only words that make me glad:

BLU-TACK.

Space

My parents drive me back to London. I sit in the front seat of the car, my arms clasped tight around Jay's jumper with a knitted heavy parcel on my lap. Jay's camera and a folder with the photographs are wrapped inside the empty woollen arms. We drive towards the city creep. The brown and frozen fields give way with every passing mile to the crush of concrete sprawl. The traffic starts to thicken tight around the car and a giant poster billboard shows an advert for a movie Jay won't ever see.

'You don't have to do this, love,' my mother says.

'Just do what feels right. You'll always have a room at home. I can come and get you any time,' says Dad. 'As long as I'm not overseas.'

'I suppose that I could stay with you?' my mother says. 'I mean, the futon's not ideal. I always said you should've bought a proper sofa-bed.'

She reaches from the back seat and puts her hand upon my arm.

'I'm fine,' I say. 'I just want to go home.'

Jay and I were standing in front of our first house. We wondered at the novelty of our very own front door. The bathroom was an orange tiled outrage and tassels danced around the edges of the lamp shades. Our flat furniture looked all wrong there; too impermanent and modern, too spaced out within in the space. We wrestled with our mattress to the bedroom in the eaves. A lamp glowed low like caramel as we sat and laughed and ate our salty chips from soggy paper bags, so hungry for it all.

The traffic stops and starts and stops. The intermittent pulse of the North Circular pushing the curdled mass of cars along the city's clogged and narrow streets. I stare at the low houses by the road, pollution streaked and mottled grey. I've never noticed them before. Bed sheets hang where curtains should, transparent, thin behind the plastic window squares. Old Mercedes sit on driveways and around the double-glazed front doors are hanging baskets hanging empty. I look for stars but they are lost inside the grimy glow of the urban orange sky.

We pull up on our street.

Not ours.

Not anymore.

Jude is waiting on the pavement near the door, the street-lamp spilling light on her. She is wrapped like Christmas, which somehow in my grief has been and gone, the celebration lost somewhere. Her wool green coat and large blue scarf are bright against the winter drab and her elbows bend to form a cradle filled with wine, some flowers and a family-pack of Haribo. She stamps her feet upon the ground, her body marching without moving in a fight against the cold.

'I wasn't really sure what I should bring,' she says, glancing down into her arms.

'Fuck knows,' I say. 'They're great.'

I try to smile, swallow hard and hear the quiver in my words. She plants a solid kiss upon my cheek, my arms still wrapped around Jay's stuff, her arms filled up with coloured gifts.

'Ready?' says Dad as he turns the key inside the lock and pushes the front door against the weakening resistance of the paper crest of piled-up post.

'Are you sure you want to do this, Em?' my mother whispers just behind me in the winter dark.

Memory

I'm home from work. The house is strange. The food shopping is packed away.

'I'm home,' I call. But the broken bird-bone scatter of my words disperses in the awful still.

I go to get some water from the fridge.

Inside synthetic light glares harsh, reflects off the plastic wrap.

The vegetables lie neat inside, the leeks like disembodied limbs.

A slash of pink. The petals cold. The dahlias are in the fridge.

And peppercorns around the room. He's filled the grinder, dropped the rest. They lie like cut-out tumours on the worktop. They're cancer spread across the floor.

'I'm home,' I try again with dread.

I hold my breath.

My heart beats loud.

I slowly start to climb the stairs.

Netflix

Upstairs I'm nestled in the pillows. It's late and everyone has left. I've made a cup of chamomile tea and Jude's flowers sing carnation bright inside a jug of water on the old pine chest of drawers. The tea smells better than it tastes, the floral scent decaying into rotten hay and saccharine which sticks to the enamel of my teeth and makes me retch.

Jay and I are watching Netflix on the laptop, snuggled in the bedding. Everything is normal, with the small exception that my husband is a photo in a frame. I've propped him on the right side of the bed high up on his pillow, the one that's made from memory foam; a foam that has forgotten to remember him and in the weeks without his weight has risen to erase his shape, undone his human dent.

'You're not actually watching Love Island, *are you?' Jay was standing in the doorway and scrunching up his forehead in a frown. 'It's not just me,' I said, 'I think the whole country is watching it.' Jay shook his head as a woman in*

a child-sized bikini began to sob on screen, her makeup staying perfectly intact. 'That doesn't mean it's any good. Can't we just watch something else?' he said, still frowning at the TV or at me.

I heave the duvet, tuck it high and tight around the two of us and binge-watch to the end of *Good Girls* series one.

'God, you'd really hate this show,' I say and click on series two.

Battery-powered golden stars gleam softly in the sealed fireplace. As the opening credits of another episode begin to play, my mobile rings.

My heart beats fast then crashes, slow. It isn't Ben.

'You okay?' The voice of Jude, concerned. 'I really would've stayed tonight. It's just the kids . . . and Rob is out with mates. I didn't want to leave you there.'

I can hear the bellow of young boys avoiding sleep, demanding stories, kisses, time. And the gentle slack and clack of chewing gum against her tongue.

'I'm fine,' I say and actually think I mean it.

I nestle deeper in the bed, bury myself beside the snapshot memory of a husband and the Netflix show he'd never watch reflecting in the glass where deep brown irises should be.

Details

For a fraction of a moment I half wake into the morning light and feel weightless, amnesia washed by broken sleep. And then a solitude as deep and wide as oceans floods over me and I realize it is morning and the earth is spinning still.

I place the photo in the wardrobe and surround it with the softness of his socks, each single sock identical to make a perfect match with any of the other socks. They create a small dark nest, black fabric feathers furling round. I miss the feet that went inside the socks, the hands that pulled them over feet, the man that walked the earth in them.

The missing is immense at once. I miss it all. The little things that make a man. The minutiae of the details.

Jay was whistling gently to himself as I sat scrolling through the morning news on my new phone. 'Want coffee, Em?' Jay asked the question that he asked me every morning, always knowing that the answer would be yes. I watched

the rhythmic tapping of his foot as he filled up the percolator.
Outside the traffic murmured. A soft blanket of sound around
our home.

I make a cup of herbal tea. I do not want to drink the tea but need something to do. I open the kettle lid and turn the tap and flip the switch. Leaning up against the worktop I listen to the deep discomfort of the water, frantic in its boiling cage, frenetic in its fight against the inevitability of steam. I wait for the surrender, for the satisfying click and sigh, then consider eating cereal. I open the fridge and find that it's been emptied in my absence. No vegetables in cellophane. No wrapped-up cheese or jars of jam. Just the sparkle of an empty fridge and three brown bottles of Asahi. I take a beer and pour the tea into the narrow gap between the empty washing up bowl and the sink.

The flakes feel rough and dry as I reach into the cereal box and eat them from my fingers without milk. I like the crunch and cracking sound they make between my unbrushed teeth, a sound that echoes in my ears. I take a swig of beer and look around. I'm not sure what to do without my mother to annoy, or the sounds of Dad, or Jude, or Jay.

There is Blu-Tack in my bag and I stick the A4 photos up in random spaces on the kitchen wall. Then I take some more and put more blobs up everywhere. I like the madness they create. The discord and the chaos formed around the perfectly framed prints and the artwork that we own. Jay liked it neat. These photos have no place among the usual order of our home but things aren't usual anymore. I take another clasp of cereal and cram it in my hungry mouth while staring at the images and trying to decipher what they mean.

I pick a photo from the wall, fixate upon the image of the door. The cereal misses my mouth and breaks onto my clothes and catches on the gentle ledge of my unimpressive breasts. I brush the mess onto the floor where it will stay. The door could be a cottage anywhere. I look around the empty room and realize that it's empty even though I'm here.

Time

Days blur, time slides, hair oil-slicks. I stay under the duvet, stash my phone away from view as Jay's birthday looms a little closer. The doorbell rings for a few days until it doesn't anymore. I text my parents and my sister every single day, sending carefully constructed reassurances to keep them from coming over. The day before his birthday I turn the TV off and put my phone away inside a drawer and will the time to pass unnoticed and the dates and days to disappear. If I just stay here in bed and shut my eyes and sleep until I'm dead, I might survive.

'Oh, Emma love. Just look at you! We never should have let you leave.'

It must be afternoon or early evening judging by the fading light that frames the edges of the curtains. My mother stands inside the doorway to my bedroom, my spare front door key in her hand.

'Noooo,' I groan. 'Please go away.'

I pull the duvet up and tuck my head down to my chest,

roll away from her and mumble to myself beneath the bedding.

'You're not answering your phone. The worry, Em. You almost scared your parents half to death.'

'Which half?' I mutter to myself.

My mother takes a measured breath.

'Right. You're getting up. I'll switch the shower on.'

I hear the shower start to run and suddenly the air sweeps in and makes me gasp as my mother pulls the bedding back.

'I'm waiting and I'll wait all day. If I were you, I'd get up now.'

I sigh deeply and slope into the shower to avoid her. This doesn't mean she's actually won. I won't use soap.

The bathroom shelves are full of all Jay's things. His shower gel, half-used shampoo, the branded plastic-bottle relics of his life. I stay under the water until the hot runs out. Back in my room the sheets are clean, the duvet changed and clothes lie fresh and folded in a pile on the pillow.

'Don't you even think about getting back into that bed,' my mother calls from somewhere else, as if she hears what I am thinking.

Downstairs my mother has achieved that thing that marks her as an adult in my mind and makes me wonder if I'll ever grow enough to finally be a grown-up too. The lamps are on, the dishes done. She's found the matches in the drawer, lit two candles on the counter.

'Bit much maybe?' I gesture at the flames that flicker-dance and fill the room with floral scent and lemon zest. She sucks the air in through her teeth and swallows hard as if she's swallowing down sticky words as well as oxygen, then goes back to chopping vegetables. I relent, pull out a chair to sit.

'Where's Dad?' I finally ask.

'In Paris until Wednesday. Is this all about tomorrow, love?' she asks, her voice much softer now.

'Ta daaaa,' I said all happy-proud as Jay opened his eyes. Balloons were hanging in small clusters, coloured orbs of joy filled with my breath. There was bunting laced around the room and presents on the table. 'Happy Birthday, Jay!' I beamed at him. He smiled but his eyes were matt. 'Give me a sec,' I said, my tampon heavy, leaking through. The gift he really wanted wasn't something I would give.

The silence that I offer is oppressive. My mother just ignores it and fiddles with the vintage radio I've always loved. She rotates the dial slowly back and forth until she finds the perfect point at which the radio submits, like the breaking of an amniotic sac, and gentle chatter gushes from the speakers and floods the room with sudden sound.

'Does it matter where I sit?' she finally asks.

She keeps on glancing at the photographs and tiny Blu-Tack balls stuck up around the walls. She chews her bottom lip as I just sit and wait for the long lecture that she doesn't give. The candle scent has been eclipsed by the strong smell of a chicken roasting in the oven next to feathered sprigs of fragrant thyme and a rainbow-spread of vegetables. The house smells like a proper home; of sweet carrots and rich peppers and olive-oil roasted herbs.

The house no longer smells like mine.

Panic

My mother says she's given it some thought. The futon just won't work, not with her back, not at her age, and I refuse to go and stay again. A compromise is reached in which she enlists Jude as my personal parole officer. She commands that I must speak to her, no matter what, each single day. I agree to make her go away.

Alone now in the house again the photos haunt my every thought.

'I can't work these out,' I message Jude.

'Go for a walk,' she writes. 'I'll pick you up for bowling night on Thursday.'

I venture out the house and down the road towards the high street. Outside Tesco I begin to feel breathless. I stand there motionless, in the middle of the pavement, my body desperate for fresh air. I swallow down deep lungfuls. But the air just tastes of cars and chaos, leaves me parched. The siren from an ambulance weaves itself into the thick and heavy sounds and makes me jump. The city is surrounding me with its lack of clear horizons. The buildings are too high, the winter sun reflecting and refracting off a thousand different windows and metallic shapes that form the steel bars of a towering and man-made cage. I unzip my heavy winter coat, feel trapped, pinned down inside a cell of constant sound.

A woman knocks me with the edges of her oblong leather bag. A man shoves past me while looking at his phone, white AirPods plugging up his ears. I feel the sharp apex as his elbow meets my ribs.

'Sorry,' he says without looking, but he's walked on by and I have no idea if the sorry was for me.

I wrap my hands around myself. Hold onto myself tight. The buildings and the people and the noises feel like they're rising up and pressing inwards, crushing all my feelings further down into myself. It's hard to breathe.

Sinking down onto the concrete, the contents of my bag fall out into the street. A 'Diva' coloured MAC lipstick rolls towards the middle of the road. It's hard to breathe, then harder still. I'm drowning in the city air, a flapping fish upon an urban shore. I squeeze my head between my knees, fixate upon the pavement's grit and grain and embedded chewing gum remains.

'Are you all right?' A woman kneels on the street beside me. I'm clearly not. I stare down at the looping laces of her Flyknit Nike trainers and try my hardest not to die. 'Are you asthmatic?' I shake my head and focus on a piece of gum that's been ground into the pavement. 'Can someone go and get some help?' she calls out to the city.

More shoes begin to circle me. A tight circumference of different matching pairs.

'I'm a nurse,' somebody says. A woman leans her body in and arches over me, protective like a cowrie shell. She tells the shoes to 'back away', to give me space, but still it's not enough. There's a paper bag over my face. I can hear the crackle and the crunch as the bag expands, contracts, expands. A metronome of panic. The smell of coconut comes off the nurse's hair and I hear the hum of people talking and the drumming of my heartbeat as I hold onto this stranger's hand.

We were waiting in the lobby. The air was warm and crickets sang along with tree frogs in the dark. A lady at reception took our luggage, looped a ring of flowers round our necks and asked if we were newly-weds. 'I can't afford this place,' Jay whispered tight into my ear. 'It's fine,' I said. 'I can bill it to the agency as research. The hotel chain comes up for pitch next month.' I lied with ease and handed the receptionist my bank card while sipping at a cocktail that smelt of coconut and local rum.

'That's it. Slow breaths.' She rubs my back more slowly than my breathing as she kneels on the pavement by my side. My breathing starts to slow and the ringing in my ears begins to fade.

'I think you're having a panic attack. Have you felt like this before?'

I shake my head to tell her 'no'.

'My husband . . .' I finally whisper in the space between each cracked and crippled breath. I close my eyes and see red roses on a wooden box beneath the winter earth.

'If you let me have his number I can call him now,' she says.

'No,' I say. 'You can't.'

February

Dance

The doorbell rings and I glance down at my phone to check the time. It's too late to be the postman. I think about ignoring it and going back to bed but I'm scared my mother has arrived again without an invite and will shortly try to break the door down. At least her leggings would be used for actual exercise for once. But it isn't her. It's Anne, Jay's mother, waiting in the winter rain. She compresses her umbrella in the doorway, wraps and binds it tight then seals it with the Velcro tab, rainwater catching in the fabric of the folds.

'Can I come in?'

I do not answer her but cross my arms and watch the rain that's falling heavy on her greying roots. The water drips are trailing down the contours of her face and the cheekbones that are Jay's. I want to tell her to 'Fuck Off' and that Jay wouldn't want her here, but it feels like more effort than just nodding 'yes' so I step aside to make some room. I watch her, silent, as she settles her umbrella up against the wall inside the door and the water slowly leaks to form a pool. She fumbles with the buttons of her coat.

'I'm sorry, Emma,' she blurts out fast. 'I never should have said those things. I just . . . It's just so hard to comprehend. But I never should have said that just because you married him you would have all of the answers.' I stare at her in silence. She peels off her gloves and rubs her hands like tinder. 'Please, Emma. Can I sit somewhere?'

I nod, but just because it's raining and the way she looks reminds me of a kitten being drowned. I keep my arms folded tight across my chest, and watch her walk into the kitchen, select the chair that Jay liked best and pull it out to sit. I flinch as wooden chair legs scrape against the wooden floor. She turns more slowly than she should and hangs her coat over the square framed back of the chair and smooths it flat. She is neat, just like her son.

The rain knocks hard against the windows as if begging to be let in too.

'I . . . I don't know exactly why I came,' she finally says. I just stand still and wait. 'I . . .' she tries once more.

'Are you here to tell me that I killed your son? Again?' I ask coldly, my lips compressed.

'No.' She shakes her head. 'No, not at all. I wanted to say sorry. I'm so angry and . . .'

She smells of strong perfume mixed with the farmyard scent that's escaping from her sodden, woollen coat.

'Well, you've said it now,' I say.

She doesn't leave but takes a breath and spins her

wedding ring in circles, the gold band loose beneath the knuckle of her thin ring finger. There is silence for a while.

'I really am so sorry, Emma. I know it's not your fault. It's just . . .' Her words drop off the cliff edge of the sentence and she puts her hand towards her hair and tries to recompose herself, to smooth the saturated strands of brown into an ordered shape.

I look at this wet woman in my kitchen, a stranger tied to me across a generation with a surname that we added to ourselves along with wedding rings. A tie that is now half undone. Her eyes sit low inside their sockets and her skin is taut and thin over the canvas bone frame of her face. I really want to hate her but I'm tired and the person I despise, she isn't here. Instead there is someone just as lonely, just as lost as I am.

'It's fine,' I say at last, possibly meaning it.

She's shaking just a little, from the cold or from the grief. I do what others do to me and offer tea, forgetting for a moment that the fridge is almost empty. She takes a beer to my surprise. I want to laugh out loud at this prim and uptight woman swigging beer from out the bottle before lunch. Anne looks around the kitchen at all the flowers in the vases and all the flowers in the sink and all the photos on the walls.

'Are those ones Jay's?' she asks confused.

She stands to get a closer look at the A4 prints tacked up along the wall in random spaces between frames, surrounded by small Blu-Tack spots. I sit and wait. She takes another swig of beer, then shakes her head a little side to side as if to readjust her thoughts. I imagine all her thoughts like flecks inside the snowglobe of her brain and wait for them to settle down, to rearrange themselves into a landscape that is new. 'But these two here are Cornwall. Why on earth did he have those?' She points towards the wooden door and the sun which hovers low above a beach and strip of sea.

How would I know? I want to say. How does she know? I bite my lip and shrug, go back to stand before the open fridge.

'I have no idea. I'm not sure what they're of, or even where. I thought that they might tell me something but I'm not sure what I thought they'd say.'

She paces up and down the room and finally stills, shaking her head in what looks like deep confusion.

'Yes, these are both of Cornwall. This door right here, it's from The Nook.'

An almost-laugh escapes her mouth. She seems slightly hysterical.

'The what?' I hold the handle of the fridge a little tighter in my hand. I can smell the kitchen cleaner someone's used to scrub the empty shelves. I stare into the artificial glow and remember the bright dahlias.

'The Nook,' she says again. 'It's a cottage down in Cornwall. Did he never mention it?'

I think about the fact that there is yet another thing I didn't know.

'No. He never said a word,' I say.

My speech sounds strangled, strange, detached.

'I didn't know he'd been there since . . .' says Anne. I hold the handle of the fridge and grip it tight. 'The cottage was my parents'. I grew up there. After Jay was born my parents let us stay there every summer while they visited my uncle. But then . . . then . . . Well, I haven't been there since Jay started boarding school. And once my parents died I planned to sell it, finally have some money for myself, but Martin thought it better that we kept it as a rental. He has managed it for all these years.'

'So, Martin knew that Jay was there?' I ask.

'No.' She slowly shakes her head. 'Jane must have given him a key.'

'Who's Jane?' I ask.

'She lives next door. She was my friend.' Anne looks back at the image of the cottage door. 'It's usually empty in the winter. No one wants to go on holiday to a seaside village in the cold.'

She laughs again. Too animated, her laughter and intensity unnerving.

'But why would Jay go there?' I ask.

'I've no idea,' says Anne, shaking her head again.

The energy seems suddenly to dissipate and she takes a seat, slumps in the chair. There are things I didn't know about her son. So many things. I wonder if she's thinking the same thing.

'But why?' I ask again, confused. 'Why there? Why then?'

'I'm not sure, Emma.' Her voice is tired suddenly, all languid, loose and slow. 'You know he didn't speak to us. The last few years . . . His father . . .' She bites her lip and a single tear threatens the tight composure of her face.

This woman who I hardly know beyond the fact that she's the mother of the man I loved is now crying silently. Her suffering is hard to watch and I wish that she'd just go away. But I find my body moving to her, folding itself round her fragile shape as she tilts her head into the cradle of my neck, her head too weighted down with feeling to hold up. We sit there with our beer bottles, swaying just a little. Two women locked inside a strange embrace; an awkward dance of mutual loss and separate loves, both grieving for the Jay we knew and the Jay we clearly didn't know.

Gift

'I'm actually going there tomorrow . . .' Anne re-finds herself. She takes a clutch of keys from the pocket of her coat, a slight tremor in her hands resonating through the metal and turning into sound.

'Going where?' I ask.

'The Nook,' she says. 'I'm leaving Martin, leaving Jay's dad.' She laughs again, that high-pitched nervous laugh that sets my teeth on edge. She fumbles with her fingers, locates a key, unthreads it in a circle from off the awkward looping ring. 'For you.' The ice-cold key is pressed into my palm and instinctively my hand contracts, my fingers curl and close to form a fist around the solid shape. 'You're welcome to come too. If you need to get away.'

'That's kind of you but I don't think that's a good idea. I'm sure you need your space.'

I'm saying no but my fingers won't unfurl. She struggles, pushing a large button through an eyelet in her still-damp coat, and rubs at her thin wrist before walking to the door and waiting rain. A sudden wave of want floods in, a wish for her to stay a little longer; this woman who shows me shards of Jay in the way she moves her hands towards her face and the way she sounds out certain words. My heart contracts against her leaving. As she leans to zip her heeled boots she winces slightly, quickly pulls her face back to a smile.

'Well, if you change your mind,' she says, 'there's a bedroom for you there. You can turn up any time you like. Just call and let me know you're on your way.' She sinks the other foot down deep into the second heeled boot and pulls the zip with shaking hands. 'I'm done with space. I've been alone since I was married. I'd appreciate the company and you might find a change of scene is good.' She looks towards the photographs and shakes her head again.

'Thank you for this,' I say, 'but I just need to be at home right now.'

A steep and frightening dizziness descends from out of nowhere and I grip onto the table edge to stop the room from moving and the ground from rising up to meet me. The world is spinning fast and I can feel its momentum.

'Are you okay?' asks Anne concerned.

'Yes,' I say. But in the mirror by the door I see myself as she sees me, a pale face with sunken cheeks and clammy skin. My stomach swims with acid bile and there's a high-pitched ringing in my ears. 'I just need to be at home,' I say again, my voice coming from far away. 'I'm where I need to be.'

Despite the words, the key stays clasped inside my hand, inside a grip that won't undo.

I do not give it back.

Nightmare

Jay is naked and entwined with Ben. Their limbs are interlocked and gleam slightly with sweat and their faces are so close that they are breathing in each other's breath.

Jay looks at Ben and grins.

That grin that makes the world wait.

And their eyes burn constellation bright with want and love and lust.

Confession

A doctor I've never met before pats the plastic-covered chair beside his desk, his eyes remaining firmly locked on a large computer screen. His desk is piled high with stuff as if a tide came in and dumped an ocean's worth of plastic round his wrists. He rubs his fingers through the scratch of greying stubble that spreads like algae at low tide covering the contours of his jaw. The room smells of antiseptic, bleach and the burning scent of dust that has settled deep behind the radiators that are always on too high. He brushes a thermometer aside and a pen without a lid to make more space to type.

'I'm Dr Jones. How can I help?'

'I . . . I . . .' I stumble over words, unsure of what to say, forgetting in the moment how to speak. The pause becomes uncomfortable.

Eventually he stops typing and looks straight at me, his eyes meeting with mine and suddenly I realize how few people do this to me now. Instead they watch the walls, they search the sky or glance down at their feet as if to check that they're still rooted to the earth. I wonder if they worry that my sadness is contagious, that some power lies inside my widow eyes, Medusa strong since they've seen death.

'What exactly can I do for you today?' he asks again.

I take a tissue from the man-sized box that lies among the debris on his desk. I scrunch the tissue, make it small and fiddle with the crumpled ball.

'My husband died. He killed himself before Christmas.'

I watch the doctor's body shift a little in his seat as he looks towards the clutter of his desk and finds the pen lid in the chaos and searches for the pen, now lost. He clears his throat.

'I really am so sorry.'

'Why do people keep on saying that?' I ask. 'You didn't kill him, did you?'

He doesn't answer, simply says, 'I can suggest some things to help.' He moves the mouse towards the left, pulling up a digital prescription screen. 'As a start I can refer you for some counselling. I'll mark it down as urgent. It's important to keep talking but the wait can be a while. In the meantime there's a support group close to here called SoBS. You'll find some people there in the same boat as you. Here. I'll write it down . . .'

I imagine a small rowing boat painted white and blue and too far from the shore. It is filled with tiny people without life jackets. They cling pathetically to each other as the ocean tosses them around, the boat a paltry plaything in the vastness of the waves. I plunge the boat down to the bottom of the imaginary sea. I sink all of the unwanted sadness and anchor it down deep. Fuck this. I didn't ask for this.

Dr Jones takes out a sheet of clean A4 from the printer tray and types something into Google. He slowly writes down 'SoBS: Survivors of Bereavement by Suicide'. He tries to craft each letter carefully, taking time to turn his clichéd scratchy man-boy scrawl into some words that I can actually read. He underlines 'Survivors'.

'Who says that I'm surviving?' I mutter underneath my breath.

'What was that?' he asks, still concentrating hard on forming letters with his pen. He bites his lip and scrunches up his pallid forehead as he writes, the effort obvious.

'I don't want to talk to strangers,' I say instead. 'I don't like them much.' I stare directly at him while I'm speaking but he doesn't seem to notice.

'Strangers are simply friends waiting to happen.'

I wonder if he read that on a fridge magnet or some revolting feed, but he looks too old for Instagram.

He passes me the paper, which I fold in half and half again, pinching at the creases with my finger and my thumb, making it small, then smaller still. I origami my avoidance. The room is minuscule and far too warm, a sealed chamber painted in an NHS mint green. Tiredness is pulling at my eyelids, pulling heavy, pulling down, and I close them for a splinter of a second.

'I really don't need this,' I say, putting the paper in my pocket. 'That isn't why I'm actually here.'

Dr Jones looks up, turns his attention from my notes which light the large computer screen. There are lines and lines of blood tests taken over years, a small red message in the corner alerting doctors to a list of allergies and a review date for the contraceptive pill. I stare into a face that looks as if it's weathered over years of listening to a litany of patients' woes. Deep crevasses of tiredness span out around the grey-green rockpools of his eyes. I open my mouth and pause.

'I just can't sleep,' I finally say. 'And when I do I have these awful, vivid nightmares.'

Cold

I open my eyes and see a mass of silvery tentacles have spread across the outside of the Velux. They stick onto the glass and obliterate the sky. Lying on the bedside table is a bottle with six tiny sleeping pills and a small leaflet on grief describing all the ways that it can manifest. I cringe, remembering the conversation at the doctor's. The awful pity. Concerned eyes. The condescending lecture on anxiety and loss. I scan the endless list that is printed in the leaflet: nausea, headaches, fatigue, a change in appetite, insomnia and disturbed sleep.

Downstairs I see the creep of frost has covered everything outside and won its war against the warmth of winter sun and the heat that's locked inside the London bricks and concrete surfaces and walls and the heat that radiates from nine million people, all living, breathing, walking, running, eating, sleeping, having sex. God, I miss sex.

We were lying naked in our bed. Jay was wrapped around my limbs, his limbs like interlocking ivy. The universe expanded and contracted and then disappeared until the only thing that still existed was our sweating bodies, starry eyes.

The frost has turned the city into something new and rarely seen. The patchwork square of garden with its worn-out grass and scratch of shrubs that crouch down low inside the safety of the brown and muddy borders is white and clean and fresh and glittering. I open a window and inhale the air. It smells cleaner than London normally does; of Jurassic rocks and metal seams and the frozen aisle in Sainsbury's. The frost looks kind, not deathly cold. I remember someone telling me that dahlias die with the first arrival of the winter frost, that the icy white turns foliage black.

I think about the dahlias left in the fridge, a portent ice-cream cone of pink, and wonder if they turned black too.

Hot

I keep thinking about sex. I find solace on the internet, in the faceless groups where widows tell their deepest thoughts to Facebook. I read hundreds of their posts but don't write a single word. For the first time in my life I'm shy. The other women write their brazen truths in endless posts and it turns out that I'm not the only one who misses sex.

They call it 'Widow's Fire'; where your body lags behind your brain and still expects your partner's touch. I find a post written by a widow who went crazy having one-night stands, shagging everything in sight to fill the hole in space and time and flesh her husband left behind. But the thought of someone else's skin and body and strange breath makes my stomach heave and twist again. I want sex but just with Jay.

I text my sister with the words, 'I'm horny and I'm sad.'

She replies straight back.

'These boys won't eat four fucking peas. Can't remember feeling horny since I had them both.' Then adds, 'Of course you're sad. I'm so sad too. It's sad. x'.

CHARLOTTE LEONARD

I slump down on the sofa, switch on the Sky box and scroll down through the endless list of things that no one ever wants to watch. The photographs loom high above my head. No matter where I look my gaze returns to them as if they're whispering and watching me and taunting me. I cannot focus, cannot think straight, cannot shush the frothing mess of questions without answers that are swimming in my mind.

My mobile pings again and Jude has sent a link to a vibrator that you can fill up with the ashes of your loved one.

'Too soon?' she types.

I laugh out loud with no else around to hear. It's really not the worst idea. I almost want to dig him up and place him in a glass dildo and keep him in my bedside drawer.

I must be mad.

Madness

'Are you absolutely mad?' Jude asks.

I'm not sure how to answer that. Before Jay died the answer always felt like 'possibly' or some days even 'yes'. But if I was mad then Jude was too, our hormonal-led insanity just the right side of normality. I rummage through the bowling balls, their familiar feel a comfort as Jude and I attempt to resurrect our Thursday-night routine and do something close to 'normal'. My mother has been nagging me for weeks and while I'd rather be in bed at least she won't be calling me. My fingers slot into the pleasing holes of a size 10 ball and I lunge to take my aim. Jude is sitting with her legs crossed on the leather bench, picking carefully through the jellybeans that she's holding in her hand.

'I mean, it's only been a month or so and you really hate the countryside. You know there's no Deliveroo? You know they won't have Uber there? Do you even own a pair of shoes that don't have heels? And what about our bowling, Em?'

The ball veers slightly to the right and clips the pins, knocks only two. I scrunch my face up like a child.

'I can buy new shoes. And I've ordered wellies off the internet. It's not that hard.'

'But Em, it's *real* countryside. You think our parents' house is rural and it's twenty minutes out of London on the train. You even say that that's too far! But Cornwall, Em?'

'It's not for long.'

I join her sitting on the bench, shuffle myself up close to her.

'But it's miles away!'

'I really need to find the places in the photographs. I need to know why he went there and if . . . if Ben was with him too.'

I glance towards my borrowed shoes, the laces long, the leather marked. We listen to the metal clunk and heave that sweeps the fallen pins aside, replacing the formation, remaking it anew. Jude chews a while then stands, selecting a size 12 and bowls a strike. So effortless.

'But being all alone? Do you really think that's a good idea? You look exhausted, Em.'

The electronic scoreboard is playing a montage behind her head of bowling strikes and celebration fireworks and dancing girls from MTV. The bright lights make my head hurt. I bite my lip and scrunch my eyes as she sits back down beside me.

'I won't be all alone,' I say. 'Please don't tell our mother but I'll be with Anne.'

'Anne? Jay's mum?' She sounds incredulous.

'Don't,' I say. 'I know exactly what you're thinking.'

'But Jay?' she says.

'What about Jay? Perhaps he had her wrong.'

'Really? I mean, he wouldn't even let her near your wedding. And she didn't ever try and make an effort with you both.'

'Well, maybe that was Jay, not her. I don't exactly trust any of his life choices right now.'

'Well, maybe not his last life choice . . .' she says, which actually makes me want to laugh.

My sister takes more jellybeans from out the pocket of her jeans. She passes me a green one and I scowl at her, leave my palm upturned until she sighs and adds a red one too.

We watch the family a few lanes down who are sprawled across their curve of bench, a jumbled mess of winter coats and bags and scarves and girls with lanky limbs. The father helps his youngest child to bowl. He guides her to the smallest ball and stands behind her as she leans, says 'Wait!', adjusts her little body to the right and watches as she takes her aim, then cheers as the slow rolling ball bounces off the barrier and finally hits a single pin. The entire family clap and laugh and squeal in their shared delight.

'Please stay here, Em,' Jude finally says. 'Just stay in London where your life is. Please?'

'I'm not sure where my life is now. Or even what it is. My entire marriage might have been a total sham.'

'I'll help with finding Ben,' she pleads. 'I'll try again. I'll try harder.'

'You've tried! I've tried! He doesn't want to talk to me. I need to see the cottage for myself. I need to figure out the reason why Jay went there and the reason that he lied to me.'

'Please don't,' she begs. 'Perhaps it's time to let it go. This is becoming an obsession. I know it's hard. I know.'

She doesn't know. She thinks she does. My parents too. I'm sure they've Googled 'suicide' and ordered books from Amazon. I'm pretty sure my mother will have contacted some helpline. She loves a brochure, booklet, leaflet, any kind of printed guide. They'll have sought advice on what to say and what to do and how to be around me in this grim uncharted territory. They'll have read the facts, the numbers, stats. But none of them can possibly know what it means to be the one who's left behind. The person left without a note, just questions without answers and a wedding ring but no husband.

'Please stay,' Jude tries again. 'For me?'

I take the jellybean that's bright and green. I hold it in between my teeth and suck the sugar from its oval shape until it shrinks to nothing.

'Maybe,' I finally say. 'Maybe.'

Distraction

It's morning and I'm hot or cold and drenched in sweat. The sleeping pills don't stop the nights from filling up with curdled dreams; vivid, viscous, violent scenes, so life-like and so powerful that they spawn new memories of themselves. The memories stick like seaweed to a salty jagged rock and refuse to dissipate despite the undeniability of dawn. Last night I dreamt again of Ben and Jay.

The two men follow me around all day. I scrunch my eyes, reopen them in an attempt to clear my mind, to reset all the things that I am seeing in my head. But the image of my husband and his lover stays: Jay and Ben, both dewy-eyed and lit up with a golden-shine. I try to do some washing, sort the lights from darks, but I keep muddling the piles up.

I rescue a pink bra that is entangled in white socks and cream tea-towels. This craziness, it has to stop. I need to concentrate and sharpen up, to focus on the photographs. I have a piece of blood-red string that links to Jay and spans across my kitchen wall and stretches far across the land and reaches to a Cornish door that's bright and blue and far from here. I need to see if answers lie locked deep inside the distant land.

I scrunch my eyes again and suddenly the sea swims in and fills my throat and I vomit all my urgency and vivid dreams and complicated feelings into the cradle-cup of my own hands. The vomit seeps. Neon orange bile mixed with spittle trickles in between my fingers and falls in mucus strands and splatters in an arc across the pile of dirty laundry. Inside my head my heartbeat sounds just like the clicking of a clock, the ticking of a hidden bomb.

I need to go find answers.

Denial

'Your sister called. You're where?' my mother shrieks.

I hold the phone further away to save the inside of my ears from the siren shrill of panicked, frantic mother-words. My breath forms icy clouds.

'She's where?' Dad echoes in the background, actually home for once.

It's 10.07 in the evening. He'll be sitting on the sofa now, his feet up on the comfy stool he's claimed as his, his eyes glued to the BBC and its stories from today. I imagine his large fingers, struggling to press pause on the remote and finally managing to freeze the TV, leaving some well-dressed woman on the screen all open mouthed without her news.

'It's fine. I'm fine.'

I look around the empty platform where I'm waiting for a taxi. The service bars are dancing on my phone; a measly two, then one, then two.

'You're clearly not,' my mother says. 'You've driven off to nowhere just a month after your husband died.'

'I didn't drive,' I say.

'That's not the point, Emma.'

'And anyway, it's not nowhere. It's Cornwall.'

'Cornwall! For goodness sake! You'll be the death of me.'

'Well, you won't exactly be the first. It seems to be a talent of mine.'

'It's just a turn of phrase, Emma. And don't be so ridiculous. The fact you even think that you killed Jay is exactly why you shouldn't be alone in some strange place. How am I supposed to keep you safe so far from home? And why on earth are you there anyway?' Her voice ascends through octaves as she asks.

I consider telling her the truth; that I really have no choice and that I need to find some answers. But the words don't come. Instead, I look around at where I am, while my mother blathers on. The station is minute. Two single tracks, two platforms flanked with slatted wooden benches and three streetlamps spread too far apart. On the platform opposite, two teenage girls with tiny skirts and without coats are sitting underneath a lamp, their bodies perched like birds on the backrest of a bench passing a single cigarette between themselves. I watch the waving orange glow as one inhales before blowing smoke plumes from her nostrils. Shivering together, the girls both wait for a train to take them somewhere that's not here.

The air smells strange and the quiet is disturbing. This had seemed like such a good idea a hundred and sixty miles ago.

'Well?' she asks again. 'What are you doing there?'

'I don't know,' I say and pull my winter coat tighter. I want to tell her about Ben and all the photographs and how the only thing I know for sure is that Jay came here without me and photographed a cottage door. I want to say I'm desperate, frantic, desperate to know why. Instead I say, 'Because Jay's mum. She gave me keys to some small cottage here in case I needed space. And, well, I need some space, I guess.'

I do not tell her Anne is here as well, cannot face the disapproval that will spill out of my mother.

'But, Emma. I'm not sure that's a good idea right now. You're all alone!' She is pleading now. The words are needy like a child's and tinged with undertones of cross. 'Oh God, Emma! Talk to your dad. You can tell him where you are.'

I hear her hand my dad the phone.

'So, Cornwall hey? What's the weather doing there? It's bloody raining here again. And freezing too.'

'Don't ask her about rain!' My mother's irritated yell from somewhere far away.

'You all right there, love?'

'I think so, Dad.'

'So where exactly are you then?'

131

Door

I'm not sure where I am. Brian from 'Brian's Taxis' drops me as close as he can get to the front door. The man looks like a seated heart attack. His reading glasses balance on his stomach bulge and he is eating crisps out of a packet that he's wedged between his swollen knees.

'I'm sorry, love. Last time I tried to drive up there I took off half the side panel. Cost me a fortune to repair. These streets were never meant for cars. Especially not at night,' he says, his local accent dense as home-made bread slathered in lard.

In the forty minutes from the station he has told me everything he knows about the village that I'm staying in; how his parents used to run the shop and small post office but it's all changed since the second-home invasion, which is why he moved across the valley to a town not far away and not at all because of the affair with Tess who owns the bakery. I know he knows that I am staying in a cottage that's a second home but it's left unsaid and I pay him cash, adding on a normal London tip. The money makes him blush and ramble out his awkward thanks through a gob of broken crisps. I wonder just how many doughnuts he could buy with what I've given him and if the number is enough to win Tess back.

In the silence that he leaves behind, my iPhone lights the steepness of the street and I climb to find the cottage door and see that it is bright sky blue and splits in two. I stand there on the doorstep, stand there staring at the door. Embedded in the top half is a small window, secure and round just like a porthole on a ship, and below there is a heavy-looking door knocker, the curving shape of a rusting land-locked fish. I shiver, take the photographs from out my bag, shine the light upon the A4 print that is this door and hold it up against the frame. I cannot tell if it's the night sea air or the knowledge that my husband once stood here but goosebumps rise across my skin and look a little like the pebbledash that's stuck fast to the old stone wall.

I run my fingers over blisters that have risen in the weathering of the paint and breathe the air that smells immaculate and frozen, clean as distant stars. The cottage has a name, 'The Nook', engraved into grey slate. In London there are only numbers that count high, then higher still which are fragmented into letters marking out the many flats. But here the buildings each have names. I circle with my phone, look around at all the cottages. Some are locked up and dark inside and some have lights that shine behind closed curtains, and in the dim I can make out 'Thread Needle', 'Crow's Nest', 'Sunnyside'.

The inside of the cottage smells of trapped sunlight, of long-lost time and well-read books, of furniture that's not been moved but moulded, melded with the walls and floors to make a real home. A table lamp has been left on and casts light upon a multitude of cushions, blankets, ancient throws and books and books, words everywhere. There are flowers pressed and faded now, the colour of a stretch of sand, the petals flat, preserved inside the chipped and golden painted frame. Jars and bottles full of shells, and wooden ships line windowsills. It feels like a calm retreat curated over generations where everything's embedded in, the fabrics smooth, the colours corn. A note is on the table, letters inked onto the back of a receipt in writing I don't recognize.

'Welcome to Cornwall. Sorry that I've gone to bed. Yours is the bedroom at the front. Please make yourself at home. Anne x'.

I leave the note and lug my bag up narrow stairs. It's warm inside the cottage, thick walls providing shelter from the cold and bitter air that bites outside. I find I do not need to hold my breath for fear of finding Jay afresh. I climb new stairs, my feet sounding a different tread, and discover two bedrooms, one with the wooden door already shut, and a bathroom with an ancient metal bath. There's a lamp on in the bedroom at the front, the one nearest the sea that faces out onto the lane, and I lie down on the floral bed with cotton sheets so washed and worn they're almost silk. The bedroom here is dusty pink. Like roses. Roses still in bloom unlike those in the photograph that Jay believed was beautiful when all that I could see was rotting petals, thorny stems.

Anne has left a filled hot-water bottle inside a knitted cover between the mattress and the soft duvet. The heat has dissipated and the rubber is skin-warm beneath my touch. I fold myself into the bed, still fully dressed, and hug it to myself. My mind is all awash with photographs. The questions they create. The multitude of missing words.

Staring at the ceiling I can see that all the angles here are odd and all the walls are smooth but full of gentle bumps. Imperfect plaster flowing over undulating curves. I get back out of bed to pull the velvet curtains closed against the dark of unrelenting country night, a darkness that is darker than any night I've ever seen before. I stare beyond the window at the endless endlessness of it. The moon and stars are hidden somewhere underneath the padded clouds which cancel out all light and leave the sky a perfect, inky black.

I leave the curtains hanging open round the white and wooden frame. No need to lock myself away. I climb back inside the softness of the sheets. I thought that I would feel fear among the unfamiliar black, here in the dark. But instead there is a comfort, an ancient kind of wrapping lending solace to the soul. There are no monsters under beds or memories waiting in the corners of this unfamiliar room. My fears have all already happened and the memories are lit up by the sludge of London light which seeps beyond the edges of each day and blemishes the beauty of the nights. The memory of a hanging man. The memory of the photographs that don't make sense. The memories of the living and the dying through the endless days and poisoned, unrelenting nights that have all followed since.

Outside, some streets away, the sea is rushing up and over sand and pebbles on the beach. I listen to the faint lull of the crash and push and pull and hush. The simple rhythmic lullaby of ceaseless waves. The cyclic sound that keeps on coming, going, rising up and pulling down. I try to stay awake a while, to keep my head above the soporific depth of sound, but it wraps itself around my bones and gently pulls me under, down.

Breakfast

'Morning,' says Anne.

'So you're Emma!' the other woman squeals.

The two women are fully dressed and sitting down at the table with a metal tin that's battered, dented over time. I stand still inside the safety of the doorframe, only just awake, and wearing Jay's too large pyjamas with a blanket wrapped around me as a sort of makeshift shawl. I wonder what the time is. I wonder what I look like now to someone I've never met. I rub the sleep dust from my eyes, 'Star dust' my mother used to say when I was small, and I wonder for a second what I'm doing here with strangers.

'I'm Jane,' the other woman says, her face all smiles. 'I live next door. I've made some cake.' She gestures at the tin.

'Come on, sit down,' says Anne. 'She doesn't bite, she's just a bit overexcited. It's pretty quiet here in winter. I'll put the kettle on. I'm sorry that I wasn't up to welcome you last night. I'm just so tired since . . .' She rubs her ringless finger as if adding up the losses on her hand.

'Not tea,' I say, too fast, too curt, into the space where words ran out.

Anne nods but looks as if her pale face might crumple up like paper if I speak loudly.

'No tea it is,' Jane rescues us. 'I'll make it, Anne. I wouldn't mind another cup myself. I'm parched from all this catching up.'

I take a seat and watch silent as Jane breezes round the kitchen like a coastal wind that impregnates the sails of ships with billowing and wild life. I've never met someone like her. She seems too good, too whole, too warm. I eye her through my narrowed eyes as she heads towards a cupboard to the right side of the sink. She finds the tea bags effortlessly and takes an ivy-patterned mug from another cupboard close to her. Anne comes back to life, returns from some dark place inside her mind that seemed to hold her hostage for a while.

'Sorry,' Anne stammers, rubbing her left wrist through her thin jumper. 'Jane is an old-old friend of mine. We lost touch but she used to keep me sane during the summers here when Jay was young. She lives next door.'

'Less of the old! We're sixty-six years young, thank you. Although those summers do seem like quite a while ago.'

'That's because they were. I hardly recognize us now.'

'Oh, don't be so ridiculous. You look just the same, whereas gravity has ravaged me. It's like everything's

138

migrating to the fucking grave and my breasts seem in the greatest rush.' She chuckles to herself then grimaces in horror. 'Oh shit, my mouth.'

I don't know if she's saying sorry for the swearing or for talking about graves. But either way it makes Anne laugh. Anne looks down at her own flat chest, her bony frame.

'At least you actually have something for gravity to work at.'

'Ha,' Jane scoffs. 'You've no idea how lucky you are. My bra puts up a daily fight and every day it loses. I don't know why I bother with the awful things.'

I cross my arms over my chest in case my breasts become the next topic of conversation.

'You're beautiful,' Jay was saying from our bed, his camera angled like a gun. 'Oh, stop it, Jay. Put it away.' He winked at me and said, 'Are you sure you mean the camera?' I covered up my chest with one bent arm and threw a pair of socks at him. 'Please, Em, just let me take a single shot. Then you can see what I see too.'

I unbury my right arm to take the coffee and the plate Jane's offering with its slice of raspberry-covered sponge. I dip my finger tentatively into the cream and suck the sweetness of vanilla from the tip. I sit with my own memory until an image suddenly intrudes, excludes all other thoughts. I can see Ben's back gently curled in the softness of some natural glow. An evening light is falling on the contours of his perfect flesh and his head is turned towards the camera, slightly coy. There's a glint inside his seal brown eyes as he stares straight at the lens.

My stomach growls in urgency and the image fades away. I feel hollow, empty, sick. I start to use my hands as if the cake was bread, break off great spongey chunks of it to fill the emptiness inside. I can't recall when I last ate, then pull a recollection from my mind of a dry and dusty sandwich filled with tasteless cheese and saltless spread from the trolley on the train as it hurtled over brown and barren fields somewhere close to Bristol. That sandwich feels like moons ago. I swallow down the sponge and my stomach gurgles its delight.

Jane stirs the tea bag in her tea with a patterned silver spoon that she's taken from a kitchen drawer, then smiles even wider as I stuff more cake into my mouth. I watch the sun stream in through the imperfect windowpanes and catch upon the particles of spinning dust which circulate around the room like small rotating planets.

'In the summer they'd be hers,' Anne says, nodding at Jane. I must look confused, my mouth still crammed with creamy cake. 'The raspberries,' she says. 'She grows them. Or she used to.'

'I still do,' says Jane. 'On the patch of land right at the top, behind this row of cottages. There's canes and canes of them up there in summertime. You'll be sick of them by then.'

I swallow down the soft sweet cake.

'Oh, no! I won't be staying long . . .'

Anne simply nods and Jane smiles wide. Jane's hair is grey and shot with lightning strikes of pure white and must reach well beyond her shoulder blades but is wrapped and bound up on her head in a tight and curving swirl like the inside spiral of a shell. There's a feather tucked into the side and I notice now the strands of hair that have escaped are dripping, soggy, falling damp. She sips her tea, taking her time and sees that I am looking at the wet ends of her hair.

'It's why I need the tea,' she says.

'Sorry?' I shake my head confused.

'She's just been for a swim,' says Anne.

'I usually bring tea with me in a flask but this morning I forgot.' She laughs. 'I forget a lot these days. Not that I'm old . . .' she quickly adds, which makes Anne smile.

I pretend to sip my coffee while the women chat of nothing and of everything. Jane's face is sun-stained in dark patches and gently creased around her eyes. At sixty-six she is the same age as my mother but she couldn't look more different. Her generous curves are stuffed inside a tight T-shirt that once was black and has faded to a well-washed grey, emblazoned with Metallica and Guns N' Roses logos. She wears baggy jeans and Birkenstocks and there are bangles, beads and rose quartz looped around her podgy wrists and a silver necklace hanging round her leathered neck.

'Is there a pool nearby?' I ask.

141

My mother keeps on telling me that exercise is good for me, especially now, especially since. Endorphins and all that.

'A pool? God! No!' Jane scoffs at that. 'I think there might be one somewhere. Saltash maybe? But the buses don't go often.'

'But you said that you'd been swimming.'

I watch a drip of water trail down a strand of lunar-hair and drip onto her T-shirt, the cotton soaking up the liquid.

'She has,' Anne proudly says. 'She's been swimming in the sea.'

'It's February,' I announce the obvious.

'Yes!' Jane says elated and laughs a wide and open laugh that animates her seasoned face.

I like her but she's clearly mad.

'Apparently it's nice,' Anne says, shrugging her shoulders.

'It is! The summer wimps are missing out. It's so much nicer than you'd think.'

As if to counteract her claim Jane shivers, wraps her hands around her steaming mug and hugs it close in a clear attempt to warm herself. Jane's bracelets slip down her goosebumped arm and reveal a tattoo of badly inked barbed wire. The green-black marking wraps around the soft part of her wrist and she catches the direction of my gaze.

'Oh that?' she laughs again. 'That one's a tad embarrassing.'

'They all are, Jane,' says Anne, who smiles.

'Fine,' says Jane, 'but that's the worst.' She turns to me. 'I became a tiny bit obsessed with *Bay Watch*.'

'In her forties!'

'Yes, okay. I wasn't all that young. But at least it was the series. The original. Not that dreadful movie featuring that vacant hunk of youth. Not that I'd say no.'

I can't help but smile too.

'But why get that?' I ask and point at the barbed wire.

'Pamela Anderson of course. I know it's not that feminist but I wanted to be just like her. She had this tattoo inked around her arm so I thought I'd get one too. Although in retrospect I probably should've thought some more.'

'I think it's called a midlife crisis,' Anne says.

'Midlife? Life-long more like,' Jane says. She rubs at the tattoo as if it may come off if she rubs it hard enough but the soft of flesh just moves around beneath her touch. 'You could come too?' she adds.

'Swimming?' I ask and laugh aghast. 'I'm terrible with cold.' I tuck my free arm back inside the safety of the blanket shawl, shuddering at the very thought of icy winter sea.

'It can help, you know,' she says. 'When things are hard.'

I look out of the window at the grey and weighty sky that's dense with clouds, watch a seagull swoop and almost graze the edges of a cottage chimney pot. The loss expands, compressing all my organs tight and emptying my lungs of air. I can almost smell the scent of him. Fresh soap and something close to cinnamon and freshly fallen autumn leaves.

'I really am so sorry, love,' Jane says to me.

'Jay came here with his camera. Anne said you must have

let him in. Was he with someone? And when exactly was that? Did you speak to him?'

Anne shakes her head.

'I can't do this,' she says loudly and puts her tea down on the table with a crash and walks out of the room, her head hung low.

The tea slips up and out the mug and puddles round the base.

'Let's not talk about this now,' says Jane. 'Another time. I promise.'

She grips my hand and squeezes hard. She reaches up behind her ear and takes the soggy feather from her hair to make a gift of it in lieu of words and explanations. I try to focus on the thing. To make it vast inside my mind in an attempt to overtake the thoughts of Jay.

The feather is bright white, the edges flicked with grey, and there is downy fluff along the base, the wetness clumping up the barbs into small and separate sections. I smooth out the individual strands to make it flat, pristine and new. And somewhere on the edge of things the sound of Jane who is saying that 'It's shit, it's awful, total shit.'

'It really is,' I finally say.

Orientation

'I'm sorry about earlier,' Anne says.

She waits while I bend down to tie the laces on my trainers that I've only ever used before for walking to the tube.

'It's fine,' I say. 'I understand.'

'Come on. I'll show you round.'

The wind outside the door is shocking. It is ionized and feral. A living, moving, solid thing that is lashing up the narrow lane. It catches in our hair and makes Anne's fan out wide, a mermaid's mane alive around her narrow face. For a moment her hair stays suspended, held up inside the whipping of the bitter wind. I wrap Jay's scarf around my neck, pull a bobble hat down low to keep my hair in place. Side by side we set off down the lane towards the centre of the village and the sea. The cold air makes it difficult to speak, it slashes at our words and so we walk mainly in silence.

The walk is slow, the details large. I try to think about

my journey to the tube and back in London, but I only find a softness and a blur. A gap inside my memory like I wasn't fully there. The specifics of the roads I walked, the things I passed, the colours and the characters of London are just out of reach or lost somewhere, fragments that I failed to catch inside the net of noticing. It's different here. Like all of life is Instagram and suddenly a filter's on demanding my attention.

'Are you really going to post that?' Jay was laughing as I photographed the Michelin-starred plate of food. 'I work in advertising, Jay. It's aspirational.' I scrolled through all the filters, chose a 'Hudson' tint. 'But does anybody care about your dinner? I mean, it really is delicious but . . .' I ignored him as he ate and changed my mind, chose 'Lark' instead.

I shudder at the very thought of checking Instagram right now. All those perfect shots of other people's perfect lives. Instead I keep my phone inside my pocket and try to focus on what's actually here. Small cottage doors, each painted in a different hue of bright despite the low of winter light, and metal key safes pinned to walls just waiting for the summer crowds. You can spot the homes of locals with their window ledges cluttered like small altars to the Gods of the Outside. There are offerings of perfect shells and vases crammed with oval stones and bottles full of sea-glass; a tumble of greens and browns and topaz blues.

At the bottom of the lane we turn and climb the steep

146

and curving hill. I can see the sea in glimpses through the back windows of cottages and every now and then the buildings break to leave a gap of stony wall or tiny square of garden lawn, like a tooth that's missing from a mouth, and the sea swells in to fill the hole; a small snapshot of water and of sky, framed on three sides by buildings and by land, that reaches up into the atmosphere of grey.

Anne leads me down a slender path onto the beach and suddenly the landscape fills with greyish sand and silvery sea. I can smell the salt and hear the restlessness of waves and the resistance of the granite rocks shot through with quartz. There is the constant churning sound of sand and stones and the loud and glorious crying of attention-hungry seagulls. But most of all I feel the sea. I feel it as an urgent urge, a pull that's deep inside of me, like a stomach that is hungry or a body lost in lust. I wonder if the water in my bloodstream and the saline of the sea have linked by sheer proximity and tied me to the winter tides.

'I'm heading back. It's freezing out,' Anne yells into the vast that is both beautiful and bleak. The wind catches at her words and carries them away.

'I'll be back soon,' I say, needing to stay.

There's a pushing and a pulling I can sense from all around that feels as if it's urging me towards the cold and salty edge.

Uncertainty

'It's just for a few days,' Anne says.

It is awkward at the table without Jane's warm energy and conversation. Between us sit two bowls of hot beef stew (at least we think it's beef) that someone in the village must have made for us and neither of us wants to eat. I thought people in the countryside could cook, but obviously not. We both play with our food, stirring absently with forks and spoons until the mashed potato marbles with the gloopy thick meat sauce.

'The solicitor in London needs to go over some things. I just want this whole divorce thing done. I'm sorry that I have to go.'

'Will you be all right? Going alone?' I ask.

She smiles with her tired eyes.

'I've been alone for years, Emma. I feel less alone than when I was living with Martin.'

I stare into the sticky stew and shred the strips of

simmered flesh with the sharp prongs of a fork. It's enough to make me vegan.

'And you?' she asks. 'Why don't you ask a friend to come and stay to keep you company?'

I think of all my friends whose lives I only follow now on Facebook and Instagram, their picture-perfect happiness too hard to face properly.

'I'll be fine here on my own,' I say.

But my stomach dips and dips and dives at just the thought.

I've no idea if that's the truth.

Hunger

I wake up, remember Anne has left and realize that I'm starving. My entire being is an empty space that food could fill. There is no Deliveroo here. No Uber Eats. No takeaway. It is breakfast but I want a vat of sickly Coke and a large burger crammed full of cheese and jalapeños with a side of spicy fries that you can only find in Five Guys, that are dusted so deliciously with salt and Cajun flavours. And maybe some of Jane's soft cake with raspberry jam and heaps of cream, and prawns sound good, and Weetabix that's sprinkled with a tablespoon of sugar and is floating like an island in a sea of ice-cold milk.

And that is when I start to cry. At Weetabix.

The final straw.

Weetabix

'Slow down,' Jude says. 'I can't hear what you're saying, Em.'

There is snot that's running from my nose and is muddling with the tears that are leaking from my eyes to form a gross and sticky mess. I shudder, heave, and try to speak through gasps of air and sobs of sounds that just keep slipping, sliding out.

'But . . . now . . . I've never liked before . . . now . . . Weetabix.'

I somehow find a way to place the words into the gaps between the sobs. My mobile phone is pressed against my head until it hurts the cartilage inside my ear and I clasp my knees up to my chest and hold them tight inside the grip of my left arm. The wooden cupboard doors are pressing up against my back. The cupboards with no cereal.

'Em, just breathe and try that all again. I can't hear what you're saying.'

'I want WEETABIX!' I wail to my sister down the phone and then I start to sob some more.

There is snot all up my jumper sleeve and mascara stains streaking the wool. My feet are sticking out of Jay's pyjama legs and are cold upon the tiled cottage floor. My toenails look like sinking suns, the orange polish that I wore before now growing out and chipping. Jude pauses for a while.

'Right.' She says the word slowed down and measured as if to give herself the time to understand the conversation. I can hear the patience of a practised mother in her calm and controlled voice. 'You need to explain more. I don't quite get it, Em. You're upset because of Weetabix?'

'Yes! Because I want it.'

My face is getting sore from where I'm rubbing hard repeatedly beneath my nose, above my lip, with the corner of my soggy sleeve.

'But why is that upsetting you?'

I start to calm now, listening to the gentle lilt and dip and dive of her familiar voice, like a beacon out at sea. I can hear myself a little more coherent, the spaces in between each sob allowing for more words.

'Because I hated it before,' I say.

'So?' she says. 'I love the stuff. You're allowed to like it too.'

'But I don't like Weetabix. I never have. You know that, Jude. And now I do!'

'Em, if you want to eat some Weetabix I would go and eat some Weetabix. It's only cereal,' she says.

'It's not. I don't know who I am right now. And there isn't any in the house.'

152

The sentence starts to rise up like the green parts of a building wave before it breaks and sounds just like a wail. I feel my face compress with heat and crumple up and crease again as the panic sets in again. There's a pause and then she whispers, 'Just a minute, Max,' to the son who I imagine is now clinging like a limpet to her legs.

'Em,' she says, 'just breathe. I know that this is difficult. I can imagine if Rob died that I wouldn't want to change at all. It's like moving on a little. And that must be immensely hard. But it's just a bowl of cereal. It's okay to like it now.'

Oh God, I'd never thought of that. And the green wave crashes down upon itself with the magnitude of its own weight and the pressure breaks itself apart to leave a white and frothing mess that is me sat on the kitchen floor.

Commute

Jude has to go but insists I try the meditation app that she downloaded on my phone for me. I open up 'Emergency Calm' and listen to a woman called Tamara spend three minutes trying to tell me how to breathe, as if I've never breathed before. Tamara is annoyingly composed and clearly isn't hungry. I'm supposed to watch my thoughts float by. I imagine a large sky with boxes filled with cereal instead of clouds. Giving up, I close the app and wash my face instead under the kitchen tap, which forces out a solid flow of silver water, needle cold.

I get a grip and make a plan. First I'll buy some cereal and then I'll go find Jane to ask her about Jay. I take a book off a shelf; a copy of *The Catcher in the Rye*. I read it once in school and pretended that I loved it. An older boy had told me it was 'life-changing'. I never actually asked him how it changed his life but I read the book and everything stayed just the same. Perhaps it will be useful now. The A4 photographs I crease and store inside the safety of the folds created by the stitched and threaded pages of the book. I take a tote I'd bought at Tate Modern and put the book inside the bag beside my wallet and a pair of slightly itchy woollen gloves that I would never wear in London.

Shore

The village shop is warm inside with tiny silver Cornish pixies in a shallow bowl beside the till. 'Lucky Pixies – Just £3' is written on a Post-it note and Sellotaped onto the side. The price of luck. If I'd only known, I would have saved the tip I gave to Brian in the cab.

'All right, love,' says the lady sitting at the counter on a stool.

She is large and round and almost glows. She looks as if she swallowed all of summer and stored it for the winter months. A light is coming off her cheeks, from off her curves and bulbous limbs. I gravitate towards her like a moth. I'm not sure what to say, the sudden thought of making small talk is exhausting and I don't know if 'All right, love' is a statement or a question or a straight hello.

'Do you have Weetabix?' I ask.

I can smell the pasties, sausage rolls, the scent of butter melted in a pan and gravy, meaty rich and strong. My hunger is now everything. It's eaten all my other thoughts.

'Just over there.' She smiles as she points towards a tiny shelf and goes back to her magazine, which appears to be a listing of the things to watch this week on ITV.

The shelf is packed with toilet rolls and toothpaste tubes, with tins of beans and bags of rice, some Marmite and some cereal. I sweep my eyes across the things and finally find the single box crammed in between two cans of tinned tomatoes and some Tampax. I grab it with a feral need and cradle it like treasure I have found.

At the till I dig my wallet from my bag in search of cash and find that I have none, just a few loose coins all dull and brown and random cards from London stores.

'Can I pay by card?' I ask, concerned.

I need to buy the Weetabix. But the lady at the counter warmly laughs as if the question is ridiculous. Her mirth sounds lighter than the air itself. I imagine it as a white balloon that rises, floats around the room and finally comes to rest beside the flour and the pasta on the very highest shelf.

'There's no reception here, love. No need to fret. Just pay me next time you have cash. I'll start a tab.'

'Oh . . . really? Are you sure? Is that okay? Thank you so much.'

I stumble over words as my fingers fumble through my bag in search of gloves and house keys, hungry, desperate to get back.

'I'm Emma, by the way,' I add, finding one glove but not the other.

'I know you are. You're staying at The Nook with Anne.'

So this is village life. I wonder for a moment if in London anyone who lives near me has even noticed that I've gone. The neighbours in the basement flat below might miss the sound of footsteps but not actually me. And the postman may have noticed that there's never any answer to his knock.

The thought is interrupted by the jingle ringing from a bell above the door as someone enters, trailing tendrils of the wind with them which swirl and dance around the place. I can hear the mournful whimpers of a dog left just outside.

'Good morning, Pete,' the orb of woman joyfully calls.

'Morning, Sue,' his gruff reply.

'Cold out today.'

'Sure is,' he says, his voice solemn.

He glances at me for a second, tips his head to say hello and heads towards the newspapers. There are streaks of white shot through his thin grey hair and a hint of sadness that hangs around him like a heavy coat.

'Well, thanks again,' I say and turn to leave while searching for the other glove that's still missing in the bottom of my bag. My fingers finally catch on empty woollen fingertips and as I pull the glove a photo falls from the book, unfolding like a butterfly in flight and coming to a gentle rest beside the old man's feet. He bends to pick the paper up. He groans a little as he stands again and rubs the muscles near his knees as if to rub some ache away. He slowly moves the photo in his hands, rotates the image round and round.

'You been photographing Porthlowal?' the old man says.

'No. Not me. Where's that?' I say.

'The next bay round, just down the lane. We're in a valley here so the next village is very close.'

'She's Emma,' Sue explains to Pete.

Sue sounds excited at the saying of my name, looks pleased at her own knowing. The creases that crisscross the old man's face crease further still and his eyebrows rise as his eyes meet mine.

'Jay's then?' he says.

I simply nod.

Jay's name is like the sudden incantation of a spell. It conjures worlds and fells them. It summons in an instant all the life I used to know, the man I loved, the man I lost, and leaves me suddenly untethered from the ties of earth. I start to float above myself, a dark and complicated mess that's tangled up and disappearing quickly out of sight. My body stands inside a shop. It's morning. I have Weetabix. But the rest of me is somewhere else. There's a ringing in my ears now and I start to drift into the dark of some immense and depthless night. A place that has no shining stars. No way to work out where is North.

Consciousness

'Emma! Wake up, Emma!' a woman calls, her voice all shrill and panicky and incredibly annoying. I wonder for a moment if my mother has appeared. I open my eyes and see two faces peering down, concerned. A round and ruddy woman who is clearly not my mother and a slightly crumpled aged man. Beyond them shop shelves rise like London buildings on both sides; the walls made up of bags of rice, Pot Noodle pots and tissues in square boxes. 'Emma!' the woman shouts my name a little louder. The faces swim, the focus moving in and out, my eyes a broken camera lens. I try to sit. The world wobbles for a while, then starts to settle, finally still. 'Are you okay?' the woman asks. She's flapping, flustered, floundering.

I recognize the face as Sue. It's Sue and Pete. I'm in the village shop.

'You fainted. You'll be fine,' Pete says, his steady voice horizon flat, without a hint of drama, as if he's seen it all before. 'Eat some of this.' He takes a Mars Bar from behind him off the shelf, unwraps it for me now with fingers deft despite his age. I notice all the flecks of paint across his hands, the colours of the sea embedded underneath short nails. The chocolate tastes like heaven must. I swallow it like star dust.

'I'm sorry,' I mumble through large sticky bites of Mars Bar.

'You gave us such a fright,' Sue says, her rosy cheeks more fully flushed.

'She's fine. These young ones just don't eat enough. Just look at her. She needs some feeding up.'

'I'm sorry,' I say again.

I'm mortified. Embarrassment is kicking in at the same speed as the sugar seeps into my bloodstream. I sit with my damp back against a shelf, an empty Mars Bar wrapper in my hand, the cereal box by my side.

'I'll take her home,' Pete says to Sue. 'And I'll call by Claire's and see if she can check on her.' He turns to me and says, 'You ready then?'

'Weetabix,' I say weakly, the only word that I can find.

Texture

'You need an arm?' Pete gruffly asks.

'Thank you but no. I'm feeling better now,' I say. 'There really is no need to come. I can make it home alone.'

'I know you can,' he says, not leaving me.

We slowly walk in silence down the lane back through the village, the sea now on the other side. The serious old man and me. As we pass a stone jetty Pete's pale Labrador bursts off towards the sea in large irregular leaps as if excited by the whipping of the wind and the demented movement of the waves.

'Iggy! Come back here right now!' Pete shouts towards the pounding swell, the dog entranced.

'Iggy?' I laugh. 'Like Iggy Pop?'

'Yes,' he says.

'Because he limps?' I ask.

'Perhaps,' he says and the corners of his mouth creep up a little at the edges.

Iggy lollops up the cobbled ramp at surprising speed despite his limp, his fur all dripping wet, and he shakes and joyfully vibrates the sea off himself, spraying cold water on us both. I laugh again at the hobbling dog's consuming joy. The droplets feel fresh and good upon my face and the sea wind blows and billows all around, moving energy and oxygen that makes me feel more awake. Less underwater. Less opaque.

'Do you paint?' I ask as we walk on.

'The wind!' Pete yells, pointing an arm towards his ear, my question lost inside the whip of air, and so we walk on up the lane in steady silence to the cottage with its blue front door, passing no one on the way.

Inside the narrow hallway the wind is left outside and there is silence and a solace.

'I won't come in,' Pete says, still standing on the doorstep.

'You're welcome to. Anne's had to go to London but I'm sure that she won't mind.'

Pete's forehead creases in a frown.

'The dog,' he says and gestures to the soggy canine by his side.

'Oh. Yes,' I say. 'Well, thank you once again.'

'I'll get Claire to come and check on you. She's our GP. You'll like her.'

I pull at woollen fingertips, removing both my gloves. Cupping my palms into a shallow bowl I blow as if to fill the hollow full of warmth. I take a breath, prepare myself.

'Jay's photo of the beach. Do you know anything about it?'

'December time,' Pete says, bending down, untangling Iggy from a loop of lead.

'I'm sorry?' I ask, my eyes widening.

'I saw him in December. Just before he died. He had his camera with him then.'

I stand stock still, as this new knowledge seeps to fill a crack inside my fractured mind. The fact that Jay was here just days before his death. Another fragment of the man I didn't know but thought I did.

I was wrestling with the twinkling lights that wrapped the Christmas tree like stars. The house smelt thick of forest walks and clouds pregnant with heavy snow. I could see myself reflected in the bauble that was hanging on a branch. I looked all stretched, distorted, strange across the curving blow of glass. 'I'll be back by Friday, Em,' Jay said and hung an icicle onto a branch I couldn't reach. 'The client needs some face-to-face. It's only for two days.'

'I . . . I . . . didn't know. I knew that he had been here but I didn't know exactly when,' I stutter. 'Where is Porthlowal again?'

'Well, I'm pretty sure that's where it's of. You can tell from all the rocks along the left-hand side. Porthlowal isn't far, it's the next bay round. You can walk it in ten minutes.' I take the box of Weetabix from out my bag, needing some-

164

thing, anything at all to hold. I hug the box into myself. 'If you carry on along the lane down past the shop. It's the beach in the next village.'

I hold my breath and count to three.

'When Jay was here, was he alone?'

Pete nods a 'yes'.

I exhale slowly in a way the lady from the meditation app would probably approve of. Pete looks down towards his dog who is calm now by his side, rubs the flop of velvet ear between his finger and his thumb and gently clears his throat.

'Take care,' he says, 'and make sure that you eat all that.'

He nods towards the box of Weetabix that I'm holding like a flimsy cardboard shield across my heart.

Kindness

'Emma dear, you fainted!' Jane just bustles in. 'Poor thing. Sit down. That's horrible.'

I've only been inside about five minutes and I've no idea how she already knows. News seems to travel faster than the wind round here. She smells of coffee beans and in the pink and silver tangle of her hair are five different patterned feathers sticking out at random angles. 'Oh, ignore the hair. I was bored and tried to dye it pink last night. I liked it on Rihanna but it doesn't really work on me.'

'It looks great,' I say. 'And honestly, I'm good now.'

'It's probably the Snow Moon. It can really mess with things. It's a very powerful moon, you know. You're not a Virgo, are you, love?'

I am saved from answering the question with something that I may regret by yet another knock at the front door.

'Oh good. She's here,' Jane says to me. 'Pete said he'd see if she was home.'

Jane goes to answer the front door and leaves me sitting

166

at the table, my gloves still clutched within one hand as if I'm gripping onto someone who has disappeared and left me only shadows of themselves in random bits of empty clothes. I feel slightly dizzy, woozy, sick now that I'm sitting inside the warmth of home. The women hug each other in a tight and close hello.

'Emma, this is Claire.'

Claire reaches up to touch Jane's hair.

'Don't ask,' says Jane.

'I didn't. Never said a word!' Claire laughs then turns to me. 'Hi, Emma. It's so nice to finally meet you. I'm the local doctor here.'

Claire is slim and dressed in yellow wellies with a heavy-duty raincoat which she hangs up on a wooden peg beside the door. The woollen hat she pulls from off her hair is furnished with a bobble made of different coloured strands just like the pom-poms that we made at primary school by wrapping yarn round cardboard rings. There is something in the way she moves, the way in which she wiggles off the wellies from her feet without using her hands and the colours of her day-bright clothes that reminds me of my sister.

'This is really kind of you,' I say. 'I'm fine, though. Honestly.'

My cheeks flush pink at the kind concern of strangers. But she just smiles wide and waves the words away into the air.

Claire dumps her heavy doctor's bag onto the kitchen

tabletop, takes out an ear thermometer, a stethoscope and pops a small white clip onto my fingertip which shows the beating of my heart.

'Right, let's take a look at you. So, you fainted in the shop then?'

She is serious and focused now while peering down the hollows of my ears. She makes no mention of the moon, which gives me some hope that she might have actually studied medicine.

'I guess,' I say.

'Have you fainted before now?'

'Only once, at school,' I say.

'Well, your obs seem fine and you haven't got a temperature.' She gently pulls the tired skin that sticks like bruises just below my eyes and seems satisfied with what she sees. 'You're very pale. You could be a bit anaemic but your eyes look good to me. When did you last eat?'

'I had some chocolate at the shop. But I haven't really eaten yet. I went there to buy breakfast.'

My cheeks have gone from pink to red. They're searing bright now, all alight. I'm horrified by all the fuss as I look down at my empty lap.

'Jane. Have you got some orange juice at yours?'

'Yes, loads,' says Jane.

'Would you mind just grabbing it for Emma?'

'I'll be right back.' Jane leaves looking immensely pleased that she can help.

The second that the door swings shut Claire turns to me.

'Emma, are you eating properly? I know you've been bereaved but you need proper meals.'

'I am,' I say. She tilts her head and looks at me intently. 'It was just today. I really wanted Weetabix for breakfast and there wasn't any here. Everything tastes different now.'

'And you feel well?' she asks.

'Of course not, no. But that's just grief. I saw a doctor back in London and he told me it was normal.'

Claire reaches out and gives my arm a friendly squeeze.

'It is,' she says slowly. 'But please do me a favour? Will you come up to the surgery after five one day next week and we'll register you here and run some simple tests? Just to give me peace of mind that nothing else is going on.'

'There really is no need,' I say.

'I'm sure you're right. But humour me? I promise that it won't take long.'

I sigh. She doesn't seem like someone who will take no for an answer.

'Fine,' I finally say. 'It will be a waste of time but if it means that you'll stop worrying.'

'It will,' Claire says. 'Thank you. Now take this too.'

'What's that?' Jane asks, walking back in with a large carton of orange juice from Asda. I had half expected something more organic or obscure here in the rural depths.

'A dinner invitation.' Claire deftly tears a mint green page from a small prescription pad and presses it inside my hand. I look to see that she has written a phone number and address in a script that's rounded, neat and clear.

169

'I know,' she laughs. 'A doctor who can actually write. That's my mobile and where we live. Come for dinner with us sometime soon? We've got three kids so as long as you don't mind chaos there is always loads of food.'

'Thank you so much,' I say, surprised by yet more kindness.

'I would love it if you came. It's not often we get new people here outside of summertime. I'll cook,' she adds.

'Oh God,' Jane laughs, her hands placed on her hips. 'Don't eat anything Claire cooks unless it's pasta. Or you'll really need a doctor.'

'My cooking's not that bad,' Claire says, pretending to be hurt. 'And at least I'll never ask about your horoscope.' She winks at me while packing up her things. 'So, let me guess, Jane reckons that the full moon made you faint?'

I smile at that.

'Yeah, yeah. When all the pregnant mothers in the county are in labour late tonight you won't be laughing then,' Jane says.

'Oh God, please no. Jake's got Scouts and Martha's friends are coming over to avoid doing their homework and tomorrow's just as bad. I could really use a good night's sleep.'

'Aren't the babies born in hospital round here?' I ask them both.

'Mostly,' Claire says. 'But the hospital's a drive away and the midwife team don't always make it here in time. So it's often left to me if I'm the closest.'

'Full moon!' Jane taunts.

'We'll see! Let's hope you're wrong.' Claire laughs and turns to leave.

'Thank you,' I call again as she slips her narrow feet back into sunshine-coloured wellies and wraps her coat around herself, stands to brace herself against the wind that is playing havoc in the lane. 'That was really kind of you,' I say.

Claire waves goodbye and as she walks away I notice that her hair is damp and dripping very slightly. Tiny droplets falling down her collar and trailing down her back.

Questions

'Jay,' I say. 'Pete said he came here before Christmas?'

Jane has dragged me home with her next door, is frying bacon for me in a pan. She takes two eggs from a wicker bowl and I notice that a tiny fluff of feather is sticking on the sides of one, a reminder of the chicken that's been left somewhere without an egg.

'I thought you knew.'

'No.'

I bite the frayed edge of the nail of my ring finger.

'He was here for a few days at the beginning of December.'

'Pete told me. That was just before . . .'

'I know,' she says.

I look up at the low-slung beams that span the ceiling of the room. They are hung with random pots and pans and onions and garlic bulbs and in between are bunches of dried herbs that flutter from the rafters like a fragrant kind of bunting.

'Oh love,' she says, turning a rasher in the pan with a pair of wooden chopsticks. 'Here, butter these.'

She passes me two pieces of warm toast, all golden brown, cooked just enough, and an oblong pack of salted butter wrapped in foil.

Jay was making marmalade on toast. Each slice of bread was toasted twice, singed just enough until each side was slightly black and the air was filled with morning smells: dark dust and melted butter, sweet oranges and shower soap. 'That toast will give you cancer,' I told him as he bit into a crunch of ash. He looked at me and laughed at that. The hilarity of the deadliness of toast.

'Did he say what he was doing here? Did he seem okay to you?' I ask.

'I wouldn't really know. I mean, we didn't chat that much. He seemed okay from what I saw. Bit quiet perhaps, but then maybe that was normal? I haven't seen him since he was a child. He was always chatty then. Forever jumping off sea walls and walking places, exploring with an old camera.'

'But what exactly was he doing here?' I ask again.

She cracks the eggs into a cup, attacks them with a whisk, throws in pepper and a generous pinch of salt. The egg falls mucous thick in jelly yellow strands between the stretch of metal prongs. She adds the eggs to butter in a pan, begins to stir them slowly in a looping swirl with a length of wooden spoon.

The motion of the movement throws me back in time. I remember Jude's soft arm inside the bathtub making swirling loops and soothing sweeps as I lie upon her bathroom floor, my husband dead, my heart scraped raw. I scrunch my eyes against the feeling that I'm back there now.

'I've no idea,' Jane says. 'He was only here for a short time but was out walking for most of it. I came to drop a cake round, but he didn't want to talk. Too much to do, he said, although he never did explain exactly what it was that he was doing.'

March

Wrong

'Sorry. I'm what?' I ask her to repeat herself.

The surgery is neat and bright and there are trees outside the window by Claire's desk. She softly says the words again, as if by lightening her tone she can lessen the deep impact of their meaning.

'You're pregnant, Emma.'

'No,' I say shaking my head, 'I'm not.'

I smile at her politely and fold my arms across my chest.

'The test says that you are, Emma,' she tries again.

'It's wrong,' I calmly say. 'It's just the shock of losing Jay.'

'Well, grief can manifest in lots of different ways. But you're pregnant too.' I shake my head. 'I really am sorry, Emma. This clearly isn't news you want.'

Claire is calm as lake water, all glossy still, professional and speaking very slowly.

'There's nothing to say sorry for,' I say brightly. 'I'm not pregnant. It isn't possible. I took the pill. I took it every single day.'

'I know this is an awful lot to take on board . . .'

'Your test is wrong. It's all a big mistake,' I say and simply shrug. Claire frowns and gently slides a box of man-sized tissues towards me. I reach out and slide them back again. 'I'm fine. I'm just not pregnant.'

I stand up to leave the room, collect my coat that's draped across a chair and wrap Jay's scarf around my neck again.

'Please, Emma. I can help,' she says. 'Why don't you come over tomorrow, when you've had some time to think, and we'll come up with a plan?'

'There's honestly no need. I've already told you that I'm fine. This is all a massive waste of time.'

I close the door behind me as I leave.

Claire is kind but she's incompetent.

Her stupid test is clearly wrong.

Tears

Claire might be right.

I'm standing in the bathroom in my underwear, staring at my stomach, my iPhone clasped inside my shaking hand. Perhaps there is an 'almost bump' that I hadn't even noticed. I Google 'contraceptive failure rates'. Outside are slanting rooftops made of chiselled Cornish slate that are peppered with small chimney pots and smoke that climbs in fluffy curls. Beyond the roofs a glimpse of sea, a streak of icy blue and grey that hangs suspended just below the winter sky. The tears I cry are quiet ones. They seem to seep from out of me.

I read somewhere that years ago people believed that human tears originated in the heart. They thought that when the heart weakened from sorrow or from sadness it would start to break apart and that the by-product was water. I wonder if they're partly right. Perhaps my heart is breaking, melting down and leaking out the corners of my eyes. I wonder if I cry enough my heart will finally

179

disappear, just dissipate, evaporate and leave me lifeless, less in pain.

An image on my phone appears of a bar graph with each type of contraception shown in a different block of colour. The bar that shows the pill is the dark purple of placenta and reaches wide across the graph to show a massive nine per cent. I read the words: 'Nine out of every 100 women using contraceptive pills as their only means of birth control become pregnant every year.' I scan the list of early signs of pregnancy: nausea, headaches, fatigue, a change in appetite, insomnia and disturbed sleep.

Things all so similar to grief.

Blue

I half-walk, half-run along the empty lanes back from the tiny pharmacy located in the next village, the test in my coat pocket. It's the same brand as the one at home that's hidden in my bedside drawer from all the many times before when Jay waited for the news I knew I wouldn't ever give him. I picture it still lying there beside the packs of paracetamol, the pens and scraps of paper, notes, postcards, old letters, a redundant Apple charger from before they changed the socket size (again) and, hidden at the very bottom, a month's prescription of the pill.

Jay was sitting at the kitchen table, an Asahi in one hand, his heavy head hung down. 'I'm so sorry, love,' he slowly said. The blue test lay between us on the table, the negative a secret battle line in a war where no one won each month. 'We still have time. We have more time,' I whispered to his crumpled form as I drank a swig of beer and tried to swallow down the guilt.

Back inside the quiet of the cottage I take the test out of the box and try to still my hands enough to read the folded-up instruction sheet despite the fact I've read the lines with Jay a hundred times before.

Pyjama legs and Marks & Spencer's comfy pants are puddled at my feet as I slouch back on the toilet seat and reach the test between my legs, my white and waxy crayon legs so slim they do not look like mine. I hold the test unsteady in the stream of piss which splashes, sprays all warm like human touch across my hand. I click the blue cap back in place and leave the test to rest upon the cistern ledge. A plastic offering placed high upon the most human of altars.

And then I wait. Two minutes. Time enough for seven hundred lightning strikes to strike the earth and ten earthquakes to shake the ground and my heart to beat two hundred beats. Two minutes that stretch out to feel like endless time as I sit pressed tight inside the space between the toilet and the sink, my back up against the wood-striped painted panel of the bath.

I push my thumbs into the hollow of my temples and rub the furrows of my forehead with the pads of clammy fingertips. Outside the bathroom window, a gull flies fast across the sky. I lean up and over, flick the metal handle of the window catch and push the pane of glass out wide. I breathe in deep as the bathroom fills with bitter cold and fresh sea air and the distant sound of winter swell that crashes on the shore.

And then it's time. And time stands still as I turn to see the lines on the pregnancy test are brilliant and blue.

And there are two.

A stark clear plus, a bright and blue addition sign, a human sized addition to my life.

No

I throw the test into the bin and push it to the bottom of the bag, then crumple up the cardboard box until it forms a small tight fist. I clear the search off my phone then sit and rip up the instructions into small then smaller pieces until I have a tiny pile of celebration-less confetti, each piece a fragment of the carefully printed truth in a range of different languages. I know the breaking of the words won't break the meaning of them too, but I find the act of shredding paper far more calming than the meditation app. It's almost on a par with rolling Blu-Tack.

I don't like babies, I never have.

I prefer shoes.

Jay always wanted children but the thought of being stuck at home like some archaic fifties housewife, changing nappies, washing baby clothes and singing boring nursery rhymes, just made me want to drink tequila. He had longed for it so badly that I couldn't bear another conversation about the pros and cons of babies versus Jimmy Choos. And so I lied.

I pretended we were trying while I carried on taking the pill. Jay lied about a lot of things but I lied too.

He would have been ecstatic at the test result. He would have grinned and kissed me firmly on the lips and squeezed me tight and maybe even cried a bit. At least I think that's what he would have done. Perhaps he wanted Ben more than he wanted this. The thoughts all start to spiral, loop and tangle up inside my mind, like the writings of a madman. Illegible, chaotic swirls.

I cannot face another thing to think about right now.

This is too much. I will not think.

Parents

The light that throws itself across the wall moves gradually throughout the day until the sun begins to sink and disappear behind the solid bank of cottages and spindly trees, just leaving shadows, shapes and shade. I'm still in bed trying my hardest not to think, which is much harder than I'd hoped. My mobile begins to ring. I'm still ignoring all my friends and so I go to turn it onto silent but see that it is Dad.

'Hey,' I say. 'Where are you, Dad?'

'At home. I'm working in the London office for the week,' he says. 'How's it all going, love? Are you okay? You promised that you'd call us every day and your mum says that she hasn't heard from you. Is everything all right?'

'I'm sorry, Dad. I'm fine. I've just been busy and the phone reception isn't great. Unless I'm in my room upstairs it's hard to get good signal here.'

I look around the bedroom, at the crumpled sheets, discarded socks and underwear and glasses dumped about the place with their different water levels and a room-cold cup of herbal tea that I made and found I hated still. I think about how much I must have worried my whole family as I stare at a slice of toast from yesterday that lies abandoned on a plate and is curling at the edges like a misplaced autumn leaf. I really should clean up before Anne sees this place.

My dad keeps asking questions, attempting to engage me in a conversation about the things that mattered once. He talks about the football scores, his Hong Kong trip next week, a new lawnmower that he read about in this month's *Which?* that he wants to buy for summer. I listen to the blur of sound as he chatters on and chatters on.

I imagine my stressed mother pressed up tight against his shoulder on the sofa, her breath held taut, collecting up my words for them to dissect together later. Some sort of diatribe about coping and not coping and the mistake I'm making being here. Imagine if they knew it all. I can almost hear my mother's brain implode in horror. A glorious squelching gory bang.

'I dunno. I guess I'm walking lots. It's beautiful round here. And I've been reading heaps.'

I look at the unopened books, a Jenga stack of ignored words beside the bed.

'You sure?'

'I'm sure, Dad, yes. I promise I'm okay. I'm sorry, Dad, I'm fine, Dad, fine. I really am. There's no need for you to worry.'

I hear a rustle on the line as my mother grabs the phone off Dad.

'Of course I need to worry! You don't answer. You don't call me. There must be a landline there at least.'

'Fine,' I say, sighing loud enough for her to hear. 'You can have the phone number if it will make you happy. Just don't go calling all the time.'

She scribbles down the number as I say it.

'Are you sure this is the number, Em?' she asks, sounding suspicious.

I hang up the mobile, call her back on the house phone.

'Happy now?' I ask, but she doesn't answer that.

'I've been reading up about this stuff. It's a very bad idea,' she says instead.

'What is?' I ask.

'You taking off to Cornwall by yourself. It clearly says in every book to avoid all major life decisions in the first year. The first year after . . . all of this.'

She stumbles with the saying of the thing, adjusts her sentence so she doesn't have to mention 'suicide' out loud. Like 'Voldemort', the word remains unmentionable. Instead she often says that we have all 'lost' Jay. I remind her that Jay isn't lost. For once I know exactly where he is.

'At least my major life decision involves me breathing still.'

'Oh, Emma. Don't say things like that.'

'There's someone at the door,' I lie. 'I'm sorry but I have to go.'

Then I stay there seated on the sofa in the dark, feeling sorry for my mother, feeling guilty for the things I always seem to say to her. Just her. I sit there waiting for the warmth to leach out of my phone, remembering my mother's hand from childhood. A hand that stayed forever warm and steadfastly in mine.

Denial

Sunshine warms the room with burnished light, all blazing yellow winter bright and wakes me in the morning. It compels me up and out of bed as if I'm tied into the weather now. The local radio plays upbeat tunes that no one young would actually know, all interspersed with local ads for farm shops and a florist. Something by U2 comes on that almost makes me sing along. The music conjures up the image of my dad with stacks of CDs sorted into racks and reminds me of a different time, this soundtrack of my younger self, a person with a looser breath and lighter step.

Anne comes back today and so I make the bed, plumping all the pillows as my mother would, shake the duvet from the corners until the surface is all smooth and neat and almost flat. My arms ache with the effort of the lifting; the surprising weight of feathers stripped of flight. The window catch is metal, old and painted thick and the swollen wood sticks to itself as I try to fling it open. I make a fist and bang against the wooden edges of the window until it finally gives and flies out wide into outside. The room fills fast with cold crisp air and wipes the scent of sleeping flesh and stagnant lung-recycled air as I rub the deep ache from my fist.

In the kitchen sink I balance all the dirty cups and crumb-laced plates. There's a comfort in the washing up. A calm in the normality. I stand and run hot water, place my face over the rising steam, watch the Fairy Liquid start to froth, the bubbles more abundant than in London, a place where everything, even the water from the taps, runs hard and unforgiving. I wash and rinse, I wash and rinse, I wash and rinse until it's done, finding contentment buried in the rhythm of the task. I dig out the brand-new wellies and stare into the dark spaces that await some feet. The wellies feel strange, all wide and loose, and they make a sort of flapping sound as I try them out inside on wooden floors. I take a photo of my feet and send it to my sister.

'Should I call The Priory?' she texts straight back.

'Oh come on, Em, let's get the train, get out of here?' Jay was holding up a rucksack and a Thermos flask I didn't even know we owned. 'We can go on a long walk somewhere. Somewhere quiet, free of people.' He winked at me with naughty eyes. I groaned at just the thought of damp and rotting leaves and sodden fields and muddy stiles. 'Can't we walk along the South Bank? Do a gallery instead?'

191

The cupboard space that's tucked beneath the stairs is reminiscent of an Oxfam shop in some small provincial town. 'Just help yourself,' Anne said when I first came, so I rummage through the random things that seem to be essential for someone living by the sea. There are musty picnic blankets, spare light bulbs, a hammer and some nails, a basket made of fraying straw, three waxy coats, umbrellas and an old and battered rucksack. I take the rucksack out. It has leather clasps that work just like the buckle on a belt and I fiddle them undone, then fill the bag with chocolate bars, my mobile phone, a water bottle and *The Catcher in the Rye* containing just the photograph that Pete believes is Porthlowal.

Outside the wind has dropped. The morning air is fresh and seaside cold and smells of wood smoke that is curling like calligraphy from chimney pots and drifting through the empty village lanes. The sun is out, the sky is bright. It makes me blink, my eyes adjusted to the blunted light that gathers thick inside the cottage walls. There are seagulls sitting on the rooftops and a cat that winds its way along the granite edges of a stone gutter that runs in gentle angles down a slope towards the sea.

I walk down through the village, past the numerous empty cottages locked up for all of winter. The real homes have curtains pulled apart to let in the morning light and I catch small glimpses of the people living life inside, the windows framing this small moment in their morning. I pass a boy sat on a sofa, his guitar balanced between his knees, teen-fingers stretched over the strings in search of chords, and a couple eating toast each lost inside their separate readings of the morning's news. Small snapshots of how life goes on. A little further down the lane I see a mother with a baby. I stop and stare.

The woman clearly needs an intervention of some kind. A large group of professionals who can offer help and gently let her know that she has lost herself. I carry on just watching through the front window. The infant is wedged into a wipe-clean seat and grasping at a tiny orange plastic spoon while the woman cajoles mushed food into its mouth with awful mimicked gapes and a strange contorted-munching face.

I glance down at my stomach and wonder if ignoring something hard enough can make it simply go away.

Twins

Porthlowal looks familiar, so similar to the village that I stay in now, as if they form two architectural twins sat side by side, cross-legged in the narrow valley on the coast. The cottages are painted in the same palette of soft sea shades; all white and cream and pastel hues with small adverts for rental websites in the windows and sills crammed with hand-made wooden boats and tiny painted lighthouses and cowries filling old jam jars. The only difference here is the presence of a pub called the Anchor Inn that sits above the curve of beach, its windows looking out towards the sea, and rocks in strips upon the shore below a set of steep concrete steps that unravel down towards the beach.

I grab the metal rail, my knuckles bleaching with the tension of the grasp as my wellies slap against my calves. I descend the sea-washed concrete steps. The sand is dry above the high-tide mark and I unwrap my woollen scarf, spread it out to make a blanket strip of knitted purls across the floor. Around me there are smooth and pleasing driftwood nubs, small feathers, coloured plastic rubbish flecks and scatterings of sea-rubbed glass. My knees fan wide across the sand like seagull wings as I open the old rucksack, remove a Twix, devour it. It feels good to sit here on the beach collecting sunlight with my face. Without the wind it's almost warm, the sun making a subtle nod towards the fact that winter isn't always here.

Beyond the beach the sea sprawls huge. It floods towards forever, the water stretching far away, shocking in its difference. It is not the same as yesterday or days before. The water is less angry now and the grey contains more blue. I watch the waves smoothed out to gentle bows which hurry up the shore in nervous arcs, retreat again, the line between the land and sea an ever-moving thing that blurs and bends and fluctuates with time.

I go to take the photo from the bag, to scrutinize the picture and work out why Jay came here.

I'm actually pregnant. Fuck.

Not thinking isn't working. I can hear the metronome of my own blood and feel the nausea fortify as I screw the photograph up small inside my hand, compress it tight into a ball of pixelated rocks and minerals that have weathered over time into fine fragments of almost nothing that are picked and moved with every tide, so small they have no choice but to submit. The image of the blue front door took me all the way to Cornwall. But now I'm here and sand is sand and sea is sea and sky is sky. There's no red string that leads from here, no massive revelation. This photo doesn't tell me anything at all except that Jay photographed the sunrise or the sunset from the place where I am sitting now. I hang my head, fixating on the sand between my legs which is interspersed with smashed and battered fragments of what once were shells.

Panic

Iggy lollop-bounds across the beach to me. He levers at my chin with his wet nose forcing my head, urging it up. He runs in circles round and round the scarf that forms a makeshift blanket on the sand and attempts to push his muzzle deep inside my bag in search of snacks. I gently push Iggy away, pretty sure that chocolate kills or makes dogs sick. I'm not quite sure. I've never had a dog. I can hear my mother now: 'Just think of the germs and all that moulting hair.' Iggy starts to lick my hand and I let him. I let his germ-filled slobber coat my fingers. The dog bows low and collects the scrunched-up photograph inside his grip of teeth, holds it for a while in his mouth as if determining its worth and drops it back, saliva soaked.

'It's not a ball,' I tell the dog. 'It isn't anything at all.'

I scan the beach looking for Pete but there is no one here except for me. We sit awhile, Iggy and I, waiting for Pete to come and join his dog. I listen for the crunch of footsteps in the grainy sand, I listen for a beckoning call. But it doesn't come and then I see. A pile of clothes; loose corduroys sprayed with different coloured paints, an over-sized brown jumper and a pair of boots, grey socks stuffed in, all folded neat and left beside a large flat rock, abandoned next to a drawstring duffle bag. I think about the quiet man who seemed so solemn and so sad and start to run across the sand.

I am standing at the shoreline, Pete's clothes clutched in my shaking hands. There's the giant swathe of water but no one out there, only sea.

'Pete!' I shout and Iggy starts to bark and limp faster along the shore, propelled to noise by the panic hooked inside my voice.

I look back towards the pub behind with lights switched off and shutters closed. There's no one here to help but me.

The sea is heavy, pressing dense against my legs. Soon the water reaches up and spills over the lip of rubber boots and floods the hollow spaces round my feet with arctic cold. Iggy thinks this is a game. He rushes to the gentle waves and barks as they attack, retreat, clearly amused. I stand there rooted to the spot.

'Oh please God, no,' I whisper to myself.

I stand for frozen time inside the shallows, my feet weighed down with water and the horror of another loss until Iggy's barks become louder still and he starts to run in gallops, moving fast between the shore and me.

At first it's just a shadow in the water, a shape caught on the edges of my sight that comes and goes from view in time with gently rising, falling waves. I strain my eyes against the sun and focus on the moving thing. I swallow my stupidity as Pete slowly appears. A head at first, a crest of wave, a swimming man, his grey hair mingling with the colour of the sea as he swims towards the shore with calm and even strokes. I take large backwards steps out of the surf and sink down onto the damp sand, his clothes still clasped inside my arms, my heart still shaking in my ribs. Iggy keeps on running, continuing to play his game against the sea as we wait for Pete who is swimming back towards the shore like something from a movie.

Freeze

He's no James Bond. I've never seen a body quite as old before. Pete stumbles on a shallow rock and staggers out of the water in his trunks, his skin all red, ablaze with cold, some seaweed and a grin on him. He's tall and slim but the tissue that was once held firm across his chest is hanging slightly loose round him as if the muscles of his body no longer have the same resolve to grip themselves onto his frame.

'Thanks for grabbing those.' He nods down at his clothes that I am clutching rigid in my arms. 'Did you find the towel by any chance? It's in the bag.'

I shake my head, still lost inside the shock of losing him and finding him.

'Were you shouting earlier?' he asks. 'It's hard to hear out there.'

He shakes his head from side to side, tips his whole side down towards the right and with his flattened palm attempts to knock the sea from out his ear.

'I couldn't see you in the water,' I whisper as I look down at the speckled sand beneath my feet and try to slow my breathing.

There is silence save the sound of water pulling at the beach, enticing sand away from land and the gentle panting of Iggy who lies calm and still, exhausted by my side.

'Ahhh. I see,' he finally says. Pete walks towards the slope of granite rock and takes a faded towel from out his bag. He wraps it tight around his torso, tucks the corner in to form a makeshift skirt like David Beckham in the nineties. I follow silent with his clothes and, shaking, offer up the jumper first, which he slips over his still-damp head. 'I didn't mean to frighten you,' he says. 'We swim here every single day throughout the year. I'm usually here with Jane and Claire.'

'Claire does this too? You all do this? You're mad,' I say.

But he's clearly heard that one before and smiles like he knows some sort of secret that I don't.

'Maybe,' says Pete. 'Perhaps that's true.'

He's clothed now, quick, well versed and nimble at re-dressing, layering himself inside the warmth that fabric gives. He comes to join me on the strip of scarf and rubs at patches of his hair with the well-used towel. The towel against his hair sounds like a pencil being sharpened, the shavings curling off with each rotating crunch of spinning wood. The worst of all the wet now gone, he slots his head inside a woollen beanie that's lined with something soft.

'It just looks horrible,' I say. 'Why would you do this to yourself?'

My feet are numb inside my rockpool boots. I pull the wellies off and tip the water out.

'We have our different reasons,' Pete says, passing me his towel and pulling a spare pair of dry socks from his bag.

'What's yours?' I ask. 'It just looks painful. And sadistic.'

'It's the opposite,' he says. He stares out across the water as he speaks, his eyes lost to the ocean. He feels so far away from here, still swimming somewhere out at sea. It's as if the calmness of the flat horizon has pervaded him. 'The cold, well, you get used to that. It's not so bad. But the feeling you get afterwards. It stays with you. It's something that is hard to put into words.'

I nod in understanding of his struggle to find words. I think of all the feelings, facts, the huge and incommunicable chasms in my life that sentences won't satisfy. The darkness I've been left without a language to explain.

Pete smiles to himself, his hand fumbling inside his bag. 'It's important to get warm quickly,' he finally says. 'After a swim is actually most dangerous.'

'Really?' I ask. 'But why?'

I try to focus only on the moment that is this. To just listen to the words he says.

'Your body isn't coldest in the water. Just when you think it's over and you're safe and dry on land, inside your core keeps cooling down. It's called the Afterdrop. It's why us swimmers wrap up fast, have tea on standby in our bags.'

He digs again inside his bag and finds his flask, unscrews

the lid and pours in the steaming liquid. He cups the lid with both his hands, holds his face over the steam which rises up into his gaze. I wonder for a moment if we're feeling the same thing, if I'm also in an afterdrop, an all-engulfing freeze of grief.

'That sounds horrible. Why would you do something that makes you feel awful?' I say.

Pete laughs.

'Well, the Afterdrop, it doesn't last for very long. And then the feeling that comes afterwards . . . Well, it makes it all worthwhile.'

Reasons

'What's this?' Pete picks up the soggy scrunched-up mess that is the picture of the sand and tries to press it flat against his skinny thigh. He rubs the paper almost flush but the shadows of deep wrinkles still remain among the wet. 'This the picture that you dropped inside the shop?'

I nod a 'yes'. Close by a seagull lands, its feathers still stained brown with youth. The eyes glitch fast and flicker in their shallow skull-sockets.

'Jay's photo of the beach,' he says.

At the saying of Jay's name, the memories of our life together rise to form a sudden threat to breathing, being, staying calm.

I was queueing with a Diet Coke and a salad from the cold aisle. A man was standing just behind me unloading fresh ingredients: bright carrots, chicken breasts and cream. I glanced at him and our gazes caught and set alight. He pointed at my shopping with a bunch of tarragon and while grinning said, 'Please tell me that's not dinner?' 'Are you offering to cook for me?' I asked and a fire spark ignited in my hungry heart.

I push the memory back into a box inside my mind.

'Well, I stand by what I said,' says Pete. 'I still reckon that he took it here. Look at that rock formation over there.'

He plunges his large hand into the sand, lifts a pile of the stuff up high into the air and lets the grains fall down and trickle through his fingers which he holds splayed wide to form a home-made hourglass where time falls through at different speeds.

'I don't know what it means,' I say.

'Why should it have a meaning? It's a sunrise on a beach. The sun sets here behind that hill.'

I look behind me at the land with its forest full of leafless trees, dark pen sketches of curving wood and sweeps of grass and empty fields of furrowed brown.

'Because I need it to. He didn't photograph like this. And he wouldn't leave me here with nothing.'

Pete doesn't say a word, just sits beside me watching the close ripple of the waves and soaking up the interlude of winter sun while rubbing gently at the belly of his dog.

'I paint,' he finally says.

'I guessed,' I say and smile, point out his paint-encrusted clothes.

'Sometimes the feelings in my paintings, they are obvious. I'm mad and paint a stormy sky. I feel content and paint a calm and peaceful sea. But it usually isn't quite as simple as all that. Sometimes I don't know what I'm feeling 'til I'm finished with the thing. And it might not be the thing I'm painting that holds meaning, but just the way I've painted it.'

'So you're saying that the subject might not be the most important thing.'

'It might. Or it might not.'

'That really isn't any help at all,' I say and Pete just laughs.

I shake my head and try to think of something else to say. Pete fills the flask lid with more tea while Iggy rolls his rotund flank, rotating it towards the sun, and one large ear falls velvety across closed eyes. I'm jealous of his gentle calm and simple canine dreams. The seagull sees the movement of the dog and jilts its wings out wide and lurches off into the safety of the sky.

'What's your reason then? You said the three of you have reasons why you swim throughout the winter. Can I ask what's yours?' There's a subtle flinch, a sudden flash of pain across his face as if he stubbed his toe but is trying not to let it show. 'Sorry,' I quickly say. 'I didn't mean to pry.'

'Four minutes . . .' he replies. 'The time it takes to fall in love.' He keeps his eyes horizon-locked while talking. 'Some scientist, he proved it back in ninety-seven. I remember reading all about it in the papers at the time. If you stare into the eyes of another human being it only takes four minutes to fall in love with them. And Evie and I, we've had whole years. Forty-six whole years. That's an awful lot of minutes.' He pauses, looks towards his dog. 'But there never are enough.' Pete shakes his head from side to side and hides his knuckles deep in Iggy's fur. 'My Evie, she has Alzheimer's. She can't remember all the minutes that we had together. But they were good. So very good.'

'I'm really sorry, Pete.'

He waves the words away, not looking for my sympathy.

'So I swim because the feeling that comes afterwards, it helps me cope.'

'But what about the cold?' I ask, my feet still aching in dry socks.

'Well, in the cold my mind shuts down and there is only swimming and the sea and that briefly lets me forget too. If only for four minutes at a time.'

Agitated

Four minutes feels like forever when all that you can hear are irritating sniffs and stifled sobs. Anne is back from London and crying in her bedroom, trying hard not to be heard. I feel irrationally annoyed with her, which could be due to hunger or to hormones from the thing I am not thinking of. I dial Ben again but the phone goes straight to voicemail. Headphones help to block out Anne, but even my favourite songs I find I have no patience for right now. I skip through tracks and shuffle through the photographs while my thoughts jump haphazardly around. They move from Jay to Ben and then to babies and then back again. A messy triangle.

I don't want to think, but despite all of my efforts, not thinking is impossible. I consider calling Jude and telling her I'm pregnant, but I know exactly what she'll say. She's always wanted nephews and nieces and apparently Rob's sister's kids don't count because they live in San Francisco. 'This way I'll get to have another baby,' was what she always said to me, 'but without the pregnancy or sleepless nights or any of the bad bits.' I would remind her that her own vagina had almost split in two but apparently that's what she'd been referring to as 'bad bits' and it was my vagina's turn to 'take one for the team'. She will be overjoyed, completely thrilled and will say nothing that I want to hear. Calling Jude is not an option.

I'm doing Kegels without meaning to and I'm definitely hungry and in need of company that doesn't need consoling. Creeping down the stairs I grab a coat, close the cottage door behind me and find myself walking to Claire's. Outside the dark turns out not to be dark at all but moonlight bright, a glowing matt and starry black. The sky is like the backdrop of a set scattered with gunshot wounds which let the stage lights shine right through. I can see my cloudy breath, the road beneath my feet, the cottages each side as I walk the hill while holding tight a bottle of red wine by the thickness of its long glass neck. I found the bottle in a cupboard in the kitchen with some brandy, sherry, old sloe-gin. I hope it's meant for drinking and that Anne won't mind. Not that I really care.

Chaos

'Who are you?' A boy aged three or four opens the door. He is wearing green pyjamas with tiny, printed dinosaurs which roam across the undulating landscape of his small and moving limbs. There are bright red furry socks on little feet and a Harry Potter cape that's fastened at his neck with Velcro tabs and in his hand, clasped tight like special treasure, is a large round ball of hard Blu-Tack. He doesn't wait for me to answer, just looks me up and down and scrunches up his bright brown eyes. 'Are you Gryffindor or Ravenclaw or Slytherin? We can't be Hufflepuff,' he says.

'Why not?' I ask.

'Because my brother says I'm not allowed.'

'I'm Slytherin,' I darkly say. 'But your brother's wrong. You're definitely Hufflepuff. I know these things.' I wink. He grins at me, a large wide grin.

'Did you bring something for me?' he asks and points towards the wine.

'I'm sorry. No, it's for your mum. But I have a lot of Blu-

Tack in my drawer. I can bring you some. Is your mum home?'

'Yes,' he says and yells out 'Mum' with endless m's. 'But I'm Otis. Just don't forget. Make sure you bring a gift for me and not for Jake next time.'

'Is Jake your brother then?'

'Oh, Emma, come! Come in! I'm glad you're here. I didn't even hear the door. I'm sorry about the chaos.'

Claire is calling out the words while rushing fast towards us both, rubbing palms and backs of hands across a limp and damp tea-towel.

'I can go,' I say. 'I just wanted to apologize and give you this.'

I hold out the bottle of dubious wine.

'Don't be silly. This is normal here and there's nothing to say sorry for. You really didn't need to bring me wine,' she says, grabbing the bottle from my hand with lightning speed. 'But I won't say no.' Otis looks bored and spins on red-socked toes and runs away and up the flight of wooden stairs. I hear his flattened feet making contact with the floorboards overhead, his footsteps louder than a man's, so self-assured and unapologetic in his youth. 'There's loads of food for dinner. Come on, come in,' Claire says again as the smell of good lasagne reaches my nose, all comfort, cheese and earthy meat, and I relent.

She leads me down the narrow hall with walls lined thick with family photographs of babies, weddings, holidays and out into a kitchen at the back. There's an Aga in the corner and school trousers drying on a complicated metal rack. The fridge is covered with bright sugar paper, each different coloured piece adorned with scribbles, drawings, googly eyes, potato prints in poster paints. They're clamped onto the door with magnets of the alphabet that form short words like 'bum' and 'poo'.

'I'm not sure if it's any good.'

'It's wine,' she says. 'It's great.'

Upstairs there's suddenly the sound of yelling and a heavy wooden door slams shut.

'MUMMMM. He's doing it again. I'm going to kill you, Jake!' a girl screams loud across the house. Claire stills herself and stands and waits, her lungs stopped full of air to listen for the killing part that doesn't ever actually come. She lets the air back out her mouth, a long slow stream of tired breath.

'That's Martha, she's thirteen,' Claire says by way of explanation. 'And then there's Jake, he's nine. They drive each other mad. And you met Otis at the door. I warned you it was mayhem here.' She deftly pulls the cork out of the bottle, takes a tumbler meant for water from the cupboard by the fridge and pours herself a giant glass without offering me any. She takes a hefty swig and sighs, sets it back down.

'Now, what can I get you?' she says.

I look longingly towards the wine and ask her for a vodka but she only laughs despite the fact that I wasn't actually joking.

Family

The bathroom mirror stares right back, confronts my gaze, offers no help. This was a terrible idea. I can hear the family round the table, the clink of cutlery and laughter and the constant bubbling chat of kids. Occasionally I hear Claire's voice and her husband's low deep tones bleed through. A family with a father. I do not even know them here, they are not friends, they've no idea. The effort of pretending to be normal is at once immense. Beads of sweat are forming on my forehead, underneath my arms and up my back.

'Fuck you,' I say into the uselessness of mirror glass.

'I'm sorry. I'm not feeling good. I need to go,' I tell the room.

The unrelenting heat is pouring from the Aga and the room is absolutely stifling. I grab my coat and hold it in my hand. The family stop their chatter, stare. All except for Otis who just carries on attacking his lasagne with a small blunt knife.

'You're mine,' he mutters to his food, his eyes intense.

'Are you okay?' says Claire, looking concerned. 'Let's get you home. You're very flushed. I'll walk you back.'

The children start to talk again and carry on their conversation as I grovel my apologies and Claire digs out some Tupperware just in case I'm hungry later.

'I hope you feel better soon,' Claire's husband Mike calls cheerfully as we head towards the door.

I almost want to laugh at that. I'm pregnant and my husband's dead and no one gave me any wine which means it isn't very likely.

Night

'I'll be okay. I'm fine alone,' I say to Claire outside the door, the shock of air a sharp relief. She ignores me, slides her arms into her coat and makes a loop with her bent arm and threads mine through to link us two as Jude would do.

'Are you kidding me?' she says. 'You've met my lot! We'll have to walk quite slowly, though. That way Mike might actually wrestle Otis into bed for once, although I seriously doubt it. And anyway, I'll feel better knowing that you're safe at home.'

'I'm so sorry about dinner,' I say again. 'It really was delicious. Jane was wrong that you can't cook.'

'No, she's absolutely right. Mike cooked tonight, he usually does. And please stop saying sorry. There is absolutely nothing to say sorry for.' We walk in easy silence for a while, the only sound our feet meeting the concrete of the lane, our footsteps perfectly in time. 'How are you doing, though? Are you okay? I've been thinking about you.'

'I . . . I took another test and now . . . I don't know how I feel.'

I unwrap Jay's scarf and bundle it a little tighter round my neck.

'Of course you don't. It's a huge thing to take in. I'd used heaps of ovulation sticks with those stupid smiley faces and I'd lie there with my legs up after sex each time. Even then, finding out that I was pregnant still came as a shock, which is ridiculous.'

We're both quiet. Both thinking our own thoughts.

'I'm not sure what to do,' I say after a while, our arms still linked.

'That's up to you. You have options.'

'I don't even know how many weeks pregnant I am.'

'Then let me arrange a dating scan. Please at least let me do that?' I nod a 'yes'. 'Emma, this would all be hard enough if you weren't also grieving too. Have you talked to anybody yet about Jay's suicide?'

'No.' I shake my head. 'I can't. There are no words.' Claire grips me tighter with her arm. 'And I keep on messing up,' I say.

'What do you mean?'

'Well, I thought that Pete, I thought that he'd . . .'

She laughs a soft and friendly laugh.

'I did hear all about that, but I think that he was mostly

flattered that you cared. He said how much he liked your company.'

'I'm awful company!'

'You're not. You're really not. You're great and you don't need to be okay for us. We're quite an understanding bunch. And everyone has something going on.'

I think of Pete, his wife still here but somewhere else, now lost to him.

'Pete told me that his wife has Alzheimer's.'

'I wondered if he'd told you. Yes, she's not in a good way. There's a carer living with them now but I don't know just how long that's tenable. It's an awful strain on him. But I'm glad he talked to you. He isn't one for saying much.'

'He said the swimming helps.'

'It really does. It helps us all!' She laughs slightly hysterically.

'Pete was telling me about the cold. He said that he forgets for a few moments when he swims.'

'It doesn't work that way for me. I don't forget. But it changes how I see things. I spend so many hours of each day stuck inside the surgery or the house. The swimming keeps me tied to the outside, reminds me just how small I am. And conquering cold water makes me feel like I'm Superwoman. Well, if Superwoman was a working mum with bad stretch marks and a pretty hefty mortgage. Either way, it makes me feel great.'

I can't remember feeling great. I can't imagine how that feels now.

As we head towards The Nook's front door we can hear the sea connecting with the shore down on the beach. The tick-tock move of sea and sand as time moves on regardless.

Claustrophobia

The waiting room is hideous. It is hot and dense with sounds and air that's almost tangible and thick to touch. It's windowless and full of pregnant women, babies, screaming toddlers and men who all look nervous, bored or revoltingly in love. I stare at all the men. Jay suddenly looms large in his vast absence as a wave of grief swallows me down and tumbles me around before it spits me back into the waiting room. A room that's far too full of couples, couples waiting for their babies.

There's a poster of a mobile phone with a giant cross over the middle of the icon. I take my phone from out my bag, see all the texts I've sent to Ben – 'We need to talk', 'Please call me back', 'We need to talk about the photograph' – and press the side to turn it off.

'Stop that!' a very pregnant woman yells at a small child as a plastic brick arcs through the air.

The corner of the room is carefully cornered off with a sturdy plastic barricade that's made to look just like a picket fence. It wraps around what once upon a time must have been a picture-perfect play house, but everything looks jaded now. The plastic fence has faded to the colour of left-over school-canteen potatoes and the house's walls are graffitied with small waxy crayon scrawls. Inside the fence is a mess of dented and discarded toys and trapped toddlers, the captured children small and wild and filled with snot.

We were lying in our garden on the tiny patch of grass bleached yellow by the summer sun. Jay rolled over, gently kissed my stomach through my T-shirt and traced a ring around my belly button with the tip of his forefinger. 'I've got a good feeling about this month. You're going to make the greatest mum,' he murmured between kisses. I looked at him and forced a smile I didn't feel.

The horror-toddler throws another brick. His mother sighs and moves to tackle and manoeuvre him. I have never seen anyone so pregnant. The woman lifts herself off her chair and rises slowly, a giant mound of moving flesh, her walk obscene. Her gait is spread and her hips have splayed her legs out wide. She shuffles to the child, slowed down by her own corpulence and the opening of her pelvis, her body clearly giving in to the imminence of birth. She grabs another brick from out the toddler's hand and sweeps him up and sits him on her buried hip. Her movements are all smooth and liquid. Loose despite her size. I wonder what that feels like; to be so full of life that your body struggles to contain it.

I lay my hand across my belly, to try out being pregnant. No one would ever guess that something swims within, a thing without a father. The warmth that radiates from my resting hand is seeping through my jumper now. I can feel it on my abdomen, which is hidden underneath green unwashed wool. The threat of tears begins to churn and build behind the tidal barrier of my dry eyes. Jay should be here now sharing this. The hand across my belly should be his.

Weight

'Emma Bell.'

I do not cry but follow the large midwife who bellows out my name. She is wearing scuffed blue Crocs and is far wider than the women in the waiting room. She doesn't turn to look at me. I follow her along a corridor that's fluorescent-lit into another room that's only walls. It makes me think of prisons and battery caged chickens.

'Stand there. No, don't just stand there. On the scales I mean,' she barks and takes my wrist and writes my weight in biro on my hand. She traces over numbers so the ink stands out. It hurts my skin as she presses down the nib. 'Just so I don't forget,' she adds.

'Don't ever write on skin.' My mother's voice echoes somewhere in my thoughts across the decades from a time when I'd return from school with teenage love hearts and textbook pages inked onto young hands. 'It's bad for you,' she'd say. I imagine all the biro ink, the toxic weight of me that's seeping down into my bloodstream and creeping through the individual pores.

'You don't weigh much.' The midwife sounds really annoyed. 'You need to eat more food. This isn't the right time to be concerned about your looks. You're pregnant now.'

'I know I am,' I say, 'or I wouldn't actually be here.'

She ignores me, yawns, not bothering to lift her hand. I watch her mouth open into a large dark hole that I would like to stuff with toilet roll. She notices me staring, snaps it closed and gestures at a plastic chair.

'Today's been long. Let's get this over with,' she says.

'The feeling's mutual,' I mutter underneath my breath.

The midwife is clearly tired. I can see it in the slow threads of her writing and the matt glaze of her eyes. She is a woman waiting to go home. She seems so deeply bored of women and their bodies and their babies, so very bored of all new life.

'Is this your first pregnancy?' she asks.

'Yes.'

She doesn't say a thing. Just ticks a box and scribbles something in my notes.

'Partner?' she asks.

I manage, 'No.'

She looks up for a second and seems about to ask a question that she chooses not to ask. I'm pretty sure she thinks she knows my story. She has filled in all the blank spaces with conclusions and with prejudice. I feel for the other women she sees here in this clinic. The solitary women: the widows, the unwanted and the ones who choose to be alone. The others that she thinks are far too young or far too old to be good mothers. I fiddle with my wedding ring, spin it aggressively with my fingers and my thumb, but she doesn't look. She doesn't ask.

'Then I guess I have no need to ask if you're a victim of abuse. We have to ask all women now.' She points up at a poster tacked onto the pale green wall. 'If you're frightened of your partner call us' is printed in a fifties pop-art font inside a bubble and mounted on a background of pink dots.

'No,' I say again.

But it feels like abuse. Her asking me. Him leaving me. Him leaving me alone here in this airless place that's crammed with pregnant women and their partners. Perfect families all gestating right in front of me.

'Date of your last period?'

'I don't know,' I say.

'What do you mean that you don't know?'

She sighs loudly, as if I've failed somehow at womanhood.

'I don't know the exact date. I was still taking the pill.'

She shakes her head and frowns, as if she's heard that one before.

'Fine,' she says. 'Take this.' She scribbles something on another form and sighs again. 'Just down the hall. The blue chairs on the left. Sit and wait right there. Someone will come and call your name.'

And I leave to go and sit along the hallway on a chair alone, like a child who was naughty and is waiting to be punished.

Rhythm

The sonographer is kinder. She sits high upon a stool, a screen and keyboard spread in front of her. It is dark in here, like being in a submarine. Only the monitor throws out a low, hypnotic, gentle light. I can see the image of some other woman's baby, its perfect body frozen in the middle of a movement on the glowing screen. The lady pulls fresh paper out over the metal trolley bed and I lift myself up, lie down still. The paper makes a crackling sound like crab claws breaking in the lock of hungry seagull beaks.

She hasn't introduced herself but I don't mind. A flick of her dark hair falls in a sheet across her eyes and she pauses for a moment to gather it all up into her hands and tie it in a ponytail and adjust herself on the tall stool. She snaps on a pair of latex gloves and takes a plastic wand and rolls a condom over it before covering it with gel.

'This might feel cold,' she gently says. 'Ready?'

'Yes,' I say while thinking *No* and staring at the thing that looks exactly like a dildo.

I was worried my vagina might have sealed up from lack of use but unfortunately it hasn't. The wand is now inside me and she's presses it into the flesh of my insides, firmer than expected. She makes slow and sweeping movements now from left to right, maintaining pressure, searching in the dark. There's a frown across her brow, like ripples in a watery pool. I close my eyes.

'Oh . . .' she says, sounding surprised. 'We won't need this.'

I breathe out in relief as she slowly pulls the wand out and I wonder if the test was wrong and my abdomen is empty. I cross the fingers on both hands.

'This might feel cold,' she says again and I feel her trail a line of gel across my stomach. There is a silence in the air now, heavy like the holding of a hundred breaths. She sweeps and pushes, sweeps some more, applies more gel. I open my eyes. She smiles while she deftly clicks between some points upon the screen, joining crosses, making links to take some measurements. I watch her as she joins up dots and think of all the photographs, of all the random bits of string that I cannot tie to any kind of meaning. 'Well, there's your baby. Judging by the size I'd say you're fourteen weeks.' I swallow hard and think of how the weeks have passed so quickly and so slowly, time a volatile and fickle thing.

'That's great,' I manage in a whisper, not actually meaning it.

She holds the screen, turns it around so that the image

faces me. And there it is. A kidney bean of baby with a silhouette of head and little limbs and shadows of small solid bones. Inside the curving shell of it a tiny light pulsates at speed.

'Would you like to hear the heartbeat now?'

Before I have a chance to tell her 'no' a heartbeat fills the room with living sound. It beats and beats with rabid speed. It sounds so loud, so much in need, a call for what I cannot be.

Plan

I have two things I have to do:

1. Get rid of the evolving cells that threaten to undo me and I wish I'd never seen or heard.
2. Discover why Jay died.

Jane's feather is propped inside a small glass jar and balanced on the windowsill like a flag that says 'Surrender' but to who or what I am not sure. On the table is my laptop trying hard to link to the 4G that only seems to come in intermittent waves. I don't want to wait to speak to Claire. Or anyone at all. I just want to get this done.

Eventually the reception lasts just long enough for me to find a coloured map of red inverted Google tears showing that the nearest clinic is just back across the border into Devon. I call the number for the place and a woman's voice answers the phone. She sounds a little like a robot that's been programmed to be kind. I answer all her questions,

228

provide her with the things she asks, the dates and weights and state of things. The woman says that there's a cancellation if I want it, that there's room for me to come today, that I'll need to spend some hours in the clinic. She mentions that a partner or friend would be 'a very good idea' but I don't have 'a very good idea' to bring with me.

'I'll come,' I say. 'Alone,' I add, and book it in.

The ending of the thing is just in reach. I look for taxi companies to take me to the train station. I don't want to chat to Brian. What I wouldn't give right now for a total stranger with a 4.8* rating in a white Toyota Prius but my search for someone else is useless. Uber doesn't work here and there isn't anybody else available today.

I meet Brian further up the hill where the lane expands to save his car from crooked walls, and slide into the back seat of his cab that smells of crisps and chemicals and strawberry-scented pens, the type I used to covet with my friends at primary school.

'You leaving here already then? Not cut out for country life?' He chuckles at the thought of that, finding himself hilarious. His giant belly rests upon his trouser-suited lap and his shirt pulls tight around it. The buttons strain. His face is red and ruddy, potted like a lawn that's been destroyed by garden moles. 'I mean, it's different in the winter. Nothing like you city lot imagine it. I'm not surprised you're not staying.'

'I am. At least for now,' I say. 'I'm just going shopping for a moon cup. It's for periods. You stick it up your . . .'

'Okay, okay. I get it. Not my business.'

We sit in awkward silence for a while.

'Actually,' I say, 'I forgot the charger for my laptop and some other things I meant to bring.' He rolls his eyes at my reliance on the city shops and I feel the secret sitting in my stomach like a smooth and heavy pebble, solid, like the stones by Brighton pier where the sea lifts up and churns the beach leaving flawless ovals everywhere just small enough to swallow if you wanted to.

I press my fingers in the dip where my ribcage butterflies apart. I press down hard, expect to actually feel it there. A perfect pebble lump of foetus. A dense mass of deception. But my fingers only find soft flesh between the splay of bones.

Pivot

The nurse holds out the small white pill. It rolls around the bottom of the see-through plastic cup as she walks across the clinic room, her arm stretched out.

'You'll need to come back here tomorrow for the next stage of the process. After that things really start. Then you'll have to stay here at the clinic until you've passed the pregnancy. That can take some time at fourteen weeks. It's all written in this leaflet here.' I take the leaflet that my mother would approve of with its bullet-pointed tips and pastel-coloured hints, a timeline and a help number. 'If you're positive you don't want a surgical procedure then you'll need to swallow this,' she says and passes me another flimsy cup that threatens to collapse within her clutch, half filled with tepid water from the tap. I go to take the single pill, to lift the cup towards my mouth.

I think of Ben. I see him at the funeral, drunk and swaying, spilling beer and leaking tears from red-rimmed eyes. I can hear Ben telling me he cannot live without my man.

Jay loved someone else, I tell myself. *Just get it over with.*

But my arm stays heavy by my side. I fixate on a plastic pot plant that's sitting on the nurse's desk. Its cheap green leaves are far too pert and vile in their brightness, a shade of green I've never seen before in nature. My throat is tight and there's a dampness spreading out from underneath my arms, along the bottom of my back and a wet and sweating stickiness between the meat that is my thighs. I can smell the antiseptic, sterile bleach and the bovine scent that's building in the hollows of my armpits.

'If you wait, your options will be limited. The timing means that you'll be looking at a surgical procedure, which you've told my colleagues you don't want.'

There's an awkward pause and I wonder if I could somehow make myself pass out, just faint, unconscious on the floor. I want to have my brain switched off. I'm jealous of the plastic plant and the ease of its existence.

'I've changed my mind,' I finally say.

'You want to keep the baby?'

'No,' I say. 'I don't want to be awake for it.'

I'm not exactly sure if I'm referring to the operation or to all of life. The nurse pauses and takes the cup, removes the pill from out of sight.

'I understand,' she says kindly. 'But we can't do that for you today. You'll need to book. You can do that at reception now or on the phone if you prefer.'

She says goodbye and as I leave without stopping to speak to anyone, the heavy fire-door slams hard. A sonic exclamation mark.

Avocado

I try to ignore time but with every day my clothes grow more uncomfortable. Two weeks have passed and I haven't called to book the termination yet. I've been busy staring at the photographs and busy staring out to sea and busy watching *Bargain Hunt* and *Loose Women*. 'All done,' I lied to Claire, not wanting any questions or her kind concern. I tell myself I'll call the clinic in the morning but the morning always comes and goes and comes again. The tomorrows keep accumulating while a solid bulge is rapidly appearing and is pressing with the force of something living, up against the constraints of my jeans. The button will no longer reach and I'm forced to leave the zip splayed wide. I hide myself in layers, smudge my contours with large jumpers, baggy cardigans and coats.

There are moments where I wonder about motherhood, where I let myself consider it for just a second as an actual possibility. I try to grasp the word 'Mother'. It feels so strange inside my brain, a word that until now has meant my mother and not me and I instantly connect with Dad as if the words are half a whole. 'Mother'. I try again to see if it can stand alone. I've no idea. Especially when the mother that I'm thinking of is me.

I'm more confused than ever and the Blu-Tack is lacking its appeal without my mother to annoy. I start to roll it anyway. I mould it into tiny balls, less satisfying than before, and stick up all the photos on my bedroom wall between small frames of pressed cowslips that have faded over time. The photo of the cottage door and the crumpled shot of Porthlowal I stick a little to the left. Two photographs I've managed to attach to a place that give me no idea of why Jay died.

I get distracted, look online. The website asks me about time. It wants to know the days and dates and in return it tells me facts in pastel pink and day-dream blue about the small dividing cells which lurk within. Apparently hair follicles have formed in patterns now and I imagine swirls and empty whirls, like water draining down a plug across translucent skin. I read that it has ears now that can hear my voice and know my sound. I wonder what it feels and thinks when in the night the only lullaby I offer is a song made up of subdued cries and desperate sighs.

A brightly coloured bar chart full of vegetables and fruit beside the different weeks clearly shows me that the thing inside is now the same size as an avocado. I Google 'avocado' and read about the trees that cannot pollinate alone. They need another avocado tree close by so they can grow. I think of all the paired-up avocado trees around the globe, both rooted to the deep soft earth, stable and solid, side by side, dependent on each other for the growing of new fruit.

Even avocado trees can't cope alone.

Jolt

Admiring the placement of the photographs I notice all the missed calls on my phone. I pray that they're from Ben and hold my breath as I listen to the voice message.

'Mrs Bell, it's Colin Stokes, the coroner's liaison officer. I apologize for leaving you a voice message but I've tried to phone on a number of occasions and I haven't had much luck in getting hold of you. I just wanted to inform you that we've set a date now for the inquest and your presence is required. If you could call me back, let me know that you've received this and discuss all of the details, that would be very appreciated.'

I think about the strand of rope, how it cut into his fragile skin. Shaking, I drop the phone from my hand. It lands right on the corner of the wooden floor with a loud crash. A crack spreads wide across the screen, a giant splinter through the glass.

'Are you okay?' calls Anne, concerned from somewhere down the stairs, and all that I can tell her is 'I broke something important.'

April

Priorities

The cracked phone works despite the fact that it is clearly broken.

'What?' I say, too curt, too fast.

'Well hello to you too,' my mother says.

'Hello,' I say all child-like and petulant.

I fold a jumpered arm beneath my chest and hold my ribs in a half hug. My forearms rest upon the growing bulge of belly flesh. The photos on the bedroom wall hang around me like a gathering of paper ghosts, the images all haunting.

'You know, I'm still not sure if being all alone in Cornwall is a very good idea.'

'I know you don't. It's partly why I'm staying here.'

'Emma. Please don't start,' she says.

'Fine,' I say, 'I promise that I'm fine. I've made new friends. I'm really fine.'

'Like who?' she asks.

'There's Pete,' I say. 'He's old,' I add before she asks.

I think of how I keep trying to avoid him since my wrong assumption he was suicidal, naked and swimming off towards his death. Downstairs Anne is cooking dinner, even with the bandaged arm she hurt when tripping on a paving slab in London. She is banging pots around and running taps. I creep to close my bedroom door against the threat of her disclosure.

'And the neighbour Jane is nice. There's the local doctor too. I've had dinner with her family.'

I fiddle with the pillow, smooth the bedding that's already flat.

'So, you're doing fine?' she asks, sounding suspicious. I look down at my changing shape that is becoming harder to ignore. I trace the places with my fingers where the 'v' of open metal zip has printed patterns on my fickle flesh.

'All fine,' I say, my voice upbeat, my throat tightening.

'Well, you can show us for yourself. We're on our way.'

'You're what?' I say. 'You can't!' My voice ascends in panic.

I haven't said I'm here with Anne. And what about the pregnancy? My mother cannot know because it then becomes too real; a thing that's true and cannot be ignored for any longer and will need dealing with immediately.

'You keep on telling us you're fine, but we still want to see you, Emma love. We miss you and we're worried. We just want to see you for ourselves.'

'No,' I say. 'You don't need to. I'm absolutely fine.'

'We're already on the M4, love. We'll see you very soon,' she says, and I can almost hear her smiling.

Movement

I hide inside the bedding like a seed that doesn't want to grow. I rip off a strip of fingernail with the sharp tips of my teeth. The nail tears too low and leaves a ragged edge and strip of raw and burning flesh. My finger throbs in time with the beating of my heart. I suck at it. The phone rings loud and crashes my awareness, breaks through my concentration. It is them again.

'There's traffic on the M5, love,' shouts Dad.

I hold the phone further away.

'I think there's been an accident. We're hardly even moving,' my mother yells.

The phone on speaker in the car distorts their voices, makes them sound as if they're trapped together inside a metal chamber deep below the surface of all things.

'Where exactly are you both?' I ask, the words slightly muffled by the finger stuffed into my mouth.

'Somewhere close to Taunton,' my mother calls.

'We might be a little while, Em,' Dad says more loudly than he needs to.

'Okay,' I say, my heart beating at running speed.

My parents' imminent arrival is as effective as three lines of coke. I attack the house with an energy and fortitude that I haven't had for weeks and do not stop until the kitchen is immaculate, the mugs washed up, plates put away. Anne looks at me bemused from a safe corner of the sofa where she rests her arm and pretends to read a book. I move through rooms, a human whirlwind, until there are no signs of toast or bowls encrusted with remains of Weetabix stuck solid to the sides like superglue mixed with cement. I air the rooms and fluff the cushions on the sofas and the chairs, just hoping that the plumpness of the shapes will somehow prove to my observant mother that I'm fine.

As I pass the mirror in the hall with its thin and gilded wooden frame I glimpse the body that is mine but not quite mine. Anne hasn't noticed anything but it's unmistakable to me, which means my mother will definitely notice too. A curve that starts down low, a small ellipse.

I run back up the cottage stairs and dig inside a drawer that's lined with floral paper and scented with small bags of lavender that crunch, the flowers dried and crisp with age, the scent still somehow hanging on like a slowly fading memory of a flower once in bloom. I forage for a cardigan. I layer up, add wool to wool, then hang Jay's scarf that falls down loose around my neck and covers up the front of me.

There is still time before they get here, and now, wrapped

up warm, I am too warm and far too nervous to just sit and wait inside the house.

'Seeing your parents will be nice!' Anne calls as I begin to wrestle with my wellies.

'Hmm,' I say.

But I seriously doubt that.

Endorphins

Sitting on the pebbles mixed with sand above the high-tide mark I take my wellies off and pull at both my socks to reveal lines of pale toes and flops of sallow cod-white feet. I lay a towel across my lap and peel down the jeans from my neglected winter legs. Long hairs have grown on my calves, my body furred in the neglect. The trousers try to hold my shape but fall and crumple into legless pools of denim on the sand. I check again to see if anyone has braved the early April beach. But no one else is here but me. I wriggle out of the layers that I've carefully used to cover up my shallow bulge of swelling cells; unwrapping jersey, cotton, wool.

Plain black pants and frill-less bra can almost pass for a bikini. I leave the safety of the towel and walk across the scrunch of bitter sand towards the ever-waiting sea. The cold wind whips across my skin, which prickles at the shock of the exposure to the air. Sea water rushes over my toes, distorts the image of my feet. There's a pause before the pain kicks in, that perfect moment in the middle when the hurt has yet to reach the brain and coalesce as feeling. Then suddenly the ache spreads out. Profound and piercing pain fanning out across the bones inside my feet. The sore is deep. It hurts and hurts. Another step and now the water reaches up around my ankles and starts to pull my lungs in tight, the cold collecting all my breath and hinting at a deeper toll. I bite my lip, focus and stride a little further till the water comes to meet my knees, the sea an almost solid thing contracting tight around the sinews of my legs and gripping round the thin of skin that prickles, burns, about my thighs.

Anyone who swims in winter must be mad. The crushing coldness latches on and won't let go. I wait for numbness to obliterate the leaden ache but the respite doesn't ever come. My feet, my legs, still fucking hurt. The pain begins to radiate towards my core and makes me feel sick inside. I give up and make a slow retreat. I pray that no one has appeared to watch me here; a woman in the water, dry above her thighs and obviously pregnant, struggling to the chilly shore without her clothes.

I'm only in the water for a minute. Maybe two. But it is just enough. As I sit upon the thinning towel and scrape the sand off my feet with cotton socks the pain turns into something else and, for the first time in a while, I cannot help myself; I smile.

Arrival

My mother picks a cushion up, re-plumps it, puts it back onto a different chair. She's looking round the room as if collecting evidence with just her eyes. Anne is nowhere to be seen.

'See,' I say. 'You didn't need to worry.'

She sweeps her fingertip along a length of wooden shelf and lifts her finger to inspect the dust that clings to her.

'Come here!' says Dad and spreads his arms to make himself wide, invites a hug.

I lean towards him, carefully arching with my body to be sure my belly won't protrude.

'Emma, it isn't all that cold in here,' my mother comments on my clothes, surveying me now that she's finished with the room.

'I know.'

'Do you really need that scarf then?'

'I've been paddling. And anyway, I thought that I looked nice in it.'

'You do look nice. You look less thin, although it's hard to tell with all those layers.' She comes to kiss me gently on the cheek, her touch just light enough to keep her lipstick perfectly intact. 'But why on earth have you been paddling in the water? It's still far too cold for that. The car said it's only ten degrees outside.'

'Because I wanted to.'

We both stand tall. I hold her gaze. This mother who is mine, who still has everything I don't, who hasn't killed her husband off, whose hair is perfectly coiffured. I run my hand through greasy strands.

'I'll grab the bags from the car. It's just out of the garage and I wasn't sure that I could drive it down that lane so I've left it at the top,' says Dad.

'I'll come with you,' I say quickly. 'Just make yourself at home,' I yell, my back towards my mother, already grabbing trainers, tying laces.

Dad and I walk slowly up the steepness of the village lane, the light departing fast behind the silhouettes of chimney pots that nestle in the valley and the windswept trees that stretch beyond with budded tips that hint at green.

'It's really good to see you, Em.'

'You too,' I say, taking his arm.

'You promise you're okay here, love? You're looking pretty pale.'

'All fine,' I say without a pause.

We pull the two small cabin bags, the tiny wheels rattling loud against the quiet of the place as they struggle to stay

248

stable faced with concrete pits and pot-holes in the rural road. Four Waitrose canvas Bags For Life crammed full of food and treats and wine hang heavy on our shoulder blades. A suitcase wheel jams itself inside a crack and makes Dad stop, so I stop too and wait in the descending dark as he wiggles the chrome handle to ease it from the grip of the road. Behind us both the last traces of daylight quickly disappear.

'I love you, Dad,' I say into the gloom.

'I love you too.'

War

'She's *my* daughter, Anne, not yours.'

We hear the shouting long before we reach the door. There are women warring, hissing words behind the walls.

'Well, I guess that Anne is back,' I tell my dad. 'I'm living here with her.'

'Oh,' says Dad. 'I see.' There is a long and awkward pause. 'Your mum won't be too happy, love.'

'I can hear that, Dad. I'm pretty sure that everybody living in the village can hear it too.'

'We could go hide in the pub?' he jokes. 'Is there one nearby?'

We both laugh in the knowledge that we never could. She'd kill us both.

'Sure,' I say, playing along. 'Tequila shots?'

He chuckles at the very thought, his laughter bigger than the night.

'I guess we should go in.'

'I guess,' I finally say.

Dad takes my hand, which is either an attempt to comfort me or comfort him.

'You know she's only angry because she loves you, Em. Anne hasn't been the best to you. To you or Jay. And your mother is protective. She just doesn't want to see you hurt, more hurt than you already are.'

'It's different now. Anne's not that bad.'

My dad just nods. We stand together side by side outside the door, still holding hands, not wanting to go in.

'Dad?' I finally say.

'Yes, love?'

'Do you think that Jay was gay?'

He is silent as the question floats and sinks and floats and agitates the air. If he's shocked he doesn't show it.

'Love, I've no idea of anything. Not anymore.' And he squeezes my hand harder. 'Ready for this?' he asks.

Departure

'I'm so sorry, Em. About your mum. She'll come round soon. She's just a bit protective and she's stubborn too, like someone else I know.'

His voice sounds sad, deflated, like a flat balloon. Dad and I reverse our journey up the lane with heavy legs, a slower pace. We place the cases side by side within the vacuumed-clean car boot and stop to rest and look out over cottage roofs towards the distant sweep of sea.

'She might be right,' I finally say.

We stare out at the morning sky that promises a stunning day and watch a slowly moving ship that's aimed at the horizon. I wish that I could be on board and flatten out the curve of the earth, head straight towards the deadly edge.

'Don't be silly, love. She didn't mean those things she said last night.'

I laugh at that.

'She really did. She hasn't ever trusted me. She doesn't think I'm capable of doing what is best for me.'

'She loves you, Em,' he firmly says, 'but love can often look like something else.'

This doesn't look like love to me. It just looks like shit parenting.

Acceptance

Iggy lollops, bounds towards my side and limps in circles through my legs, his body curling round my calves, his paws leaving small imprints of attention on the sand. I stomp across to Jane and Pete who haven't noticed I am here and are busily unpacking bags and finding towels and folding clothes in readiness, their minds already focused on the sea.

'I want to swim. Don't want to talk,' I say too loud, abrasive, harsh.

They turn around and look, surprised to see that I am here and willing, wanting suddenly to join them in the water when I've never wanted to before.

'Right,' says Pete.

He lays his socks beside his boots and puts his flask of tea on the top corner of his towel, finds three more pebbles, weighs it down.

'I knew you'd come. You've chosen a good day for it.' Jane grins at me.

She's wearing a blue swimsuit with a bobble hat and giant robe that's made of two large towels sewn together at the seams. The towelling flaps about her in the air like blackbird wings. If she wasn't quite so big I'd worry that she might take flight as she walks away across the beach, her wide bare feet unbothered by the pebbles and the small sharp stones mixed with the sand, to clutch a random feather that she's spotted, almost camouflaged against the ground.

Claire is in the distance now and walking fast with giant strides towards us all and waving with her frantic hands to tell us that she's coming, wait, she's on her way. The women wave silent hellos as Jane returns to tease the feather treasure that she's found into the grip of rubber band that keeps my greasy hair held high. The sun is low, the shadows springtime long and I can see the feather sticking like a magic talisman above my smudge of shadow head. I grin my thanks at this small gift that feels like acceptance to a club.

'Sorry that I'm late.' Claire joins us round the patchwork square of laid out towels and Iggy goes to lick her hands. 'It's jam,' she says. 'It's everywhere. Otis thinks he's old enough to make breakfast without help and now the kitchen's like a crime scene. I need a swim to wash it off.' She turns to me. 'You're here! Well, welcome to our crazy group. Have you come to cheer us on?'

'We're not the crazy ones,' says Pete. 'The swimming keeps us almost sane.'

'Almost,' grins Claire, who stands and licks a smear of jam from the knuckles of her hand.

'Was it nice having your parents down?' Jane asks. 'They didn't stay for very long. I was hoping that I'd get to meet them too.'

'She said she doesn't want to talk,' says Pete, who glances over.

I am grateful for this gentle man who seems to understand that words can have their time and place, that language doesn't always work. He looks so proud to harbour me from conversation.

'Actually,' I say, 'I want to swim.'

I was laughing as Jay hobbled over Brighton stones to reach the shelf of sea. 'You're mad,' I said. The sunlight bounced across the surface of the water and reflected in my eyes. 'Come on, Em. Get in!' he called. 'It feels great.' I loosened my bikini strap, searched for the Prada sunglasses and a novel hidden somewhere in my leather bag. I rolled away and tried to find some comfort on the lumpy towel.

'You'll love it!' says Jane.

'You sure you want to do this now?' says Claire. 'It's still quite cold in there.'

'I know,' I say.

'Well, come on then. Just keep it short. At least at first. It'll take quite a few cold swims for your body to adjust.

People usually start in summer but you're willing and you're here, so long slow breaths. Just keep on breathing in and out. And don't forget to actually swim.'

Initiation

Claire pulls herself from out her jumper by wrenching at one baggy arm and squirming till her head appears and then wiggles out of her trousers, which she leaves in an unfolded mess of jumbled, jam-stained fabric on the towel. I take a breath and awkwardly remove my own clothes too, peeling off the safety of the individual layers until I'm standing on a Cornish beach, my shape exposed.

The Lycra edges of my swimming costume cut sharp into the creases where my hips meet thigh and dig deep at the shoulder straps. I grab the front and stretch it up and try to pull the sides down low, to make it bigger, make it grow, to cover up a little more, now that there is more of me to cover up. The friends all waiting cannot help but drop their eyes down low to where the beacon of a bump protrudes, now obvious and clearly there, a thing that cannot be ignored.

I wait for them to say something. Claire's mouth has fallen wide open but no words come out and the others all stay silent too. There is just the sound of padding Iggy, panting Iggy, lapping sea.

'I . . .' I stammer. Lost.

The silence lasts for far too long. Pete finally nods and says to all, 'She said no chat.'

Claire frowns and looks at Jane, who is now frowning too. I take a breath of metal air that's salty clean and granite cold despite the sun's attempts at warmth.

'I only want to swim,' I say to break the awkward silence.

'Okay,' Claire slowly says. 'But it's important you don't get too cold, especially given that you're still . . . Well, there's a real risk of hypothermia. The sea is only about ten degrees so you have to keep it very short. At least at first.'

'You done?' says Pete and Claire just nods, her face all frown.

Leaving piles of towels and clothes and bags and flasks of tea and conversation on the shore, we turn ourselves to face the sea. The seasoned swimmers move to form a line with me stood in the middle. I'm awkward on the stones, the underbelly of my feet softened from years of city living. I stagger, tentative and lumbering. The others do not pause. They face the mass of water as if it is an enemy, like soldiers setting 'self' aside and storming forward, strong and brave with leathered feet. They meet the sea, the sea meets them and still they do not slow their strides but keep on moving through the water, their feet taking large steps across the bottom of the seabed until it's finally deep enough to lift their legs and start to swim.

259

I hesitate and falter on the seashore. The air is cold. Jane kicks herself onto her back and calls to me to 'Just get in'. She makes it sound so simple. The group tread water in a clutch, make sweeping movements with their arms to keep them floating in one spot while grinning as they watch and wait, the sunlight dancing on the surface and catching in their eyes.

I start to stride.

'Don't think!' yells Jane. 'Sometimes I find that singing helps!'

She begins to make a sort of sound which is shocking but she seems to think is singing. It runs all over octaves and combines the lines from different songs. There are some I think I recognize and others which I'm pretty sure she just made up.

'I'd tell you to stop singing but that isn't even singing, Jane,' Claire calls across the whipping sound and frothy loops of winter waves, the frown washed off her face.

Jane yells again, 'You just have to get in, Emma. What's the worst thing that can happen?'

I look at three bright bobbing heads, their eyes aglow, their smiles wide, and take a step into the froth.

'Just swim,' calls Claire, shaking her head in what I think is resignation. 'And for God's sake, please don't drown.'

The ache appears inside my feet, as if the bones are vascular and bleeding out or bruising deep. I try to crush the pain down small, to make it into nothing that needs noticing, a thing that is compact and neat and easily ignored.

I try to focus on the heads and Jane's bright furry bobble hat that floats there in the water like a rescue buoy just yards away but out of reach.

It doesn't work, the pain won't shrink but looms up large and fills my head and spills into my thoughts like the silver spread of mercury. There's nothing left to do but let it win. So I lose the fight, accept my loss, invite the aching pain right in.

Come on then, sea, I want to shout. *What have you got? Dead husband pain?*

Staring straight ahead I take large steps into the sea. I will my feet to walk into the pain and all the water rises up, around my ankles, round my knees, and up and up until it hugs my chest and suddenly I'm out at sea, my feet untethered from the floor, the cold at once a crushing pain, exquisite and encompassing, delicious and ethereal in its all-consuming magnitude. It hurts so much it's a relief. It's a physical and simple pain and there's comfort in the knowledge that to end the pain you simply have to swim back to the shore.

Or.

I'm suddenly aware that my breathing is too fast. It's as if my body wants to trip me up, expel the air and fill my panicked lungs with salt.

'Just in and out. Breathe slow and long,' calls Claire who watches, seagull-quick in her attention.

I focus on Jane's pink and wet tinged hair and try to slow the dragging of the oxygen into my nose, expand my chest against the weight of sea water before I kiss it slowly out through puckered lips in a slow hiss. I focus on the different sounds. The whooshing and expanding then the deeper sound of letting go. Tamara from the meditation app would be so proud. There's a light that plays across the water as the ripples catch fragments of day and splinter out across the sea, a giant moving art canvas that only we can see. My breath is slow and steady now. The heads are grinning, pleased with me. A sudden gust of air flicks salty spray and licks our land-locked faces fresh.

'That's long enough,' Claire calls to me.

We sweep our arms in giant scoops against the mass of water to turn our bodies, face the beach. The village looks so different from the water. There's a distance here. A wider view. I can see the cottages stacked side by side, the sweep of undulating countryside that forms soft shapes and gentle curves impossible to see when locked inside the land itself. And I like the space between my body and the shore; a giant salty barrier of blue. There's a power in the backing off. The knowledge you can swim away, to gain perspective, find new ground when not on ground. I look around and there they are, three smiling heads. We grin in silence, joined together by our mutual joy and joint accomplishment as we all swim back, a line of four towards the shore, swimming as a unit side by side.

Glow

My body is aglow with cold. It's red and pink and patchy bright.

'Put your clothes on quick.' Jane finds my towel. 'And drink this too.'

She places a small metal cup of steaming liquid from a Thermos into my cold hands. My fingers are slow, my movements sluggish from the chill.

'Is this warm orange squash?' I ask, the cup smelling like childhood as I take a swig of hot, sweet drink.

'Yes. But with lemon juice and honey too.'

'It's good,' I coo, my hands wrapped tight, my head tipped down to meet the rise of golden steam. As I swallow I can feel the hot liquid passing down my throat and through my core, something that I haven't ever been so conscious of before. Claire dips into her green rucksack and pulls out some plastic Tupperware which reminds me of the plastic gifts left on my doorstep back in London. Containers full of casseroles that say it all, nothing at all.

I realize that when swimming thoughts of dead husbands, expanding cells and angry mothers briefly left my mind. For a second I was empty, still and sea-washed clean of any sadness. The Tupperware is full of cake.

'Martha's latest thing to stop herself from revising for a science test. She's baking all the bloody time. And she's shit at washing up. On the plus-side we get cake . . . I think.' Claire picks a piece of chocolate slab, rotates it in her hands and takes a sniff. 'Or maybe these are brownies and not cake?' She sinks her teeth into a piece. 'Who cares. They're really good,' she muffles through a mouthful.

'She takes after her father then,' Jane says, grinning at Claire.

'You promise that you didn't bake?' Pete asks, one eyebrow raised, while pulling on thick gloves and breathing warmth onto his wrinkled hands.

'The cheek!' Claire says and laughs. 'You're safe. I'm actually grateful that she doesn't get her skills from me.'

The brownie is delicious; sugar, goo and thick syrup that melts to soft inside my mouth and coats my teeth with chocolate tack. The swim has made me starving. Claire rushes back into her jam-stained clothes.

'I need to hurry home and grab a clean outfit before my clinic starts. Oh God, is that the time?'

She bundles up her scattered things not waiting for an answer, her hair still wet with water dripping down onto the shoulders of her coat, and says goodbye and hugs us all and turns to me. 'Don't forget about the Afterdrop. Just wait a while before you have a shower or a bath. And Em,' she says and waits until I catch her eye. 'Please can we talk? Another time?'

I nod a 'yes' while thinking *No*. She'll make me talk about the thing. The thing that's hidden in the darkness and is best if I ignore.

Naked

'Dear God, Emma! You're pregnant!'

I am standing in the metal bath, the hand-held shower in one hand and water streaming in warm streaks down naked breasts and thighs. Anne stands unmoving, frozen still inside the doorframe, gripping at the handle with a sort of desperation as if the handle is her new best friend. The morning sun shines pale through the window and illuminates the woman with her unset hair and bandaged arm and gaping mouth. *Don't stare. It's rude. You'll swallow flies,* I think but do not say aloud. I look down at my engorged breasts that I'm actually quite impressed with and the bulge of growing belly that I'm less impressed with and clearly shows I'm pregnant.

Anne doesn't move. She just keeps hold of the door handle as I switch the water off and try to lean towards the bath towel which is folded and just out of reach on the tiny bathroom radiator. It's far too far and so I attempt to cover up my grotesque trunk with spindly arms. The water gurgles loudly as it vortexes away.

'Some help?' I say.

She eventually moves, her mouth still vast as if it is a wound that is just waiting to be mended. The towel is warm in patches where it's been in contact with the heat. I wrap it tight under my arms, tuck in the corner neat between my breasts to cover up.

'Emma?' she says again. She is clearly waiting for the answer to a question that she hasn't asked.

'Yes?'

She's pale and she's shaking. I sigh and sit down on the bathroom floor and lean back against the wooden panels of the bath. The ribs of wood support my spine and keep my backbone straight and tall. She doesn't move.

'But how?' Anne asks.

'Really?' I ask.

'I meant is it Jay's? You're absolutely sure?'

I bite my lip and hope Anne bleeds.

'Of course it is,' I say and use the bath to pull myself to standing.

'But did he know?'

'No,' I say. 'His timing was impressive. And before you ask, I didn't have a clue either before he . . .'

The grouting round the bathroom floor is peeling off in places, like bandages coming undone, and what was white is yellow now with tiny grains of sand trapped in the shallow dents between the tiles.

'Oh, Emma. That's amazing news.' Her face morphs into what looks close to happiness. 'How far along?'

I shake my head.

'I'm twenty weeks. And it's not amazing news. It's really not. I'm going to book a termination.'

'No!' she says, her face falling, her voice desperate. 'Don't say that, please? You're carrying my grandchild. The only one I'll ever have. That baby is my only link to Jay.'

'I'm not a human incubator. And you're not the one who'll have to raise this thing alone.'

'You won't be all alone. Stay here and live with me? I'll help,' she offers and she pleads.

I shake my head and think of Ben.

'I think it's better off sucked out.'

I regret the words immediately. I did not mean to be so cruel. Her face flushes.

'Get out,' she tells me in a voice that's only slightly louder than a whisper.

'But I'm wet and in a towel.'

'GET OUT!' she shouts.

In the bedroom that's no longer mine I grab my things and tear the photos off the wall. The Blu-Tack rips the paint away and leaves patches of bare plaster.

Just like my mother warned it would.

Jane

'Of course you can stay here.'

'But won't Anne be mad?' I say. 'She's your friend too.'

My eyes are rimmed with red and I'm chewing on my bottom lip.

'You're right. She is. But so are you.'

The strengthening April sun illuminates the shape of Jane as she stands there in the kitchen in bare feet, a small hand towel still wrapped around her hair which today is nightclub-green.

'I . . . it's just that I . . . I don't know how to be a mum. I never wanted children.'

A flash of pain runs through Jane's face. In an instant she replaces her expression with a smile.

'There's nothing to explain, love. It's your body. Would you like a mug? I've just been for a swim, I'm warming up.' She lifts the chocolate powder up. 'Or just a hug?'

Jane reaches out a squishy arm to draw me in and instantly I start to cry. The plastic carton full of milk rests heavy on

my back. I do not mean to cry but cannot help myself. My
emotions seem to lurk beneath the surface of myself. I used
to keep them deep within, but my outer shell is porous now,
as if my body has absorbed some of the sea and attempts to
give it back at any moment in a steady stream of salty tears.

'Come on, let's get you settled here.'

I pull myself together, wipe my eyes.

'Anne?' I say. 'I'm worried. She was so upset. I've never
seen her shout like that.'

'Don't you fret. I'll check on her. I'm surprised she hasn't
guessed before, given that you've been living there. But I
suppose in that huge jumper that you always wear it's
hard to tell. You should let me wash it for you. You don't
need it in this weather and, if I'm honest, it's a little grubby,
love.'

I shake my head at just the thought of washing out faint
scents of Jay that are wrapped up in the fibres of the wool.
My hands shake as I take a seat and watch Jane fill a pan
with milk and light the flame that burns low blue and stir
the milk like melted moon.

'Do your parents know?'

I make a sound that's something like a laugh or bark.

'I didn't get a chance to tell them. My mother's fucking
furious already. She doesn't think it's good for me to stay
with Anne . . . not that I am.'

I bite at nails that are bitten to the quick. I gnaw at flecks
of flaking skin. The room smells cocoa rich and biscuity
and dairy thick and reminds me of my childhood.

'She's your mum. She'll come around. You should tell her that you're pregnant.'

'I can't,' I say. 'She'll kill me, Jane. I don't know what to do.'

'Of course you do.'

'I don't.' My voice is firmer, scared, my panic giving words more weight.

'You're doing it already, love. You're doing what I never could.'

Journey

Today is not a day I want. I wish that it was over, done, or never needed to be done at all. The wheels clack against the track. The churning pace of speeding train. I like the repetition of the sound and the constant moving window blur. I do not want the train to stop. I want to stay in stasis, moving fast between the stations that I've never even heard of and won't ever actually stop at, so I'm never really anywhere at all.

The clacks spread wide. The train slows down. I look out of the window and see that this is Bristol and the platform here is heaving, people-crammed and monstrous full. The train doors open all at once and people spill into the spaces of the carriage, spread out and fill up seats. I move my bag that's on the seat beside me, the one that really should be Anne's if we were actually speaking.

A mother with a baby tied across her chest in wraps of fabric sling sits down. She dips her eyes and beams at the small sleeping head and strokes some strands of hair that have fallen lightly in a fuzz over the crescent moons of lightly closed eyelids. I watch her sniff the little scalp and see her almost glow as she tucks a tiny hat down over perfect whorls of baby ears. She seems so satisfied and still. Like a woman who is all filled up, who has no hunger hiding anywhere inside of her. She must notice that I'm staring.

'When are you due?' she says, all smiles.

I really can't do this today.

'When are you due?' she asks again, annoyingly persistent, as if I haven't heard across the rumblings of the train and the noises of the carriage.

She rubs the sleeping baby's back that rainbow curves beneath her palm. There are faint smudges of tiredness under her smiling eyes and her pretty hair shimmers with just the slightest sheen of grease.

'Oh this?' I say, my hand pointing towards what used to be my flat stomach. The train is slowly revving up, it's gaining speed and gaining ground. The platform edge drops steeply off, then disappears from out of view. 'I'm not pregnant,' I finally say while smiling. She looks confused and stares down at the bump. 'I know it looks like it but it's just a giant tumour.'

'Oh God!' she says. Her face turns in a moment. She looks shaken and slightly grey. 'I'm so sorry. Oh, that's awful. Gosh. I really didn't mean to pry.'

'It's fine,' I say and grin a bright and manic grin, convinced that she'll be quiet now. The woman turns away and stares down at her baby, the smile fallen from her face.

Outside the moving train window, the cityscape gives way to open fields that are vibrant green and potent, lush. The trees are hinting at new leaves and hedgerows flood with blossoms. I stare out of the window at the moving land as she holds her baby even tighter in her grip.

Crowd

The gap between the train and platform edge looms large and suddenly inviting; a dark and quiet space that waits to swallow ankles, lives and save me from my mother and today. The air smells heavy, thick with city dust and chemicals and concrete crush and dirty, breathing human sprawl. There's a pushing and compression at my back as shoals of people swarm along the platform down towards the ticket gates and the people waiting, taxis leaving, destinations further on. My canvas bag is held out in front protecting the small bump that now protrudes, as the woman with the baby hurries off into the safety of the crowd. I pass my ticket through the scanner, push the slow revolving metal bar, being careful not to knock the stupid thing.

The crowds are shocking. I haven't seen this many people now in months and the mass is overwhelming, suddenly too much to bear. Too many bodies all alive around me, breathing, sweating, talking, loud. I close my eyes and try to see the gentle lapping of the sea but the sounds of people on their phones, announcements, trains and traffic jams break through and splinter all my thoughts and drown me out.

I know the stranger has a Big Mac even with my eyes shut tight. The familiar stench of salty meat and tang of sauce and sticky smell of plastic cheese. I open my eyes to see a man beside me on my right with his briefcase clasped between his feet, his ankles locking it in tight as he stands there watching the large screen that shows a list of destinations. He takes another bite from his large burger. A single drop of liquid grease runs from the corner of his mouth. He mops it without thinking with a wedge of doughy bread and crams the rest between his lips.

Jay was waiting in the service station queue. 'You sure that you don't want one, Em?' I laughed and told him I was fine. I stabbed a lump of salad with a spindly plastic fork and swallowed down a mouth of fridge-cold salmon. 'It's horrid, right? Eat this!' He passed his burger over, grinned and took a spare from out the bag. I unwrapped it like a Christmas gift. 'I knew that you'd want mine,' he said and winked at me.

I hear them first before I see them. Dad's low-pitched call from far away.

'Em! Emma! Here!' He waves at me above the heads from the far side of the station.

I watch my parents weave their way towards me through

the moving mass. My mother wears a brand-new coat that's tied in tight around her waist and makes her look officious. My breath is held inside my lungs, my body trying to stay buoyant in anticipation of my mother's heavy disapproval. She stops and stands a foot away and I watch her eyes widen to giant pools of unknown depths. I wait for her to tell me off, to tell me that I'm awful and have absolutely no idea exactly what I'm doing with my life. The things that I already know.

But the words, they do not come from her. They never come. She is silent as she almost runs to grab me in her arms. It's the most exercise I've ever seen her actually do and for once, ironically, she isn't wearing leggings.

'Oh, Emma sweetheart, Emma love. You didn't say.'

She is being kind and hugging me, which is shocking and intensely strange.

'Well, no,' I say confused. 'You would've only made things worse.'

She looks as if I've stabbed her in the centre of her heart, but she only says, 'Oh darling girl. Does your sister know?'

'Not yet,' I say.

'How many weeks?'

'I'm twenty-one.'

'Oh love, and you've managed all alone with this?'

'I guess,' I say, frowning, flummoxed.

'At least tell me that Anne has been there looking after you.'

'Umm . . . about that . . .' I look to Dad who is staring

at my stomach with a sort of semi-grin slapped on his face. 'Well, no actually. She threw me out.'

'Whatever for?' Dad frowns and speaks, suddenly paternal and protective.

'I told her I was planning on having an abortion.'

'And the woman threw you out?' My mother's voice is getting louder with each word. 'She offered you a place to stay and it's your choice, Emma. Your body is all yours. That woman, she can . . .'

I stop listening as she carries on her rant. Some sort of primal mother thing is happening before my eyes. My mother looks as if she wants to kill someone or hurt something. And amazingly for once it isn't actually me.

Meat

The bump has partly neutralized my mother's acid tongue.

'I need a burger first,' I say.

My dad looks pleased, my mother obviously displeased but silenced by my current state.

'You never used to eat that awful stuff.'

Her face is pinched and pulled in tight.

'I actually did. And anyway, I think I'm craving meat because I'm pregnant. Which you might have known if you hadn't had a strop and left me there in Cornwall.'

'I've already said I'm sorry, Em. I really am.'

Her lips are pursed as if the words are hard to form properly. Watching my mother saying sorry is the most fun that I've had in weeks.

'Are you?' I ask, seeing just how many sorries I can get from her.

'Of course I am. But you shouldn't really eat that stuff. Especially now.'

'I'm not keeping it. I still have three more weeks where an abortion is an option.'

My parents don't say anything, but Dad puts an arm around my shoulder and my mother reaches out and takes my hand.

'I'm just trying to look after you,' my mother says, sounding genuine. 'There's this documentary on Netflix. I thought that everyone had seen it. I think we're going vegan soon.' Dad looks at me in horror and my mother chooses not to see. 'Well, perhaps after the end of June. The Burgesses are staying then and I'd planned on doing lamb. I'm not sure I can change things at this late notice.'

'It's only April now,' I say and roll my eyes towards the roof with its antique arches, curves of glass.

'All right, you two. We don't have long,' says Dad, pointing up towards the station clock. I don't know if he's referring to the time we have to make it to the inquest or the days when burgers are allowed.

Dad takes my bag from my hands and heads towards McDonald's.

'Your clothes will smell of burgers,' my mother warns.

I glare at her and fold my arms.

'You really think I care?'

I eat it like it's all that's left. My death row meal. The final feast. I stuff it fast into my face, inhale the greasy burger meat and lick the salt from my lips. It reminds me slightly of the sea; the salty trace, a saline kiss. Dad sits across from me without a burger and assures me that he's 'fine, just fine,' but he cannot keep his eyes off the cardboard cup of salted chips as if he's not eaten for days. I pick a chip and hold it out, an offering he clearly wants, but my mother mouths a 'no', so Dad says, 'No, I really can't. Thanks, love, but no. Cholesterol. Apparently I need to be more careful with my diet.'

My mother watches like a hawk, ensuring Dad doesn't give in and eat the things he wants to eat and live his life the way he wants in case he dies and leaves her all alone and lonely. Just like me. The whole thing makes me laugh out loud.

'What's funny, love?' Dad asks, his eyes still firmly on the chips.

'You'll just eat burgers anyway when you're away with work. And we could leave the station now and all get smashed up by a speeding car. What happens then?'

'I can't control that, Emma.' My mother's voice sounds hurt and sharp. 'But I can control his diet when he's here at home. And if it keeps your dad alive for longer then I don't see what's so wrong with that.'

'I'm sat right here! Can we please not talk about me dying?' Dad pleads with both of us. He fiddles with his navy tie, unknots the neat and perfect knot, then, dissatisfied, reties the thing. 'Just one won't hurt.'

He stretches out his arm and takes three chips. My mother looks physically pained, as if she's fractured some innocuous bone. She reaches for her handbag, grabs the handles, pushes back the chair.

'I guess we're going, Emma love,' says Dad. 'You leaving those?'

He points his finger at the chips, the ones I've left that are now cold, and snatches a handful, stuffs them in.

'So good,' he says and grins.

Crime

It's not a trial but all around I feel blame, the nerves, the guilt, the sweating palms where beads of fear accumulate along the creases of lifelines. The fact the room looks like the court rooms on TV doesn't help. There are wooden panels, formal chairs. I'd imagined something friendlier. A head teacher's small office space or a local London library with an air of underfunding. I hadn't thought the place would look like this; all clean and doleful polished shine, professional severity. The sudden realization that I'm sitting here and this is actually happening and that Jay is dead and I am here and waiting for a coroner brings panic with it, awful panic. I want my sister, want her hand which is stuck soothing my nephews and their chicken-poxed small bodies.

I just want everything to stop but nothing stops and people carry on arriving, filling up the seats as if it's church or some anticipated theatre show. I press my bitten nails into the soft flesh of my palm. The nails leave small marks, little purple indents in the skin. There are people here already but I scan the room and can't see Anne and can't see Ben. Angela, the police liaison officer, the one whose name I wish I didn't know, is chatting with her colleagues all in uniform. Their bodies are upright and still in sombre stance contrasting with their faces which are animated as they chat and wait to do this thing that is a job to them. Another day. Another death. Then sitting on a bench beside the paramedics and a student nurse I suddenly spot Anne. She is sitting next to Martin. She is even thinner than before and she stares ahead, unseeing; her face ashes, her eyes matt dead.

We wait for things to start. I sit between my parents who both hold my sweating hands. I keep glancing at the door until I finally see Ben walk right in and take a seat. My body fizzes frantic with anxiety and my heart beats louder in my ears and my head hums loud as queen-less bees. Ben squirms and fidgets in his skin as if allergic to himself. He avoids my desperate searching eye. The sight of Ben physically hurts and I spin my wedding ring around my finger with my restless thumb. The metal clicks against the glittered curve of my engagement band which spins round too, the rings both loose on widow hands, as if my finger flesh has shrunk to give some distance from the band in the knowledge that our marriage vows have been broken.

Death did 'us part'.

Or was it Ben?

Verdict

A silence suddenly descends as the coroner arrives. I hear the large potted plant that's sitting in the corner actually wilt. A leaf cracks off its fray of stalks, escaping from the torture of forget and the unrelenting heat from the radiators which suck the water from the air and suck the life from the plant. The leaf breaks free and flutters down all dried and crisp and lands with a soft scratch of sound upon the shiny wooden floor.

The room is interrupted by the voice of the court coroner who addresses all of us at once.

'We don't apportion blame here. Our job is simply finding answers, ascertaining exactly how Jay died.' The coroner explains to all, looking at me. 'I understand that many of Jay's family and his loved ones are here with us today.' I turn around and glance at Ben who is sweating, staring at the floor. 'I apologize if the questions that I ask are difficult to answer but they do need to be asked. Now let's begin . . .'

Undone

'It's all right, love, it's over now.' My mother hugs me limpet tight. I cling on hard and bend my head into her chest, searching for solace in the very scent of her. She has her arms around me, holds me, doesn't for a second let me go. 'You're okay, love. It's done, all done. I'm sorry, love.'

I cannot speak. The memories of his hanging frame, his brokenness, his heavy bones. I'm folded in, a flesh conch shell, the only sound the sea that echoes in the depths of my own ears.

'Let's go,' she says. 'Come home and stay with us, at least until you feel a little better.'

I nod a 'yes' and my mother grips my hand so hard it aches in the compression of her hold.

'I didn't know,' I whisper without moving, my face still pressed into her chest. My dad stands round the back of me and makes a parent circle with his hug. I shelter in the middle of the closed ring of protection.

'The finding was a suicide,' Dad says to me. 'We knew that would be the case.'

'But . . . he was seen along the railway . . . and all the medications for depression. I didn't even know those things.'

'I'm so sorry, love,' my mother says.

'I could have helped,' I say, in a voice that's barely audible.

'He didn't let you. He clearly didn't think that you or anybody else could help. Those things he didn't tell you, that was his own choice. It's not your fault,' my mother says, her voice firmer.

My mother's wrong. Of course it was my fault. There should have been a sentencing for me. I want someone to take me down, to lock me up and punish me for all the things I didn't do and all the things I didn't know. I want the gallows, want to be left hanging too. A human flag out in the wind.

The words keep circling round my brain. The things that other people said:

'Seen along the railway.'

'Stopped by someone while standing on the platform for too long.'

'Medicated for depression for two years.'

'The business was really struggling, things were bad.'

'A mounting debt.'

The sentences all swirl, whirl and rush around the insides of my head. They echo back and play again. I hear the things I've learnt about my husband's hidden anguish and the many things my husband didn't share. The words crash loud. They mount a swell. I drown in all the words I've heard.

'I'm so sorry,' I finally say to no one and to everyone but mostly just to Jay.

My mother pulls my body off hers and holds my shoulders square and firm and looks me in my salt-blurred eyes.

'You've nothing to say sorry for. I'm the one who's sorry, love. I should have been there all along. I should have been there for you both. Come on. Let's go. Let's get you out of here.'

My parents pull me down the corridor and out into the street. They propel me with momentum. A rain shower breaks suddenly and water streams down from the leaden city sky. Dad walks ahead to hail a cab and my mother stays and opens up a large umbrella to shield me. She holds my hand in one of hers, just like she did before I learnt to safely cross a road. A grip of love so tight it hurts. I stand beside my mother, let her keep me dry and hold me still. The world around us spins too fast, too full of people, too alive. I close my eyes against it all.

Inside the dark I hear footsteps on rain-washed stone before I actually feel him; a quiet breeze, a whispered hush of gentle warmth. He brushes up and leans in tight, puts his lips close to my ear and says the words so quietly that I don't know if they're real.

'It was me he really loved,' he murmurs deep into the centre of myself.

'What was that?' my mother says, spinning around.

I open my eyes to see Ben's body moving fast along the street and disappear into the throng of people and umbrellas.

I cannot say the words out loud that I know now to be true.

Stars

I'm back beneath the constellations of my childhood. The ceiling is the same but the room looks different from before.

'It's "Borrowed Light",' my dad explains. 'Your mother spent a whole day painting tiny patches on the wall. All those colours looked the same to me. And that paint's a bloody fortune too. Five pounds for just a tester pot!'

But it isn't quite the same colour. It's new and fresh and the crack that spanned the distant wall is painted over, finally gone. There's bedding too I've never seen that's bright and bold, a print that's Japanese and blue and looks like stitching, evokes small waves. My mother sweeps in motherly and flurries round the bed to switch both the bedside lamps on and pull the curtains shut across the dimming sky. The light glows up the bedroom walls, casts golden shapes across the space. I slump onto the corner of the bed. I'm spent. I'm done. I'm dry of tears.

'I'll run a bath,' my mother says.

I mutter thanks and lie down on the pristine bed, roll over onto my left side and clutch a pillow, draw it close. I pull it tight into myself and hug it like it has a heart. It smells of fabric softener and ironed cotton, airy clean.

A text alert lights up my phone: Jude sending love from far away.

'How did it go? I'm sorry that I wasn't there. Bloody sickly kids. I can't believe I've got it too. The itch is mad. The spots are everywhere and I mean *everywhere*. I love you heaps.'

It pings again. A long list of emojis. A line of yellow faces, each surrounded with small perfect hearts that aren't the same as being here.

'I'm pregnant. Jay loved Ben,' I type and the phone begins to ring immediately.

Distortion

I look down at the steaming bath that's bubble filled. The room smells safe and soft, of lavender and calm. Uncomfortable, I perch my bottom on the narrow lip of the roll-top bath and pull the chain that clinks, wrenching the plug from out its seal and watch with satisfaction as the water drains itself away in perfect clockwise circles. I wonder if it's really true that half a world away water will create a vortex that is opposite to this one. I wonder if I'm upside down, the wrong way round or if it's just a story.

'Emma? You okay in there? I just ran that bath,' my mother calls through sturdy walls and bathroom doors.

'I'm fine,' I shout. My favourite word. 'I just really want a shower, not a bath.'

I hear her sigh and mutter that 'Hot water isn't free, you know.'

The truth is that the bath water looks comforting and more than I can cope with now. I don't deserve the niceties of warmth. I think my husband must have killed himself because he was in love with Ben and couldn't find the words to tell me how he really felt. I need the shock of deep cold sea, the painful freeze, the raw release. The sea. I miss the sea. Warm water finally empties out and leaves a trace of bubbles on the inside of the tub just like a high-tide mark left on the beach, a line that tells us where things used to reach and how they change. They always change.

The shower streams a steady jet of household cold. It trails saltless down my curves, it runs around the edges of my bump and hugs itself against my hips. The cold is nothing like the cold I'm craving now but it will have to do. Small prickles rise up on my skin like barnacles along a boat. An 'O' escapes from my mouth, the change in temperature enough to jolt my brain and make me notice for a second that I'm still inside a body, a body that belongs to me. Well, not just me. At least for now.

I turn around, the shower head still pumping water, and catch sight of myself in the mirrored bathroom-cabinet door. The bump protrudes from low and stretches up and reaches out. There's nothing that will hide it now. It seems to know I'm looking, wants to let me know it's here so jabs a nameless limb out hard behind my splay of ribs. I gasp again. Another 'O' at the shock of being kicked from the inside, a strange sensation that keeps on resonating through me like an echo travelling through a cave and reminds me that the core of me is moving, growing, molten, soft.

'Please don't,' I say aloud. 'I'm not the one who needs kicking.'

I'm talking to a mass of cells, conversing with an unseen thing that's almost there but not quite there. I look away. The mirror mocks me with a body I don't recognize. My skin is stretched, my breasts are patterned with blue veins and my nipples are as dark as Oreos. I shiver, shake. The thing within kicks hard again.

I switch the shower stream to off and hold the wall, steady myself. The towels in reach are soft and large and all brand new like sheets of cloud. The labels read 'White Company'. My eyes roll high. Of course they are. Expensive. White. Ridiculous. I make a point of rubbing at my made-up eyes. Mascara smears leave smudgy marks across the fluff. The towel looks like a sweep of snow with tyre tracks careering off towards the edges of the thing, the markings of a deadly crash. I imagine the police putting up those small signs everywhere that ask for any witnesses; a human who corroborates the things they must already know. And Angela just sitting there telling some other family, 'I know how awful this must be.'

'Have you got everything you need in there?' my mother shouts as if she somehow hears my thoughts, calls out the fact I find her towels ridiculous and find her life ridiculous and see death waiting everywhere, even in the most mundane.

'No,' I say. 'I'm still missing a husband and some answers.'

'I was talking about towels,' she says.

I grab a second clean white towel and rub mascara over that one too.

May

Squash

The South West train rocks steady on the tracks that hug the coastline back to Jane and Claire and Pete and perfect icy swims. I take the pictures from my bag, the ones that haven't yet made sense. I'm not sure if I even care about figuring them out. It's not as if he loved me. So why does missing him still hurt so much? I spread the photographs out flat, push the creases with smooth hands. My hands remind me of Jay's hands that will never get to age now. Hands that knew Ben's body.

Outside the sea sweeps high and close to meet the track and greet the metal side of the train. I breathe out deep, the vast expanse of salty view, a promise and a homecoming as I dial Jude.

'You almost there?' she asks.

'About halfway.'

'I can't believe you lasted with our parents for a fort-night.'

'I didn't really see them. I mostly stayed in bed and

watched Netflix and the food was good. How's the chicken pox going?'

'Like an evil game of dominoes. Just as one of us recovers the next one starts to itch. I really wish I'd had it as a child. I've never been so ill, Em. Imagine thrush but worse.'

'But you're okay?'

'Except for all the awful scabs. I look like a Victorian whore.'

We both laugh at that, remembering her misspent youth or well-spent youth, depending on perspective. There is an electronic swoosh of opening carriage doors as a tall man walks through carrying large bags and looking for a place he'd like to sit. He looks around, avoids my stare, seems dissatisfied with what he sees, keeps moving further down the train. He hits the button, moves on through as the second set of doors seals shut behind him, leaving me alone again.

'Are we going to talk about it, Em?' she finally asks.

'Talk about what?'

'The abortion. It's two days away. Are you okay?'

'I'll be fine.'

'Mum said you wouldn't let her come. Just tell me someone else will be there to look after you.'

'I haven't told them yet, but Claire or Jane, I'm sure they'll come.'

'And you definitely want this?'

'Jude, I'm pregnant with the baby of a man who didn't love me and conveniently isn't here for me to kill. Yes, I definitely want this.'

Outside a wave comes from the sea and grows in height, then throws its weight against the train. The salt sticks to the moving glass and the train tilts slightly on the tracks so I weight the pictures with my phone and the cardboard-collared coffee cup. The cottage door, a sunrise and a stupid bit of wall. And then a sweep of paleness: all blurry smear, a dot of brown. And the photograph inside my mind. Of Ben. Of Ben. Of Ben.

Jude has to go so I wrap my Beats headphones like an Alice band around my head to block out any chance of conversation, show others that I won't engage if anyone was actually here. There isn't any music playing in my ears and the bump is pushing on my bladder and pressing on the table edge. I lift my top to look at it. There are fine and downy hairs that look disturbingly as if my skin is furring into cowhide.

I search my phone for facts about a twenty-three-week pregnancy and an image of an ordinary squash fills up my screen. The thing weighs half a kilo now. The exact same weight as twenty slices of burnt toast or fourteen pairs of empty socks.

Ache

I must have slept a little while, the train window a glass pillow of changing patterns and rural threads. Saliva has run from out the corner of my slack and sleeping mouth and left a viscid trail down the left edge of my chin. A sudden pulling in my stomach drags me up from dreamless sleep and shakes me wide awake. I adjust the headphones on my ears, which have bruised the cartilage inside with their tight compress of soundless hug, and then pull them down around my neck to form a leather dog-collar, a car-crash brace. Instinctively I start to rub the solid lump of abdomen. There's no one sitting by my side and the carriage is still empty and everything is quiet save the gentle clack and click and clack of train that's rolling over track.

Then suddenly another twinge that's sharp and strong and feels as if a human hand has reached inside and tried to grab my organs, wrapped its fingers through the loops of bowel and made a fist and squeezed it tight. I try to breathe but make a sound I do not know. It is wild and low, not something that I've ever heard. I breathe in slowly through my nose, attempt to recollect the things that Claire and Jane and quiet Pete said on the beach about the vast and icy sea and how to cope with the pain of cold submersion. 'Breathe in and out.' 'Breathe long and slow.' The pain subsides as suddenly as it arrived. For a moment, when it's gone, it's easy to imagine that the pain was just imagined too and that nothing's wrong.

My phone is full of texts from both my mother and my dad to see if I'm all right and asking if the train is full and if I found a forward-facing seat. Dad wants to know exactly what the weather's like outside of London where apparently it's drizzling.

My palms are clammy, slightly cold, unlike my face which flushes hot. I find Claire's number, want to call, but don't know what I'd actually say. 'There was a pain and now it's gone?' Instead I go to Spotify, decide distraction might be best and find an album that I liked when I was young and still naive enough to think that death was something distant; a destination far away, reserved for just the elderly and those unlucky ones who suffered awful things, huge tragedies. Unlucky ones who were not me.

Again

A song is playing in my ears. I skim through tracks on Spotify. I'm searching for my childhood in carefully curated sounds. Then suddenly it comes again. The awful squeeze. The low-down pain.

'Oh fuck,' I mutter through pursed lips and wonder if wishing away a pregnancy can actually work.

The train is crossing the long bridge that links the land and marks the place where Cornwall starts and Devon ends. The water flows beneath the train, the river wide and swollen, gushing out towards the waiting sea. I grab my phone and listen to the dial tone.

'Are you okay?'

Claire sounds surprised to hear from me.

'I don't think so. It really hurts.' My voice cracks like an iceberg. 'Something's happening,' I say again, frightened.

'Where are you now?' she asks with calm.

'The train. Saltash. We're almost there, stopped on the bridge. This hurts, Claire. Please.'

'Get off the train when it pulls in. I'll meet you there.' I can hear Claire breathing faster now and the muffled sound of metal as she grabs her keys. 'Stay on the line.' Her voice sounds serious and urgent.

'Okay,' I manage as I stand and grab my bag and stumble to the nearest door. The train is motionless upon the bridge and a voice comes through the tannoy and carries down the carriages to say, 'We're sorry for the short delay, we'll move in a few minutes more.' I wait by the train door with its clearly illustrated instructions showing how the window must be lowered and the handle opened from outside. It would be easy just to open it, right here, over the river.

'Emma? Emma, are you still there? Can you tell me if you're bleeding?' Claire's voice breaks through the dark of thoughts and brings me back.

'I've no idea. My stomach hurts.'

'Is the pain constant? Does it come and go?'

'It comes and goes. Oh fuck. Again.'

I hold the phone away and press my hand against the carriage wall to hold my body up, erect. I want to fold myself in half, to crouch down low and curl up small upon the scuffed and dirty floor. It's only a few seconds then it passes by like weather. I pull the phone back to my ear.

'Another one?' I hear Claire ask. 'An ambulance will take as long. I'm almost there. Ten minutes more.' She's calling loud into the phone. 'Just fucking move,' she says, and I can hear the beeping of a horn. 'Not you, Emma. The car in front. Just move.'

The train stays motionless, suspended on the bridge over the river. I watch the water underneath. The mass of it a slick and solid grey, sliding and slipping fast away beneath the bright blue sky and white puffed clouds.

As the train begins to slowly move another pain begins to squeeze from the inside and pushes out the breath held stagnant in the furthest corners of my lungs until it seems they start to flame and burn, like diving in the deep too long. I focus on the rhythm of the click and clack and the building sound of movement, wheels on metal ridge of track. The train is finally moving now and soon the station will appear and hopefully Claire, although the person who is waiting should be Jay. Especially as this is his fault.

Tremors

'I called ahead. She has no notes,' Claire tells the midwife on the ward.

Her hands or midwife hands reach out to help me from my coat and cardigan and loose T-shirt. Small bumps of flesh rise up despite the heat inside the ward and spread across my naked arms as they're slotted through a mint green gown. The women get me on the bed, remove my shoes, adjust the pillow round my head. The bedding smells chemically clean. I close my eyes, surrender, drown in their compassion and attention.

'I really shouldn't be here. I'm wasting both your time. It's stopped. The pain's already stopped.' But I stay there on the wheeled-bed and let the midwife move her magical machines and strap two lengths of stretchy belt around the tightness of my girth to read the secret language that's transmitting tremors from inside.

'I'm Patience,' says the midwife and I wonder at the woman's name. The potent power of a name. 'And you're not wasting anybody's time. Let's see what's going on in there.' Her voice carries a gentle lilt, exudes a power and a calm. She readjusts one of the belts and suddenly the monitor begins to print a paper strip that's covered in small seismic waves. Nobody moves as the midwife stares at her machines and reads the electronic shapes that ebb and flow in scratchy lines across paper written in a language that I do not know. 'Can you feel that?' she asks. I open my eyes to see hers flickering between my face and the steady paper printed churn. I open my mouth to tell her 'no' but then the tightness starts to come again and then the spreading ache begins to rise and I wonder how on earth she knew.

'Where does it hurt? Exactly where?' she asks.

I point towards the front of me, the dome of flesh that towers up, eclipses long-forgotten thighs. I look from Claire, to Patience and then back again to Claire. The women catch each other's eyes. They glance away, bury their gazes deep inside the undulating inky lines that keep on printing shock waves.

'Can you feel it across your back or down your legs?' I shake a 'no'. I look at Claire to see if I have answered right. I cannot tell. 'Emma, it's possible you're going into early labour now. If that's happening we can try and slow things down and we'll need to give you an injection to help your baby's lungs along. At twenty-four weeks each day counts.'

'It's only twenty-three,' I say.

Patience pauses, shakes her head.

'I don't think so. Not according to the measurements.

You look exactly twenty-four to me, maybe almost twenty-five.'

'I can't be. No!' I panic say. 'I had a scan. They told me I was fourteen weeks.'

'That's a little late to do a dating scan. They become less accurate as time goes on. I think they got it wrong. Did you have a twelve-week scan? They're more reliable for dating.'

'No,' I utter. 'No. I just can't be. I'm not.'

I reach for the recycled cardboard bowl beside the bed in case I actually vomit. I'm too late for an abortion. I swallow down the sick while Claire holds my clammy hand and strokes my head like I'm a child. This can't be happening. It simply can't.

I think of Otis dressed in his bright dinosaur pyjamas, small fingers wrapped around Claire's own. And my mother too. I attempt to see her pregnant, young and lying on a bed inside a hospital. Or at home, a corpulent hormonal mess, undone by something on the news. But the image will not clearly come. Instead I see her neat like she is now, kneeling pregnant over fabric with a dress-pin pursed between her lips, arranging paper patterns on a fold of Laura Ashley print. And my dad happy and proud watching his young wife cut out a dress, the room filled with their mutual hope and the satisfying crunch as fabric relents to the sharpened sewing shears.

'Don't go?' I say. My voice sounds small. The fear is large. It shrinks the words, compresses them.

'I won't,' says Claire. 'I'm going nowhere.'

'But your kids, your work . . . I'm sorry, Claire.'

'They're all sorted,' she says. 'You're the most important thing right now. And anyway, the kids are off to friends when school is done. The mothers help each other out. "It takes a village" so they say and, well, we actually live in one. You have a village too, you know.'

Patience stands to pull the thin blue curtain round the bed and shuts out the empty-bedded ward.

'Now just relax your legs,' she says.

My legs are probably the least relaxed that they have ever been as I grit my teeth while a stranger's latex-covered fingers reach inside the depths of me. She twists her arm and shifts herself. I breathe in deep. Claire grips my hand a little harder and I close my eyes against the deep discomfort of it all.

'Well done, it's done.'

The midwife pulls her hand from out of my insides, pulls off the gloves that snap back like the breaking of elastic bands.

'The good news is your cervix is still long and closed and hard to reach. I want to monitor you for a while, but you don't have regular contractions. I think you're just experiencing Braxton Hicks.'

I look to Claire. I've read no books. I don't know what on earth she means.

'They're like a practice version. Just your body warming up,' Claire says.

'But all that pain?' I say.

Again, the women catch each other's eyes and share some knowledge I don't have. Claire looks almost close to smiling.

'Well, they can feel quite uncomfortable and some women are just more attuned to feeling them than others. As long as they're just Braxton Hicks and nothing happens overnight you can go home in the morning. Your baby seems quite happy there for now. There are no decelerations on the trace.' Patience feeds the reams of wavy printed lines through her deft hands. Her brow is slightly smoother than it was and I feel like I've passed some kind of test that I didn't know that I was taking. She helps me pull my knickers up, tucks the blanket in around my legs, pulls back the curtain loosely wrapped around the bed. 'I'll be back to check on you. Just press the buzzer if you need me in the meantime.'

'Oh God,' I say and start to cry.

'You're fine. The baby's fine,' Claire says, in an attempt to reassure me.

She doesn't understand that that's exactly why I'm crying.

Alone

Claire has to leave. Patience goes home. The night ahead is stretched and lonely, silent, long. I lie in bed and try hard not to panic. I cannot be a mother. The monitor stands beside me in the semi-gloom like a strict soldier on sentry duty. Wide elastic straps are tightly tied around my bump, digging in and leaving imprints on my skin. My bladder's full, uncomfortable, but I do not press the help buzzer that the night midwife's left in my reach. Every time I think about the pregnancy I hear Ben telling me that Jay loved him, not me, and for a moment I stop breathing.

I attempt to find some calm, to fixate on the feeling of the blanket in my red-tagged hand. I stroke the individual indents and the texture, which is soft, as if it's been washed half to death. It's far too light across my legs to bring much comfort to my limbs. The colour must have once been white but isn't now and reminds me of the shades of paint my mother loves, with stupid names like 'Skimmed Milk White' and 'Ammonite'. I flip my phone from front to back and front to back, obsessive and repetitive. I run my finger down the crack that dents the glass.

As if she knows I thought of her, a text comes through. 'Are you safe home? Love Mum x,' it reads.

She still signs off each single text as if I wouldn't know it was from her. I flip the phone again, screen down.

The thing inside my belly stirs within the depths, dives somewhere down. Or is it up? The pillow crunches round my head. It feels like plastic, smells like fear and chemicals and far-from-home. Sleep is elusive in this strange place with its synthetic lights and beeping sounds and footsteps loud and voices on the telephone. I try to close my eyes but feel too terrified to sleep, unlike the unborn thing which has now settled in some part of me.

A woman joins me on the ward led by the night midwife. She cowboy walks as if she is a man with balls of heavy lead between his solid legs. She holds her stomach, pivots her hips, her breathing thick and laboured with the effort of just moving. She looks enormous. Vast. Obscene. I breathe a little deeper, grateful for the distraction that her presence now provides.

The moment that the midwife leaves the woman pulls the curtains back from round her bed. She's brought a bag that's crammed with clothes and drops it on the plastic chair. The bag tips up and retches out its contents on the lino floor. A phone charger makes a loud crash, white cable trailing from the bag, and lands beside her pink and nylon slippers that look flammable, as if they should have been replaced some years ago but are too loved, a part of her. She breathes out slow, lethargic breaths. She bends her swollen knees and retrieves the charger from the floor. I shut my eyes, pretend to sleep but just too late. She's spotted me.

'Your first?' she calls across the room, from in the dim of enforced night.

'Umm, I guess so. Yes,' I say, not quite sure how to answer that, not wanting 'yes' to be the truth.

She laughs as if I've told a joke.

'My fourth!' she says triumphantly. She rubs the giant bump that swells inside a loose T-shirt then grins at me as if she's pleased with all the reproducing that she's done. She looks too young to have three kids, her face too smooth, not creased with age. I watch her as she reaches up and moves a hair band off her wrist and pulls her hair up tight and high. 'You want some gum?' She waves what must be chewing gum.

'No thanks,' I say.

'Me neither. What I really want's a cigarette.'

I can't tell if she's serious, if she genuinely wants to smoke.

'I could actually drink a Mai Tai now,' I say and bite my lip so hard I hope it bleeds. She nods at me as if she knows.

'So what they got you in for then?' She lies back on the pillow.

'I had some pains,' I say. 'They thought I might be going into labour.'

'How many weeks? You don't look big.' I look down at my own round bump. It's not as big as hers but I feel grotesque and huge.

'Twenty-four,' I say. 'I thought that I was only twenty-three . . .'

'You cross those legs and keep it in! That's far too early for a baby to be born. And anyway, at least inside they're quiet. 'Cos once they're out, however much you want to, you can't shove them back.' She laughs again. I shiver, feeling cold despite the stagnant warmth. We stay there for a while, both together but alone. 'This baby thing is knackering,' she finally says. 'Your bloke the helpful kind?'

The air escapes from out my lungs.

We're interrupted by the automated sound of air that fills the fabric cuff around her arm that's measuring her blood pressure. I watch the band expand, depress and suddenly alarms go off.

'Oh not again. I'm sick of this.' Her words are slightly sticky, slow. The beeping sound is high and shrill, an urgent call. 'My blood pressure is way too high. I keep on telling them of course it is with three small kids but they just won't . . .' Her voice fades out, as if she were the ending of a pop song from the eighties which doesn't know how else to end.

A midwife I haven't seen before comes through the doors at speed, walks briskly to the woman's bed and silences the high-pitched sound, checks the numbers on the monitor.

'The room looks sorta fuzzy. I don't feel too good.' The

woman slurs the lengthened words as if she's actually found the Mai Tais.

'Hang in there, Trish,' the midwife says. 'That baby's coming out today.' And suddenly the ceiling lights are flicked to full, the room becomes fluorescent bright and sleep is cancelled for us all as the ward fills up with people rushing in to lay Trish flat and hang up drips and keep on saying, 'It's okay, Trish. You'll be okay,' as if the words will make a difference. I grab my phone and clutch it hard until my fingers start to hurt. It doesn't matter what they say, that lady doesn't look okay.

Time

My phone shows 3.03am, that dreaded hour we rarely see that sits between the end of night and start of day and doesn't seem to follow all the normal rules of passing time. Instead each minute at this hour is warped, protracted, slowed right down as if the world can't face the day so lingers, like it's hanging tight onto the moon and isn't ready to let go. In the gloom my waking thoughts grow larger than a nightmare. My husband loved somebody else. I am pregnant and he left me here. I stare up at the ceiling squares and will this night to swiftly end.

The city lights were sparkling all around us, as if the sky had shared its stars and littered them across Moroccan rooftops. I could smell the dust and fabric weave, the lemon-sweet of food and the stale sweat that seemed to rise from the buildings. 'Marry me, Em?' Jay crouched down on one knee and held out a glistening ring. There were stars above and stars below and stars inside my head and heart. I hoped the sun would never rise.

My phone shows 3.04am. The other beds are empty still. That woman, Trish, has not come back. I want to know what happened. I hope she's on another ward and feeling well, the baby that she wanted wrapped up in her arms, her partner there to tell her that it's all okay. But every time I close my eyes I see her ashen face and hear her swollen, heavy malformed words and I feel a terrible jealousy. I imagine awful, awful things I wish were happening to me, not her.

I am a perfect monster.

Metal

I text my mother with, 'I'm good. Sorry I didn't text last night. Fell fast asleep.'

The reply comes back with rabid speed: 'Was worried. Glad you're back and safe. Love Mum. x'. But I'm not at Jane's. I'm far from good. I didn't sleep. Another text arrives from her asking what time I'm booked into the clinic and whether I'm absolutely sure that I don't need her there. I just ignore that one. A small woman with short black hair arrives at dawn, the stinging stench of bleach surrounding her like a bright aura. She kicks a plastic bucket on small wheels, shoves the thing aggressively across the floor in front of her, wielding a mop as if it is a weapon.

'You mind?' she asks and mops the floor around my bed without bothering to hear whether I actually mind or not. The water sloshes in the bucket, the grey and muddied colour of the Tamar. It slips and slides, like sugared tea. Outside the safety-locked windows the sun is slowly rising.

I listen to the splosh and splash, breathe in the scent of chemicals and coffee made from granules. At 8.00am Patience appears.

'I hear I missed a busy night,' she says to me.

'Is she all right?'

'I'm sure she's fine.' Patience provides no reassurance with the words she says that sound as if they're hollowed out, too light and lacking the essential weight that truth denotes. She flicks a switch, moves a machine. 'Now, let's do one more trace and then if that's all good the doctor should discharge you when she does her rounds.'

'Can I wee first?' I finally ask.

'Of course!'

She takes the trace leads off my middle and offers me a solid arm. I pull my trainers on my feet, attempt to hold the awkward gown that seems to want to flap around, determined to expose me. My bladder feels bursting full. I waddle fast and worry I won't make it to the bathroom down the hall.

I realize as I sit there on the toilet that to stand again is almost more than I can manage. The drama that was yesterday, the awkward bed and sleepless night and knowledge that I'll have to be a mother now compounds and settles down inside my limbs and makes a home inside my bones beside the constant missing feeling. It is a deep exhaustion unlike anything I've felt before. The tiredness pulls at me with the weight of all those metals that we learnt about in school with pretty names that don't seem plausible: iridium, plutonium, uranium and osmium. I brace to stand.

Despite the fact I hate it here, I weirdly can't face leaving. I want to stay here in the bed that crackles when I move and not get up and have kind Patience rally round me every day to check on me and make sure that I'm eating well and make sure that I'm sleeping well and make sure that I'm breathing still. Perhaps there are some magic drugs that can put me in a coma or just keep me on the edges of unconsciousness, at least until the baby's grown and ready to come out. And maybe even then the doctors could just let me sleep, not wake me. Bring me round when it's an adult, when it's grown up and I am old and someone else has raised it. Someone capable of parenthood and with a better track record of keeping all the ones they love alive.

Done

'Well, that's good news.' Patience seems genuinely pleased with the reassuring trace and with the doctor's strong agreement that the baby is not coming now and I do not need to stay here any longer.

'Is it?' I ask.

'Of course it is.' She looks confused. 'You get to be at home where you belong and keep on growing us that baby 'til it's ready to be born.'

I guess I don't look overjoyed. She looks at me again as if she's trying to decipher all the thoughts I hide behind the features of my face.

'Is everything all right, Emma?'

That's a question with an answer that is decades long or very short and simply 'No.'

'Can I just wait here 'til Claire arrives?' I ask Patience instead.

'Of course you can. Why don't you put your clothes back on? Shall I help you with the gown?'

I feel like a little girl as she carefully unties the fabric bows that are knotted at my neck. My teeth are coated in a film of sticky scum and my eyes are full of morning grit. I run my tongue around my teeth, follow the contours of each individual molar and incisor. My whole human identity is written like an ancient language engraved into their ridges and their shapes. We learnt in primary school that teeth can last thousands of years, even when all other body parts have long since decomposed.

'But I haven't cleaned my teeth yet.' I was holding my hand flat over my morning mouth in mock protest. 'You really think I care?!' Jay gently pushed my hand away and leant down over me and grinned. I raised my head to kiss him. He tasted of rich coffee beans and mint toothpaste and he smelt of morning air and sweat. 'I need to get out of these running clothes and take a shower first.' I arched my eyebrows, smiled and said, 'You'd better hurry then.'

There's a makeup bag stuffed somewhere in my holdall with a white toothbrush and small hairbrush, deodorant and mascara from the MAC counter in Selfridges; the things I need to make myself respectable, presentable, that show the world I'm coping still, I'm Emma still. The bag stays zipped. My fingers form a makeshift comb that catches in the snags of hair and I doubt has any impact on the way I look; a pregnant harpy with hair gone wild.

'Is everything all right? You know that you can talk to me?' Patience tries again.

I think about just telling her. Describing Jay. Describing Death. Describing Ben. Confiding that I don't want this, any of this, that I don't know what to do.

'There isn't anything to say,' I say instead.

'Morning!' says Claire, her voice all floaty, light and bright. 'No one called me in the night so I take it you're still pregnant then!' She grins, as pleased as Patience was. 'So, are we heading home now?'

She sounds so happy and excited that it's all okay. The thing inside me kicks my ribcage hard and quick and I breathe in dagger-sharp and short. I close my eyes. Ignore them all. I'm done with speaking, done with words.

Silence

'Emma, please say something? Say anything at all?' Claire begins to beg again.

She's tried engaging me in conversation for the whole drive from the hospital, back towards the headland and the village and Jane's cottage by the sea. Now Jane is trying her best too. But silence is a thing that I can do. I've had years of practice with my mother and with Jay. This is a game they will not win.

'Oh come on, Em!' Jay was trying to appease me. 'I didn't mean to get that drunk. We just lost track of time.' I scowled and sulked, ignored his offer of some toast, stayed silent as he rambled on. 'It was all Ben's fault. He kept on getting beers in. I didn't mean to worry you at all.' I grabbed the toast off his plate and took a bite, swallowed my words.

'Just tell us what you're thinking now. We'll try to help,' says Jane, tucking a wisp of purple hair back in a messy bun.

I'm thinking they should all shut up. There is nothing anyone can say to make this any better. I cannot have a termination and raising the child of a man who is dead and didn't love me feels totally impossible. How can anybody help? I am stuck, stuck inside this body and this life I never asked for with no options left.

'We're worried, Emma. Please just talk?' Claire tries again.

I do not talk.

I take the book filled with the photos from my bag and place it on the pillow, leave my trainers by the bed and shelter deep beneath the duvet with my clothes still on.

'I have to get to work right now. Jane is staying here with you and I'll come and see you later. And I'm sure that Pete's around somewhere.'

I do not talk. I do not care. Outside I can see chimney tops and slate roof tiles but mainly sky from this low angle on the bed. Small clouds are drifting over blue. It feels as if the clouds are actually mocking me. I watch them playing, dolphin-racing, surfing on the gentle wind, oblivious to everything.

'Just rest,' says Claire. 'You must be absolutely shattered.' I hear her say to Jane in whispers, 'Will you be all right with her?'

'We'll be just fine,' Jane reassures.

I roll over in bed with just my eyes above the duvet. Jane aimlessly picks up *The Catcher in the Rye* as if her hands need something to amuse them. She flicks through all the pages. The photographs fall out like leaves streaming down from autumnal trees. She takes one sheet of paper in her hand and bites her lips as if to keep the words from falling out of her too fast.

'This one . . .' Jane finally says. 'This wall right here. I think I know what this might be. There's something you should know.'

June

Torment

I consider looking for the wall, the exact stone, the precise place, but it all feels so pointless. There are endless walls that run around the village, each full of nooks and rugged cracks that could cling onto a secret. The beach is packed with children on half-term and visitors that fill all of the cottages, the village swollen with young families that I cannot stand to see. Instead I walk onto the headland with its forest full of silence. Inside the quiet I hope to find an answer to a problem which is hopeless and insolvable. There's a menace in the arched cocooning of the heavy trees despite the lush of June that's broken through the earth beneath. Everything is scraps of darkness, scraps of light. I stomp along the footpath that is lined with ferns, their feathered leaves each whispering.

I was tracing hands over Jay's flesh, exploring all the places that were his. He breathed softly with his eyelids closed as my thumb trailed his eye socket. I stroked the scar beneath his right eyebrow, a silvered imprint in his skin. 'And this one here?' I asked, learning his body like a language. I felt him tense beneath my touch at the asking of the question. 'From falling off my bike when I was ten,' he said, his eyes still closed. 'An accident.'

The air smells of flickered sun and forest floor and minerals locked in fathoms deep inside the ancient sea. Tree trunks rise around me, dense ivy suffocating bark. Occasionally a smudge of sea and fleck of sky shows through the cracks above and lets me glimpse the pale underside of open seagull wings.

I walk until vast sky appears. A reach of blue. The tunnel starts to open up as linking trees loosen their grip and the foliage becomes more sparse, filtered and thin, thick leaves replaced with open space. I look down at the cliffs below, the appealing crags of sharp dark rocks that would obliterate a body and leave it pulped and pulverized. It hurts that he didn't simply talk to me. That he never actually said.

My stomach walks ahead of me, now large and round, tightly defined inside my T-shirt. A woman with a red backpack and tiny shorts and walking boots appears along the path that bends just up ahead. She sees the bump and smiles wide, nods her head at me. I try to smile back and dip my chin. There's a reverence for what we've found, the coastal path our chosen church, and we do not break the mutual silence, do not fill it with a crass 'hello'.

I hear her footsteps fade away behind me as I waddle, stomp from out the shelter of the forest onto the open headland. Here there are no trees, just brash sunlight and shrubs that crouch down low and cling onto the exposed earth. There are rabbit holes around the place and patchy grass that's worn thin as linen. Far below the path the sea rears up and crashes on the coastline, Medusa wild with waves for hair. The impact of the sea and rock makes a loud bang, throws up huge spray. I stand there in the drenching.

There's no one on the headland here, just a rustic wooden bench embedded with a metal square and the words inscribed in old italicized Vivaldi font that says this was 'Bert's favourite view' and he will 'Never Be Forgotten'. I wonder who remembers Bert and if Jay needs a bench somewhere and what the hell I'd put on it, given that I didn't actually know him. Perhaps a plaque placed on a folding seat inside the local cinema – 'Jay's favourite place to watch *Star Wars*.' I imagine it all sticky from the frequent slushie spills and popcorn curls and wonder if he ever went to see *Star Wars* with Ben.

So what do I do now?

Decision

The clarity that comes from eating chocolate is surprising. The chocolate bar tastes heavenly. Of childhood and holidays and syrup-coated happiness. It smells of cocoa, sugar, joy. I let it melt inside my mouth, mop the sweat from my forehead, sip some water from the plastic bottle that pollutes and contemplate my coming death. My mind is made. My death is imminent and unavoidable. I feel bad about my sister and my parents who all have no idea I'm still pregnant. But Jude, she has a family of her own and Dad has work. My mother will be very unimpressed but I'm sure will find comfort in the purchase of soft furnishings, new cushions and some cashmere throws. I can't see another option. Dying is obviously the only way to undo this, to make it all just go away.

And suddenly I feel better. The consolidation of the thought bringing an unexpected happiness. A sheer relief that everything will finish soon. I wonder if perhaps I should just do it now. There's no time like right now. I venture closer to the edge. The rocks are almost whispering, hypnotic in the glory of the violence they offer up. I take a step and stare ahead, horizon-lost, a deep yearning for oblivion. A butterfly flits into view and disappears, a flagrant flash of colour that disbands the spell of luring rocks, distracts my thoughts just long enough. I look around, can't see it now so sit down for just a minute.

The butterfly appears again. It flutters, quivers, flickers like a glowing flame along the path in front of me and disappears behind a stone. I roll myself onto my knees and heave my heavy self upright to carry on the walk.

For now.

Wings

The Nook next door is locked up with the doors all shut and curtains closed. The front looks sad, just like a pale face with pennies on its corpse eyes. I struggle to untie my trainers in Jane's cluttered living room and eventually pull out my swollen, sweating feet. I don't know how it got inside. Yet there it is. Its wings are folded tight and tall, an upright book. At first I think it's a trapped moth. The outside of its wings are black, a shade that's darker than the night and makes me think of fathoms deep, of underwater crevasses and gorges that are unexplored. It sits soundless on the glass, its still and gathered form so strange a sight to see inside. I crouch down close to watch it there. My breath is loud and fills my ears. The windowpanes are licked with salt and sticky on the outside from the times when clouds have burst like overstretched balloons, the water pouring down before the sunshine reappears and turns the rain to salty residue.

Up close the wings aren't actually black, but feathered

brown with flecks of grey. They're marked like bark on ancient trees. My face is near the windowpane and I try my best to barely breathe for fear of frightening it away. It slowly opens up its wings, spreads flat and wide, revealing peacock scatterings of vibrant orange, black and blues that look like eyes upon each wing. All-seeing eyes. The butterfly begins to flap and flutter hard, to beat itself relentlessly against the thing it doesn't see.

I cannot bear the quiet thud of beating wings. A flickering brutality. I find a dry and empty glass and an envelope and catch the self-destructive thing and take it to the cottage door. Outside the sky is dazzling blue and clouds float past, the pale colour of clotted cream. The sun feels warm upon my skin. I tilt my head up to the light, up to the sky. Holding the glass, I remove the envelope. The butterfly stays very still as if it doesn't recognize its freedom, then tries to fly away again and finally escapes from out the open cage of bevelled glass.

Turning back inside I find the butterfly has flown back and landed, softly, on my hand. I try to hold myself entirely still. The creature slowly opens up its wings, revealing all the colours that it keeps inside. It stays for just one second more, then flies away.

Jay, was that you?

Visitors

'I keep seeing these butterflies,' I tell them all.

'It's a sign!' Jane firmly says.

'Oh, don't be so ridiculous. You'll fill her head with fluff and stuff.' Pete shakes his face into a frown and takes a sip of steaming tea, too warm for this nice weather.

There's a knocking and Pete grumbles, shuffles from a chair to get the door. I hear Claire's voice and the ruffle of a hug and the muffle of a greeting.

'I just don't know . . .' I say to Jane.

'What don't you know?' Claire says, entering the room and going to take another mug from out of Jane's cupboard by the sink.

'Jane is telling her that Jay is sending messages by butterfly. Please just tell them it's ridiculous.'

'Well,' says Claire, 'I know it sounds illogical but there might be something in it. Who are we to say what's possible?'

I'm surprised to hear this come from Claire.

'Oh, not you too,' Pete loudly groans.

'Well, my dad always loved ladybirds and in the months after he died I'd find them hiding everywhere. Inside the house, on window frames, on cupboard doors. I'm sure that they were sent by Dad. And I have a patient too who swears that when her daughter died she kept on finding small white feathers in her path. She brought them with her to the surgery. A massive bunch of them. Like flowers. So, you never know. I just don't know.'

Pete grumbles underneath his breath.

'What?' Clare kindly asks.

'I said that "Dead is dead". That's what I said.' His voice is loud. He sounds school-teacher cross with us.

The thing inside moves suddenly as if disturbed by the strong sound or the strong meaning of the words.

'Do you really think that's true?' Jane sadly shakes her head at Pete and goes to put the kettle on. 'Poor Evie. When she dies she'll have to hit you round the head with something like a hammer or a giant rock just to make you pay attention, Pete.'

Scratch

I try to wait the days out. But my head is filled with photographs, of small deep scars, dead husbands and of naked Ben. Thoughts of motherhood and imagined infidelity feel like insects crawling everywhere inside me; stinging, itching with an awful scratch. My stomach grows with swelling cells. The grief floods in as giant waves as dark as tar and catches me off guard sometimes, knocks all the air from my lungs and barrels me around, away. I can't control it when it comes. I can't abide it anymore.

Soon, it will be over.

Empath

'I need to swim,' I say to Jane. 'What's with the hat? It's really hot.'

Despite the glorious sunshine and the beauty of the day, Jane is wearing a thick knitted hat with feathers in, the one she wears for swimming. Her AC/DC T-shirt clings to her large breasts and she is covered in white flour.

'It's a universal barrier.'

'I'm pretty sure it's called a hat.'

She laughs at that.

'I know it's called a hat. But I'm an empath and it's made of wool. The natural fibres help to keep the feelings of the world out. It really helps. Especially when I'm feeling porous like today. I can't quite put my finger on it but something feels really off.'

I must look a little sceptical as my friend, the human sponge, yells, 'Wait,' and starts to rummage through a kitchen dresser drawer that's crammed with batteries, pens and empty envelopes and Post-it notes that have long since lost their stick and random gloves, a woven belt. She pulls a hat from somewhere at the back.

'Here. Try this. It's all wool too. You look like you're in need of it.'

The hat is grey and slightly saggy and misshapen, and it looks more like a tea-cosy than something one would actually wear. But I take the hat and pull it down over my ears.

'Thanks,' I say and cannot help but laugh out loud. 'How does this work? I think the problem's in my mind, not coming from outside.'

'It creates a sort of barrier. Some empaths surround themselves with potted plants, or even pictures of their pets. But I find that wearing wool works best. Especially on my head, that's where the energy is most absorbed.'

She might as well be speaking Mandarin, but the hat feels good and Jane feels good and the cottage feels cool inside and the light is soporific. There is shortbread baking in the oven that is almost done, and the sun is shining down outside. For a single moment, for just a fraction of a second, I feel something close to calm.

'And your midwife says it's fine to swim?' Jane looks a little nervously at the scrunched-up towel that's ready, tucked beneath my arm. She rubs the flour off her hands and leaves a dusty palm print on the apron that she's wearing.

'Of course,' I lie. I've no idea. I haven't seen a midwife since the long night in the hospital. 'And anyway, it's June.

The whole village is swimming in the bay. There are tiny kids in there. I just really need to swim right now. Are you coming too?'

She sighs, defeated by my obvious determination.

'Fine,' she says. 'Just let me take the biscuits out. They're almost done.'

She kneels down to peer through the warm oven door, which when opened fills the room with the aroma of fresh golden baked vanilla pods. She slips her hands into some oven gloves and takes the shortbread biscuits out. They are the colour of large hay bales in summer fields.

A smile rises on my face, despite myself.

Indent

We click and clack together up the narrow lane, rubber flip-flops snapping at our feet. The whole village is buzzing, humming, full of half-term visitors and throngs of local schoolchildren, unleashed for just a single week. A group of teenagers wearing wetsuits and wet trainers run together past us up the hill towards the jumping spot, leaving foot-prints on the warm tarmac.

'How many weeks are you right now?' Jane points towards the bowling ball of flesh that sticks in front and hides my toes from my own view.

'Twenty-seven weeks,' I say, solemn.

Jane pulls a face and tries to smile.

'That's further than I ever got.'

I'm about to ask her what she means when she suddenly stops walking and starts to trail her right hand over the high stone wall that curves beside us down the lane.

'It was here,' she says. 'Jay's childhood accident.'

I look at where she's pointing, at the stretch of wall that

has a tiny indent and a single rock that sticks out further than the rest.

'Here?' I ask. 'That looks just like the photograph.'

'I walked past here that day after they left. There was blood streaked on the wall still and I never saw Jay's bicycle again. Martin said it would be better if they went straight back to London and Jay saw their doctor there.'

'But they could have stayed and seen a doctor here.'

'I know,' she says, her gaze now somewhere out at sea. 'Looking back, the way they left so fast . . . But, I always thought that it was Jay just telling tales. He was very young, and children, they have big imaginations.'

She sounds as if she's speaking to herself, convincing her own conscience.

'And you never said a word to Anne?'

I look at the section of wall that looks almost identical to every other Cornish wall.

'I didn't ever get to see her. They rented out the cottage every summer after that. I kept it clean and changed the beds for visitors, but Martin was the one who dealt with everything. I didn't hear from Anne again until Jay died.'

'Are you going to speak to her?' I ask. 'Will you tell her what Jay said to you?'

Jane slowly shakes her head.

'Even if I got it wrong, Jay's gone. It doesn't change a thing.' She rubs the wall with her right hand. 'And anyway, she's back living with Martin now. There seems no point in dragging up the distant past.'

345

Swim

A young family of tourists walk past us as we stand there by the wall looking crazy in our summer dresses and woollen hats. The children prance ahead, clearly overjoyed by the novelty of carless roads, each sucking on an ice-lolly.

'Hello,' the parents say politely and smile massive smiles that reek of holidays and happiness. We smile back and say 'hello'.

'Come on.' I take Jane's arm and drag her from the wall, along the lane. 'What did you mean exactly when you said you never got this far?' I ask in an attempt to change the subject, bring her back to me. Jane glances down towards my bump.

'Oh, that?' she says. 'That was in another lifetime. Before I even came to Cornwall.'

I focus on the slipway that rolls down towards the beach and which in the evening launches Dragon Boats; huge teams of people armed with oars who race across the summer seas while the locals watch with icy cokes and cold ciders. The beach pebbles push up under the rubber flip-flop soles and

346

massage my expanding feet. 'Free reflexology,' says Jane, who takes my arm on the uneven stony ground. We thread between the towels, towards the left hand of the bay where the sun is trapped against the cliff and heating up the slabs of stone and rocks below. She sighs deeply.

'I'm sorry if I made you sad,' I say at last.

'Don't be silly, Emma love. You don't make me sad. Quite the opposite.' She pauses, says, 'A million moons ago I tried to become pregnant, but the babies never stuck in me.'

'God. I'm so so sorry, Jane.'

I think of how I plan to end two heartbeats in one go. I am a dreadful human.

'No need to say you're sorry, love. However hard it was for me it clearly wasn't meant to be. And the man that I was with back then, he would have made an awful dad.'

Jay was tumbling over Max, scooping him up inside his arms. They wrestled on the carpet like a small pile of pandas. 'Watch the Christmas tree,' my mother warned, eyeing her precious baubles. Max squealed, yelped with toddler joy, jumped up onto Jay's back. 'You can have him any time you want,' said Jude, stroking her baby bump, slumping back onto the sofa. 'I think he loves Jay more than us.'

I dig my nails into my palm, pull the hat that's far too warm to wear further down to cover up my ears.

We lay our towels out on the balmy sand, sit with our bodies propped against the rocks that form a natural back rest. The slabs of stone have been collecting sun all morning long and now radiate it back, imbue our skin with warmth. The simple pleasure of the heat and bright clear sky makes my muscles loose, relaxed, and makes me sigh out loud. I close my eyes and soak up sun.

'Is that why you came here?' I ask her, curious, my eyes still closed.

'I had bad taste in men. And a dad who liked his booze. Cornwall was the furthest place that I could get to on the train. Now it's been my home for almost forty years.' She laughs, lost in her memories, and I open my eyes to listen to her talk. 'I love it here, but I always thought I'd meet somebody, settle down and have a family. Sometimes that makes me slightly sad. But the village stops me being lonely.'

'Was there ever anybody else?'

'For a while there was Brian . . .'

I scoff at just the thought. Brian? She must be mad.

'You're kidding, right? The cab driver?'

'He wasn't always overweight. In fact, when I first came here he was young and handsome, always swimming out into the bay, kayaking and fishing in his little boat for mackerel. He didn't have that belly then.'

I try to see Brian as slim and Jane as young, the two of them together, active, both outside. The image is improbable, the thought of them together totally impossible.

'About ten years after I arrived there was an accident. I was cycling down the lanes near here and turned the corner, saw a car in front of me and squeezed the brakes. I squeezed too hard and flew over the handle-bars and landed in the road.'

'Oh God,' I say, praying that she'll just shut up. All I actually wanted was a peaceful swim.

'A farmer found me with a badly broken arm.'

'Oh Jane,' I say.

'These things all happen for a reason. If I hadn't broken it I'd have never started sea swimming. The pain was like a prison and the water gave me an escape. It helped me get my strength back too. I'd come alone here every day and Pete would be here on the beach walking the dog. Five years ago, the day Evie was diagnosed with Alzheimer's, he came down to the beach like normal and he didn't say a word. Just stripped off to his boxer shorts and swam out to the buoy with me. We've swum together each day since.'

'And how did Claire start swimming too?'

'Claire? She thought it looked like fun and asked if she could join us. She fell in love with being in the water all year round and has hardly missed a day since then. I think it helps to give her space away from work and that big family that she has. So it then became the three of us. Now four with you.'

'Hmmm,' I say, watching a toddler watch a couple skimming stones. The young boy takes a handful of small pebbles mixed with sand and chucks them at the surface of the sea, then claps with glee.

'Well, almost five.' Jane points at my large stomach. 'I guess you count as two now.'

I smile and say nothing. I will soon become a zero.

Sign

The water in the distance is a sheet of glass. A few people are swimming and young children splash along the shore in short wetsuits. In the middle of the beach a man is struggling to inflate a giant pink flamingo with a foot pump. I stand in my cheap flip-flops on the brightness of the shore and watch a seagull mirror-fly across the spread of turquoise blue.

'Nice swimsuit.' Jane is looking at my brand-new polka-dotted patterned bulge. I've given in and ordered a cheap costume off Amazon designed for pregnant women. My old swimsuit is way too small and my bikini is obscene now. I tried it on inside the cottage earlier and flesh escaped from everywhere and the fabric cups that used to cover up each breast now look like nipple stickers; burlesque gone badly wrong. I am grotesque, my body far too big to fit inside my normal clothes. 'Don't lose your flip-flops. The tide is coming in. Leave them high up or they won't be there when you get out,' Jane warns.

My heart is racing, beating fast, in deep anticipation of the water. I take off my flip-flops and throw them further up the beach. They land among the scattered pebbles and the sand like red and rubber flotsam. I start to wade.

'You coming then?' I call to Jane over the gentle rumble of the water pulling pebbles.

'Faster than you!' she jests, raising her eyes at my slow and awkward ramble in the shallows. I lose my footing on a stone and stumble to the right. I catch myself but not before I'm almost totally submerged. The sudden dunking leaves me shocked and breathless, laughing, cold and drenched. The salty water stings my eyes. I gasp in gulps of sea-clean air.

There is only cold and sea and salt, the vast horizon and the shore, the trill and shrill of whistling birds and Jane whose face looks terrified.

'I'm good,' I laugh, still rubbing at my salty eyes with salty hands, which isn't really helping. 'I'm great,' I laugh, enlivened by the water.

I've never held my head under the sea before and the thrill of the sensation is incredible; an icy liberation from my burning thoughts. It feels like I'm washed away. A momentary cleansing that occurs beneath the surface of the sea.

No one can see I'm pregnant now and the water takes the weight of me. I pull the sodden woollen hat off my head and throw it back towards my flip-flops on the beach. I drag a soggy hair band out of my hair, twang it around my wrist and pinch my nose and breathe the air out of my lungs so that my body becomes heavier and sinks towards the bottom of the seabed where the pebbles are replaced with sand. I sink down, imagine drowning. My hair floats up as a flaming siren mane that searches for the surface.

Deep underneath the sea there is no sound at all. Just a hint of heartbeat beating in my ears. The water gives me quiet and the cold compression of my skull freezes everything that was before and what might come to be until what's left is now. This single moment. Only now. My lungs begin to blaze from lack of air and I push against the soft seabed and reappear bedraggled with my hair dripping in briny ropes.

Jane is floating buoyant on her back, fanning her arms with slow strong sweeps to keep her body flat. Her feet stick out above the sea, a sea that is so still it holds the sky in its reflection.

'Come on, you water baby,' Jane says and flips herself onto her front and begins to gently breast-stroke glide towards the distant swimming buoy and the faraway horizon line.

We normally chat, but something in the still today calls for silence and reserve. We're heading for the orange buoy. Two boats have anchored further out, both sailing boats with sails tidied neatly away, the masts vacillating slightly. Jane gets there first and hangs onto the seaweed-coated nylon rope that keeps the buoy from drifting off. She turns to face the village and I watch her beam as she surveys the beauty of the Cornish coast where we are living and the bustling summer beach. Two strokes and I have joined her too.

'Just look,' she says, her eyes still locked onto the land, and we both tread water with our feet, our bodies buoyed up by the buoy.

'It's beautiful,' I whisper, the sweetness of secret good-byes making it sweeter still. The colours of the village are soft pastel shades, the trees and land are toddler hues of vibrant greens and primary blues. It looks just like a post-card of a place you'd always want to be, someone who isn't me. The sound of people laughing carries out across the water.

'Are you okay?' Jane asks me, looking concerned.

I nod a 'yes'. I think I am, I thought I was, but realize that I'm crying marble drops of briny tears that mix into the salty sea.

'You should've kept that woolly hat on for protection.' I can't quite tell if Jane is serious or just teasing me in an attempt to make me feel less. I smile through the salty blur. 'Come on, let's go and get an ice-cream, love.'

But I do not want to leave the buoy. I want to stay here tethered to the firm seabed, buoyed up amidst the beauty of it all. The thing inside me gives a hefty kick under my ribs and in the corner of my view a shape appears; a flash of colour, splash of pigment, streaks of bright.

'Oh God,' Jane squeals. 'Is that . . . ?' It settles on the surface of the orange buoy and gently opens up its wings.

'Oh wow!' Jane says again. 'I wish that Pete could see this too. Don't tell me that that's nothing!'

I rub the tears from out my eyes to get a better look at it. But I don't know what it really means. Or if it's just a butterfly.

July

Lightning

This is the day but hours still need wasting before darkness comes. Butterflies pervade my thoughts. They flutter through my consciousness. I take my phone and find some total lunatics online. There's a site that's dedicated just to messages sent from the dead and a book that's cheerily been named *Hello from Heaven*. It sounds just like a low-budget TV show that airs during the daytime on a channel with as many digits as a phone number. There are Kates and Marys, Johns and Joes who all have anecdotes of recently departed loved ones and a butterfly. The whole thing sounds like utter shit.

I shut the tab and Google 'suicide' instead. My screen is filled with numbers, statistics that are haunting. These men, they are all dying. It's an epidemic. Everywhere. In England sixteen people kill themselves each single day and mainly men. Three out of four. So many men. I type in 'Why are men more likely . . .' and before I finish tapping in the sentence Google offers up the question 'Why are men more likely to be struck by lightning?' I scroll down through the articles on lightning storms and frightening skies and find a study proving that men are five times more likely to be hit and killed by lightning strikes than women. Men seem to be more prone to death.

I never should have loved one.

Then I never would have lost one.

But it's not just men who kill themselves.

Goodbye

Jane is in her bedroom watching old episodes of *Friends*. Outside is almost dark, the last summer rays trying their best not to let go of day. I hold onto a cheap biro, go searching for some paper. How do you write a note with words to say goodbye when all that language offers up seems trite and wrong, not quite enough? How do you write a letter when the only person that you really want to write to is too busy with the process of decaying in the ground?

A corner of a book sticks out from underneath the bed, my copy of *The Catcher in the Rye* that has slipped onto the floor. I reach an arm into the darkness to retrieve the thing. The floorboards underneath the bed slats are covered in a film of dust. I think of all the particles of plant pollen and human skin and human hairs, small fibres from the blankets and the curtains in Jane's cottage, the flecks of sand and soil and minute specks of meteorites that lost their way and burnt through the earth's atmosphere; cremated ghosts of distant stone from deepest space. I pull the book out from the lint, dust off the grains and remnants of all passing time.

I cannot bring myself to tear the pages out, to break apart the story, even if it didn't change my life. I guess there is the inside of the box of Weetabix I keep in Jane's small kitchen, but that somehow feels all wrong too: to leave my final words on torn cardboard breakfast scraps. The only other paper I can think of are the photographs of Jay's that have travelled between houses, across counties and been stuck to different walls with an impressive stack of Blu-Tack and now hide inside the novel in my hand. The paper is as thin and soft as bed sheets from a marriage that has lasted for a lifetime. I stare at all the images in turn, trying to choose my stationery. I pick the photo of the sunrise which seems bitter-sweet for a goodbye.

We were standing holding hands before the registrar. Jay wore a well-cut suit that hugged his perfect form and he smelt of ancient oaks and lemon rind and summer rain and something that was only him. I grinned at him, tried not to cry with happiness, as he slipped the golden ring onto my finger and made firm promises to love me for a lifetime.

I take a pen and write the only word that comes to mind, which isn't what I want to say but is all that I can think of. It's ironic that it's all I have, given just how much I hate it for the things it doesn't say. That stupid word that's offered time and time again but never seems to say enough. A leaking vessel of a word. A cup that cannot hold the weight of meaning that it should convey.

'Sorry.'

I scrawl the word in blue biro and sit back on the bed. I cross my legs, rub foot on foot imagining that one is Jay's, not mine, and that he's sitting next to me. For a brief moment I consider that I might be wrong and maybe this isn't the answer.

I look at the five letters. They are rounded, neat, and look like writing crafted carefully by a child obsessed with pens and stationery who adds small love hearts above 'i's' and uses scented highlighters. The 'sorry' looks ridiculous, my penmanship not worthy of a word that marks the end of words. The curving 'y' curls down low and spirals back around itself to form a perfect hanging loop, a thin-lined noose. There's a stirring in my stomach. A gentle movement. Subtle twitch. I add an inky cross of kiss.

Jane's TV is silent now so I creep to leave the photograph face down upon the kitchen table and weight it down with a half-filled glass of water that leaves a soggy curve of damp, a crescent of weeping moon that seeps the colour from the ink and hangs above the single 'x' illuminating nothing. My old trainers are in the hall. I take my time to tie them tight, being careful to stay silent, and then close the door behind me.

I know that Jane will find the note. I feel bad for all the worry that I'll cause her. As I stomp towards the beach I wonder for a moment if I should go back and add another 'sorry' for the 'sorry'.

Complex

Despite the summer month the Cornish nights are cold. The beach is now completely empty and the dark wraps round the land providing perfect solitude. There is no one left to interrupt this private act. The waves are lulling, heavy, strong. They crash down on the tideline with the weight of water mixed with stones, small rocks that have been hauled and dredged up from the soft seabed. The noise is like a hurricane. A deep and hungry thunder.

So this is finally it. The feeling is of deep relief. There's a comfort in the knowledge that it's almost over, almost done. The waves are like a meditation. The roaring is a calling. I look around the beach at the abundance of pebbles. Rocks, at different stages of destruction, that have originated in far places that I've never been to and now never will. I take the largest I can find. The thing inside kicks hard under my ribs again and I wonder why it has to wake up now. It reminds me if I swim out now beyond the buoys that it comes too. We still are one. We're both alive or both undone.

'I'm sorry.' I whisper out the words and they are carried off for no one and for nothing else to hear. 'It's for the best. There isn't any other way,' I mutter underneath my breath as I run my fingers over pebbles, my only wish that none of this had ever happened in the first place. I should have swallowed down that pill and engineered a simpler ending all those months ago. I place one hand over the bump to say goodbye. 'I can't do this, I can't be here and I promise you don't want me for a mother.'

Practicalities

A pocket full of pebbles. Just how many does it take? I'd like to ask Virginia Woolf the number that she crammed into the pockets of her winter coat before she waded out into the water. Was the fabric bulging at the seams? Was the coat so loaded with small rocks that all the individual stitches started fraying with the weight? How did she know how many stones would tip the balance of the scales and plunge her down towards her death? And how did she approach the river? Was she tentative with neat small steps or resolute and striding, fast? Was she still wearing her leather shoes, the ones she always kept for best, and did she waver for a minute, pulled by strands of love from all those she would leave behind, or did she only think ahead to the cool and silent ending that she'd craved and craved and always craved?

I should have done some research. Found some helpful hints online. I didn't Google 'drowning' like my mother would've, which in retrospect was probably a big mistake.

I could really use a leaflet now with clear instructions, helpful tips. The practicalities of death are suddenly so complex. I am bothered by my trainers. Do I leave them on or take them off?

I was sitting on the edge of a cold chlorinated pool. The swimming teacher shouted as we lowered ourselves in. Thin cotton PJs, light and harmless on the land, were suddenly all water-clogged, wet fabric weighting down our lanky frames. 'This is stupid, Miss,' Jude yelled while treading water with her skinny legs. 'We'd better hope that if we accidentally fall into a river or a pool it's just at bedtime. If we're wearing jeans and shoes we're screwed.'

The larger stones are scattered scarce across the beach. I start to search for them, to feel out the heavy ones with fingertips, to sift them from the cold, damp sand. They're hard to spot here in the dark. These rocks that are innocuous in daylight are now weighted down with meaning. I seek them out like treasure that is terrible and take them stone by stone by stone and make a pile. A pyramid of deadly rocks, a totem to an ending. I can hear the rumbling threat of sea and hear the chatter of my teeth that seem to shake and clatter up against each other, helplessly.

I need more pockets, practical zipped places to secure all the stones I've found. The waterproof that's in the hall, that would have been so useful now. I fill the places I can find. I even cram my bra with stones. My breasts hurt from the cold hard rocks that dig into the tissue that is soft and swollen, hormone soaked. My body starts to give them warmth, accepts them as a part of me, and soon we share a temperature and I hardly notice them at all. They are welded to the skin of me. I am a woman, partly stone. The sea is loud and the chatter of my teeth is loud but the voices in my head are even louder than the sounds that are competing all around; the boom and smash, the heavy thunderclap of waves that sound just like a crowd left wanting at a concert, stamping feet and smashing hands, demanding the final encore.

I focus straight ahead of me at the saline-scented promise of an ending.

Pause

I'm sitting still upon the beach. Time soars and dives and disappears and minutes stretch and hours compress and stars must move across the sky. I shiver, feel the wetness from the tide-drenched ground begin to soak slightly into my clothes. I wait inside the memories that are good. The ones that hold on tight as barnacles on rocks in storms. His face, his eyes, his firm embrace, the smell of home that was the curve of his strong neck.

> *His broken kneecaps.*
> *Crooked neck.*
> *My broken heart.*

I scrunch my face and blink away the awful image that still lingers close to everything, that is always near the surface. I search for better moments. Swim down deeper for the memories.

We were drinking at a London rooftop bar. The place was far too full of people who were beautiful or dressed to look more beautiful and the summer sun was lingering above our heads. I was happy, drunk and dancing to an easy beat that echoed all Ibiza. I spun around and there he was, still watching me, his glass held close, his eyes fixated on my curves. I danced for him. For only him.

I am sitting on the beach still. I am waiting for the moment still.

Ben was poised and perfect in the photograph. The sunlight streamed in torrents down his dark brown skin and set his body all ablaze. I dropped the camera from my hand. It landed on the bed unscathed but left my heart completely broken. I did not know my husband.

It is time to stand.

Now

Standing takes a comically long time. It is inglorious and awful. I have to roll onto my knees, move to all fours, use my forearms for support. Especially with the added weight of pebbles in my pockets. It seems I am a giant cow; large swollen belly, flooded tits. A vivid light illuminates the dark and my iPhone simultaneously pings. I roll back over, sit down again and sigh from the great effort.

I open my phone which lies abandoned on the shore. There is a text from Ben.

From Ben.

I hold my breath.

'I saw that you were pregnant and I need to tell the truth. The photograph of me was mine. I used a timer in the studio alone. I don't think Jay had noticed it was ever there. I wanted his attention. I was jealous. I'm so sorry. I just loved him too.'

I wait, completely frozen. The phone displays a tiny line of dots that flicker, showing me he's writing more. I can't remember how to breathe.

'He only ever wanted you,' the next text reads.

I stare out at the dark of night as the world rearranges.

'What?' I finally type with hands that are now shaking hard.

'I'd hoped the photograph would show Jay that I loved him. I'm not good with words.'

I take a breath and breathe out slow.

'Are you fucking kidding me?' I type.

'I thought you'd want to know.'

I press the button, switch the phone off and throw it down onto the sand. The baby moves within my belly and I wrap my arms around my girth and hug it tight. The guilt is all-encompassing. What did I nearly do?

Time dives and dips, and sinks beneath the surface of distorted thoughts, floats easily then drags like lead and disappears. The seconds and the minutes all compress while hours stretch and clouds above begin to lighten to soft grey and hidden stars, they fade away. I'm cold. My pockets full of stone. With no idea now what to do.

Rise

The sun appears like the opening of a blinking eye, a tiny slit of golden light above the sea.

Jay and I were sitting on the top of Parliament Hill after the clubs had closed. He handed me the bottle and I gulped down wine in large acidic mouthfuls. It tasted of beginnings and of lemon trees. The sky began to light in increments as the sun pulled up above the bar chart of grey buildings. A man jogged past, his shorts so tight his flaccid cock and compressed balls jiggled with every pounding step. We laughed at wobbling testicles and at the miracle of brand-new days.

'Emma . . .' I think I hear my name, but it is caught up in the sound of waves and reaches me in fragments, like the remnants of a ripped-up quilt. 'Emma?' But maybe I'm imagining things. I carry on staring ahead and listening to the pebbles and the stones which pound the shore more gently now.

371

The sun continues to rise. There are no buildings here to muddle up the skyline and the sunrise is more glorious in its stark simplicity. I breathe the salty brine-soaked air.

'Em.' The imagined voice is louder now. I rub my eyes. 'You're up early.'

The voice is male, older than Jay's and followed by another noise that floats above the gentle wind. Iggy appears first, barking a low and excitable hello, his old arthritic limbs running in uneven circles, orbiting my huddled frame. I grin and wipe the corner of my eye.

'You laughing or you crying there?' Pete sounds concerned, his feet making loud crunching noises as he comes closer to where I sit.

'God knows,' I say, turning to him.

His face crinkles more deeply as he frowns. He pauses, takes a breath of air and inhales all the beauty of the sun which rises slowly up into the sky.

'Can I sit?' he asks, taking off his hat and waiting for an answer.

'Please,' I say and pat the pebbles by my side.

Pete takes his time, struggling with joints that have stiffened over years. He lands upon the beach, sits heavily, inelegantly, and lets out a small grunt.

'I do that too,' I say.

'I'll never come to terms with age,' he says, rubbing his palms over his thinning thighs, 'but I suppose it is a blessing. This . . .' He waves his hand towards the sun and sea and empty beach. 'It's such a privilege.'

I reach out and hold his forearm with ferocity, while still staring out to sea. I cling with fingers to his jumper. I'm holding on as if he is the only thing that's keeping me from falling off a cliff edge and I cry without making a sound. He doesn't say a word, just reaches over with his other hand and places it on top of mine. We stay that way as the sun continues rising. Iggy whimpers slightly and comes to lay his head across my legs as if saddened by my sadness.

'I miss him so much,' I finally whisper. 'I don't know how to live.'

Pete inhales sharply, taking in the crying me, the lumpy clothes and the icy feeling of my fingers.

'Emma, you need to talk. You need to talk about what happened.'

'I can't. I don't have words,' I say between small sobs.

My mouth clamps cockle tight. He waits until the tears begin to dissipate, undo themselves.

'You will,' he says. 'You'll find the words in time and there'll be lots of us to listen.'

'But living is so hard,' I say.

He laughs the kindly laugh of someone who's been told something he knows too well.

'Yes, Emma. Life is hard. Living is really hard but it is always, always worth it. You never know what's waiting for you just around the corner, all the things that will come afterwards.'

I put a hand over my stomach. Feel the heat seep through

and warm my hand. I detach myself, unclasp my hands, and stare towards the sun which has cleared the clutch of the horizon. The ball of light looks flushed with independence.

'What time is it?' I ask.

'Early,' says Pete. 'I couldn't sleep.'

'Are you okay?' I ask, wiping the snot that's trailing from my nose with the back of a cold hand.

'It's you who should be answering that.' I stay silent for a while and wait until he finally says, 'Evie's not good. The last few weeks she hasn't recognized me anymore. And I don't recognize her either. It looks like Evie but her . . . I don't know what to call it, I guess her "Evie-ness", it's disappeared.' He pauses for a while. 'I miss her,' he finally says.

'I'm so sorry, Pete.'

He coughs as if dislodging a sad feeling which is stuck inside his throat.

'I also miss my bloody space. The house is full of these kind women with their endless chat, strange-smelling foods and cheerful smiles. I just had to get away from them. I never thought I'd be complaining about too many women in my house!'

He laughs an empty laugh that feels just like sorrow.

'We make quite a pair,' I finally say.

'That we do,' he says and offers me a folded cotton handkerchief with an embroidered 'E' just like the ones my dad keeps in his suit pockets. 'E for Evie and for Emma. I always carry one.'

'Just in case you find a crying girl sat on a beach whose name begins with "E"?' I ask.

'Exactly!' He laughs again at that and this time the laughter sounds more real.

Confession

We watch in silence as the sun continues to climb higher in the sky. Iggy runs down to the water's edge and plays a game of cat and mouse. The morning waves rush fast towards the limping dog, then career backwards as the tide chases the indents of his paws.

'I thought that maybe I should join him.'

'Join who? And where?' Pete asks. 'You don't mean Jay?'

I shrug and shake my head and gesture vaguely out to sea.

'Is that why you're all lumpy?'

I reach my hand deep in my pockets and pull out a load of random stones. They clatter to the ground, making a noise that sounds like summer rain.

'They're even in my bra.' I laugh slightly hysterically and reach inside my jumper and pull the warm stones out from each bra cup. I throw them all away from me. A seagull further down the beach turns sharp, unsettled by the sound. 'It was stupid. For a second I was positive. But then Ben

376

texted me and it turns out everything I thought was wrong, so very wrong. This morning I don't feel that way. So what if . . . '

'What if . . . ?' Pete gently prompts.

'Jay photographed a sunrise. What if he'd only waited for another one? Or what if I had texted Jay that very minute or got home a little earlier or if I'd asked a different question or said something, anything? He might have suddenly felt differently. He might still actually be here.'

I take a pebble from my pocket and brush away small flecks of sand.

'Emma, Jay made a decision. And he acted on it in that moment. You can drive yourself completely mad with "whats" and "ifs" but those questions cannot ever change the awful thing that happened. It is very sad. Desperately sad. But there's nothing you can do to change it. All that you can do now is survive each day yourself.'

I look up at the sun which is suspended in the sky like a child's illustration of a perfect day. And then I look down at the bump which is warming in the morning light. Somewhere inside of me a small limb shifts or an elbow or a foot and it presses out against the taut of skin which is perfect, smooth and round. It is the same shape as the rising sun.

Panic

'Emma! Pete! Emma!' Jane is wearing pink pyjamas and trying hard to run across the rocky beach, her boobs walloping around. Running really doesn't suit her. Just behind her I see Anne.

'Oh no. Not her,' I say to Pete. 'Not Anne. Not now.'

Jane looks mental, mad and wild. Her arms are flapping out around her and Anne's face is pinched in tighter than a fist.

'Emma!' Jane shouts at me again.

Her voice sounds crackly, feral, scared. She reaches us and drops down to the sand, sweating heavily and breathing hard from all the exertion. Her thick arms wrap around my body which the morning sun is slowly warming up. Anne kneels down and holds me in a bony clutch.

'I'm so sorry, Emma,' whispers Anne.

She is angular and spindle thin, a fragile thing attached to bones. Her eyes are dull, as if she's sunken somewhere deep into herself and lost some part, lost all her spark.

'Oh thank God, thank God. I found your note. I thought . . .'

'I'm sorry, Jane,' I say and hang my head.

'I thought you'd done something completely stupid.'

Anne grips my hand and squeezes tight. I have no energy to stop her.

'Well, she definitely did that,' says Pete. 'She sat here through the night putting pebbles in her pockets and contemplating swimming off to nowhere in the dark.'

'You didn't try . . . ?' Jane's words trail off.

'No.' I shake my head. 'Someone got in touch just when . . . Well, then I got cold feet. Not actual cold. I mean, I didn't even make it to the water. I'm so sorry for scaring you.' I look down at my feet and wiggle my dry toes inside dry shoes.

'Oh Emma, Em,' Anne whispers and Jane holds onto me so tight it's hard to breathe. The air is forced from out of my lungs and I think that she might kill me, which would be deeply ironic.

'The baby,' I gasp, uncomfortable and breathless. Jane loosens her strong grip but only by a little.

'Emma,' Jane echoes Anne. 'You were out here in the cold all night! You should have come to me. Or any of us. Emma . . . We all care.'

Both Pete and Jane wrap arms around my shoulders while Anne grips my cold hand with hers and I sit tight in the middle of their joint and circular embrace.

'I'm sorry. I really didn't mean to worry everyone. I

promise I won't do anything like that ever again,' I tell them all. The tide is inching back away from us and I watch a cormorant land on a jagged rock and still itself. 'I guess I'm going to be a mother now.' I stare down at the bump, rub the elbow or the foot that is pushing out against my ribs as if objecting to the confines of its shrinking space. It moves around inside and there's a pressure on my bladder which could be a head. I try to swallow down my guilt.

We sit together in a row soaking up the morning rays.

'Anne has something that she wants to say,' Jane announces firmly.

Anne keeps her fingers linked with mine.

'I'm sorry. I really am so sorry that I threw you out,' she says now, rubbing at my knuckles with her thumb. 'This isn't an excuse but I haven't been too good. Martin, well, he . . . It doesn't matter anymore. It's all my fault. I'm so incredibly sorry, Emma.'

'You left me on my own,' I say, leaving my hand in hers.

'I know. I never should . . .'

'And my body, it is mine. Whatever I decided . . .'

'I know, I know. I was just so happy at the thought that Jay had left some part of him. And the thought of you not wanting that . . .'

She doesn't finish what she wants to say.

'It's far more complex than you'll ever know.'

The sun is higher in the sky and a woman that I've met around the village turns towards the water at the far end of the beach and throws a ball for her small dog. The dog careers into the water, creating ripples as it swims. Anne's jumper sleeve has risen up and small purple-green bruises, the size of a man's fingertips, are running up her arm in a piano scale of pain. The bruises make me want to cry again. I look at Jane and see that she has seen them too. The last remaining colour drains from Jane's face as Anne quickly pulls her sleeve back down.

'Forgive me?' says Anne.

'I do,' I say to Anne and mean the words. After all, I did far worse. I somehow let her son die.

The world is waking up now and the sound of lapping waves is soporific. More people are appearing on the beach and a grey-haired man with goggles is already in the water, swimming to the buoy. I fail to suppress a yawn.

'I really need some sleep. Could someone help me back to bed? I've never felt so tired.'

'See, was that so hard? Asking for help?' Jane says to me while staring straight at Anne who will not look at her.

The thing inside shifts its little body to the right. I place my hand upon my stomach and trace the individual vertebrae beneath my skin.

'Oh God. I'm going to be a mother.'

The realization hits me like a wave. I spin and spiral, tumbled by the terror of the thought. I have no clue which way is up and the panic leaves me breathless.

'Yes, my love. You are and you're going to be just fine,' Jane calmly says.

'We're here for you,' adds Anne.

Pete nods to say he'll be here too.

I am shaking at the very thought of motherhood as I empty out my pockets, forage in every crease and crack I've crammed a stone into. I leave the pebbles on the beach, except for one. The one I picked up first. A perfect oval stone as large as my whole palm which in the morning light I see is ringed with sparkling quartz. A lucky band of mineral shining in the light that reminds me of my mum.

Visitors

I wake up sweating, panicked, scared. It's dark out now, I've missed the day and night is clinging to the glass. The bedroom curtains have been drawn and the soft glow of the lamps throw gentle geometric shapes across Jane's wall. Anne is dozing at the bottom of the bed in a small armchair. I roll my whale-large body, the simple act of rolling over now complex and exhausting. A sigh escapes my mouth. Like a lighthouse keeper watching, waiting, Anne quickly opens her eyes and carefully sits herself down by my side.

'I'm sorry, Anne,' I say. 'I didn't mean to frighten everyone.'

She reaches for my hand and I rub her fingers slowly with my own.

'I'm sorry too. It's all okay.' Anne starts to stroke my head and I let her.

'The baby? Is it . . . ?' I feel panic rising as I realize once again that I'm going to be a mother now.

'The baby's absolutely fine. Claire said the heartbeat's strong and a night sat on a beach won't do a baby any harm.'

'I really didn't want to hurt it. I just wasn't sure if I could . . . I thought it was all for the best. I never should've . . . I'm so sorry, Anne,' I repeat. A single tear leaks from the corner of my eye and leaves a damp patch on the pillow.

'I'm sorry too,' Anne says again. 'I never should have thrown you out. I shouldn't have gone back to London or to Martin.'

Our voices wake the sleeping Jane in the bedroom down the corridor. She stumbles in wearing a large Nirvana T-shirt with her orange hair wrapped high and missing all its feathers.

'I'm sorry, Jane,' I say.

'Oh sweetheart. No need to say you're sorry, love.'

'I don't know what to do,' I say, propping myself upright on the pillows and fiddling with the duvet.

'For a start you need to get some proper care, start going to appointments with the midwife,' Jane says, sounding so sensible.

I shake my head from side to side.

'I don't know how to do this.'

'We're going to help,' the women say in unison.

Jane strokes me like the child she never had the chance to raise and Anne stays by my side as I lie back down and gently close my eyes. And a tiny part of me, compressed and small, hears the words that form a life ring out at sea, and hope glimmers, a hope that things might actually be all right.

Light

I wake to find that it is morning once again and the night spent on the beach recedes a little further like a bad dream that disintegrates with every hour of daylight. The sun is streaming in now through the thin veil of curtains. Anne is nowhere to be seen but Jane is right there at the bottom of the bed all curled up; a large and well-fed cat, limbs compressed inside the armchair. The light is warm and catches on the motes of dust that bounce and float about the air like small illuminated sparks of stars. I can hear the weight of seagulls marching up and down the grey slate roof above my head and the screeching of their greetings to the day as if delighted that the sun has risen once again, a miracle they never took for granted.

A knocking at the door wakes Jane. She rubs her face with both her hands, says, 'I'll get it,' as she wrestles herself out of the chair. I smile a meek thanks.

'The note,' Jane says. 'We had to call. Whatever's happened in the past, she is your mum.'

Mothers

The room is full of mothers now. I am flanked by mothers on both sides. Both Jay's and mine who have arrived together, an unlikely pair. My mother rushes at me like a spring high tide and grabs me with ferocity. She holds me close, as if she wants to gather every part of me into her arms, and squeezes firm while breathing fast. She holds my head against her chest and I hear the hectic beating of her heart.

'Oh Emma, Em. Oh Emma love. I love you, Em.'

'I love you too,' I tell her now. 'Where's Dad?' I ask.

'In Italy. He'll be here soon.'

'It's fine,' I say. 'I just need you.'

Fuck. I actually said I need my mum. I must tell Jude. I actually want my mother here, which is shocking and surprising. This messy knot of pregnancy and longing and of loss. It feels like women's work.

'And you and Anne. You're both okay?' I look suspiciously between them both.

My mother folds her silken scarf into a smart and tidy rectangle and lays it neatly on the bed. She pats it down. They both nod 'yes'.

Anne perches on the other side of me. She barely makes an indent on the bedding, almost nothing left to weight her here.

'I reacted unforgivably. I know,' Anne says and gestures at the rotund bump.

'And I wasn't any better when I knew that you were staying here with Anne. We've all done things we're not proud of,' my mother says.

I lift my T-shirt up and take a hand from each of them. My belly is a golden ball. Soft hairs cover the skin and a darkened line of pigmentation has appeared right down the middle, an equatorial marking on a planet of its own. I press my mother's hand and Anne's down flat across the mound of flesh and suddenly from deep inside there is a kick, as if the baby is annoyed somehow that its warm and coddled sea is being cooled from the outside. Anne jumps in shock. Her shoulders shake. She pulls her hands away at speed.

'Oh God, it kicked. The baby kicked.'

'It did!' I smile, proud as if the kicking is a trick that I have magicked up.

Anne's eyes grow wide as my mother spots the spread of bruises near her wrist. She gently takes Anne's hand and puts it firmly back onto my belly-ball, places her own hand softly on top. I press my hands on top of theirs and

underneath our mutual hold the baby kicks and elbows us.
It wriggles and it squirms.
   The mothers grin.
   All three of us.

Bonding

We are sitting in Jane's cool kitchen, the two mothers, Jane and me. The cake is crammed with Jane's own raspberries and with cream, the sponge as light as baby's breath. The tang of lemons mixed with sugar cuts into the kitchen air. I close my mouth around the fork, I close my eyes, the taste is bliss. The women smile at my obvious delight.

'This is the best breakfast,' I say.

'When I was pregnant with your sister, I didn't really get cravings. But with you I had this thing for oranges. I just couldn't get enough of them.'

Jane's eyes flash with a spark of pain but her mouth continues smiling.

'I'll be back,' Jane says, heading quickly for the door that leads to the small courtyard.

I cannot speak, my mouth is full of raspberry sponge, so much it's hard to swallow down.

'The times your dad drove round and round in search

of oranges for me. It wasn't like today, with supermarkets open at all hours.'

The smile lines around my mother's eyes crease up a little deeper and trail off like kite tails on a distant wind as the happy memories play out somewhere on the inside of her head.

'Oh no!' says Anne. 'Not vegetables. Not even fruit. I was just like you, Emma, I craved good cake. I couldn't even bear the thought of anything too healthy. I only wanted sweet things. Not that Martin was too pleased. By the time I gave birth I was absolutely huge.'

I catch my mother's eye knowing that she's thinking the same thing. I'm pretty sure that Anne's idea of 'huge' differs to ours. Anne is long and thin and even before Jay died she was a tiny thing, so perfect in her self-control, not one to give into her urges or to spread herself beyond the boundaries of what's just enough.

'Did you feel sick with Jay? Like me?' I muffle out the words through cake.

'With Jay . . .' She pauses, stops and takes a deeper breath, steadies herself as if the very saying of his name has knocked her off balance. She smooths a lock of hair that isn't out of place. 'With Jay . . .' she tries again. 'I felt incredible. Most days I felt so well that I'd forget that I was pregnant.' A tiny laugh as thin as glass comes tumbling out her mouth. 'That's how I got the burn across my stomach. I was ironing and forgot about my bump and burnt myself with the hot edge.'

I want to ask her if that's actually true but just say 'Ow' instead. 'That may explain why Jay was so averse to doing any ironing! I never saw him iron anything at all. For a man who was so neat he really hated it.'

'I didn't know he hated ironing,' Anne says, cherishing this new-found fact like pirate jewels. 'There's just so much I didn't know, so much I missed.'

Jay was opening the post and making paper piles on the table. 'Well, what about inviting them for dinner?' I tried again. 'Dad won't come and Mum . . . I doubt it, Em. I mean, they hardly even spoke to us at Grandad's funeral. I'm their biggest disappointment. Their embarrassing drop-out.' Jay bit the bottom of his lip. I watched the sharp white edges of his teeth sink deep into his flesh. 'You're not a failed anything. You're perfect as you are.'

Mum reaches over, takes Anne's hands in hers and eases all the fingers out that are curled tight, the ragged nails digging in.

'I missed so much,' Anne says again. 'His father was so stubborn, couldn't ever let things go. When Jay dropped out of Leeds there was a fight about the money that we'd spent on the tuition fees. Martin warned Jay that if he didn't finish his degree he wouldn't ever be forgiven, and the bastard kept his word.'

'But you're not him. You're not Martin,' I say.

'No,' she says. 'I'm not.' She drags the words out long

and slow as if she's only understanding now the funda-
mental truth of them. 'But my husband wasn't someone
that you'd ever want to anger, and he insisted that I stood
by all of his decisions. Even if that meant abandoning
my son.'

Anne shudders slightly, pulls her hands out of my mother's
grasp and clasps at her thin ribs, hugs her arms around
herself. She takes a lock of hair from back behind her ear
and rubs it with her fingers. I can hear the hair crackling
like dry kindling.

'Well, Martin isn't here,' my mother firmly says.

'And you have us,' adds Jane, coming back in through
the wooden door, her arms full of more raspberries. Anne
shakes her head aggressively as if to shake away the
sympathy, unwilling or unable to accept our understanding.

'But I should have left him years ago. I should have found
a way to choose my son. I was just so very frightened . . .'
She shakes her head again. 'But now there's nothing left to
be afraid of.' Anne rubs her arm while beads of sweat begin
to gather on Jane's forehead and her cheeks look far too
flushed. 'No amount of breaks or bruises can ever hurt as
much as losing my own boy.' She pauses, swallows hard
before she carries on. 'My boy . . . I can't believe I didn't
leave when Jay was young. I can't believe that I went back.'

'Do you know if the divorce papers have been agreed?
Has that solicitor got any news?' Jane asks, while looking
firmly at the floor.

Anne shakes her head.

'It's really not as simple as all that,' she says. 'He's still demanding that I sell The Nook. I'll have to go to London for more meetings with a mediator. I just hope we don't end up in court.'

I notice that Anne's wedding ring is absent from her hand. The golden band that chained her to a man is now replaced with pale skin and the narrowing of flesh that comes from years and years of being chained too tight to someone else. I wish that Jay was here right now to hear all this. He'll never know how much his mother always loved him.

My own mother reaches over for the burnished silver knife and slices at the semi-circle moon of sponge. She lays a slice down on its side on a pretty china plate that's ruffled at the edges like the petals of a flower. I watch her gently push the plate so that it slides over the tabletop to Anne.

'It's time to make your own life now,' my mother says. 'The one you had before has gone.'

And I wonder if it's Anne that she is talking to, or me.

Link

The following day is hot and bright and glorious. I hold my arms like triangles and both the mothers thread their arms through both of mine. We walk, a wall of women, linked, down narrow lanes in syncing steps towards the beach. I'm tired and my balance is now really off, but the mothers keep me stable. We turn the corner to the sea and a welcome breeze whips up and swirls light and fast around the three of us and catches at the edges of our clothes and makes the fabric flutter, fly. Anne stops and pulls us to a still and stands and stares out at the beach and out towards the clear horizon where blue meets blue and sky spreads wide with clouds the colour of skimmed milk that race each other past the sun.

The air smells of July, of sun-warmed stones and heated sand and salty sea. We breathe together in a line. We saturate ourselves with air. Anne's footsteps feel firmer and more self-assured.

'You both okay?' Anne asks, unlinking arms, dancing away. It's as if the beach has stripped off years and suddenly eroded time. My mother and I stay linked together watching her peruse the pebbles and the sand, her eyes scanning the shoreline. She stops to slip her shoes off, bends down near the clear water's edge just out of reach of lapping waves. Her hands pick through the pebbles and the sand, her fingers wandering and searching, filtering the pretty grains that show their vast array of colours in the light. She picks up something small and clasps it tight inside her hand and wraps her fingers round it.

'What's that?' my mother asks as we finally catch her up. Anne unfurls her thin fingers and offers up a palm of different coloured glass. She grins like a small child, proud.

'Sea-glass,' she says. 'Jay's favourite thing to do when he was little.'

'He never told me that,' I say.

Anne prods the riches that she holds, sifts through the sparkling shapes.

'The blue ones are the rarest but Jay loved the clear ones most of all. I think because they're hard to spot. It made them feel special even though they're the most common. Here . . .'

She picks out a piece that's almost white and almost clear.

'Thank you,' I say, taking the sea-glass and placing it inside the safety of the pocket of my sundress. There's the gentle clink of stone and glass as it falls into the fabric and it knocks against a heavy thing, a solid thing. A single stone from that long night, a stone that made me think of Mum and I can't seem to let go of.

Hands

I focus on the sound of sea, the rhythmic soothe and constant ebb and gentle flow and the voices of the mothers as they fuss about me, mother hens, concerned that I'm too hot, too cold, too everything, too anything. Their voices rise and fall, an echo of the background waves.

'I'm good,' I say, batting a lightweight cardigan away that they try to drape over my sun-bronzed shoulder blades. There's silence for a while, save the constant chatter of the sea, then, 'Anne, I don't mean to sound rude and I know that you've said sorry, but I have to ask . . . are you only here with me because I have to have this baby now?'

'Emma!' my mother says, all stern and cross.

'It's fine,' Anne says. 'I don't blame her for asking.' She turns to me and takes my hand. 'The last time that we properly spoke I threw you out the house. I'd be wondering the same thing too.'

'Well . . . ?' I gently say, still waiting for an answer.

'I'd be lying if I didn't tell you just how pleased I am that you're still pregnant. When you said you were unsure, it was a second death. That baby is the only grandchild I'll ever have, the only thing Jay left. The thought of losing all that too . . . of losing you . . .'

The mothers clasp each other's hands.

'I'm sorry,' I say again.

I hold my bump and feel the guilt as if it is a solid thing lodged sharply in between my ribs.

'It was Anne who called,' my mother adds.

We're interrupted by a child walking past carrying an ice-cream with a chocolate flake, large creamy drips running in sticky globules down her hands. Anne waits for her to walk on by.

'I've been back here staying at The Nook for the past week. I wanted to come and speak to you, to try and make things right. I suppose I was still waiting for the perfect time, but then Jane called and said she'd found a note from you and I found your parents' number stored inside the house phone at the cottage. It was me who had to call your mum and tell her that you'd left a note behind and we weren't sure . . .'

I bow my head down low, unsure of what to say. My mother rescues us.

'Your father was away, Emma, and Anne was awfully kind. She came and got me from the station in her car.' Mum finds a piece of brown sea-glass and adds it to the pile on the blanket but doesn't look at me. 'I couldn't drive. I thought you might . . . I thought it might have been too late.'

She reaches out her hand for Anne and they clasp each other tightly, bound together in a way I cannot fully comprehend.

Tribe

'Is that them there?' my mother asks, blinded by the strength of sun, lost without her glasses. She gestures at the fast-approaching shapes: two women and a man who is trailed by a limping, golden dog. Iggy overtakes and greets us first. He runs in small excited circles on the blanket, leaving dampened paw-marks streaked across the pastel print. My mother shoos her arms around but Iggy simply carries on. He licks her hands and wags his tail, oblivious or unaccepting of her obvious dislike.

'Ughhhh,' she squawks and tries to sweep the sand that can be seen and the germs that can't be seen off the surface of the rug while Iggy tries to lick the flush that creeps across her cheeks. She squeals, clearly mortified.

'Come here, you silly dog,' I say, grabbing hold of his thick collar. He settles down now next to me, his breathing slowing as I rub the soft fur of his head and watch his belly rise and fall. A droplet of saliva slowly dribbles down his jowls. My mother regards him in horror, rummages inside her bag and finds a bottle of hand-sanitizer which she rubs herself with liberally, massaging the gel across her hands, smoothing it across her forearms and up into the creases of her elbows. 'Really?' I say. 'It's just a dog.'

'Exactly, Emma,' she retorts, waving her glistening arms around. 'It *is* a dog! You know I don't like dogs.'

'Well, I like him.'

'Of course you do!' She shakes her head and sighs at me.

I notice Anne, sitting quietly just watching us as if we are the entertainment for the day. Her hands are buried deep inside the pockets of her wide-legged linen trousers and she's smiling as we bicker, as we always do.

'Ladies,' says Pete, nodding his head.

Anne rises to her feet and plants a solid kiss on Pete's left cheek. She holds him by the forearms, looks at him and doesn't seem to want to let him go. They smile at each other.

'I'm staying here for good this time,' says Anne to Pete and something passes suddenly between them that I cannot put my finger on.

'Come here!' says Jane, barging between the two of them and wrapping up my mother in another warm embrace, the fourth since they had breakfast. 'Oh, Emma's mum. Your aura! It's so dark still.'

'You know that you can actually call her Carol,' I say, laughing.

Pete gruffly says, 'She thought she'd lost her daughter, Jane. Were you expecting rainbows?'

My mother looks uncomfortable at the very mention of

her aura. Jane might as well have said 'vulva'. She stiffly pats Jane's solid back until she's finally released. Pete offers out a formal hand which my mother shakes, looking relieved.

'It's great to meet you, Carol,' says Claire, raising a hand. 'Wow! You two are so alike.'

'Really?' I say. 'I always thought I looked like Dad.'

'No! No!' says Claire. 'You can't see it? It's in the chin and in the nose. You really are so similar.'

I mutter underneath my breath, 'God, no,' and wonder if I'll soon be wearing leggings too.

'Thank you,' my mother says to everyone, suddenly all serious. 'Thank you to all of you for caring for my daughter.'

'No need for thanks. It's what friends do,' says Claire to Mum. 'She's one of us.'

Admittance

We are back at Jane's and the sound of Jane running the bath tumbles down the stairs and fills the cottage with a reassuring roar. The air is hot and humid and seeped in floral hints of lavender and something that I can't quite place but reminds me of a holiday. Bougainvillea perhaps. My mother fills the kettle at the deep white sink. I watch her place it on its plastic stand and flick the switch to on. Outside the light is faltering. There's a window in the kettle that is Perspex-clear and lets you see the water inside and the multitude of tiny bubbles that begin to rise towards the surface like an underwater exhalation of a breath. My mother sits back down again.

'We need to talk,' she says. 'Just you and me.'

The kettle clamours, shakes and rattles loud behind her like a thing that is possessed.

'We really don't,' I say and lean back hard to tilt two of the kitchen chair legs up. I wobble, swing, precarious. My mother pulls a disapproving face.

'Please stop that, Emma. That's dangerous, love. Are you okay?'

'Yes,' I say. 'I'm absolutely fine now.'

The kettle clicks to off and calms. She waits until I stop myself from rocking on the chair legs.

'Really? You're fine?' she says. 'You haven't talked to anyone about Jay's death and Jane believes you've only seen a midwife once since you arrived here. But more than that. You left a note!'

She folds her arms as if that's it; the note something I can't deny, her irrefutable evidence that I'm not all right. If she had the paper in her hand right now I'm sure she would be waving it in front of me, accusatory.

'It was just a note, a stupid note. I didn't actually do it.'

'But you wanted to.'

'And now I don't,' I quickly retort. 'And anyway, I realize that I still have you. And Anne and Jane and Claire and Pete.'

She breathes out slow, a long, exasperated stream of air that hisses, mimicking the sound the kettle made as it was boiling.

'That's great, love, great. I'm glad you feel supported. I really do. But none of us are qualified for this.'

'For God's sake, Mum, Claire's a GP.'

I stroke the bump that is now so large it looks almost impossible.

'Emma, please? Can you stop being defensive for a

moment? You just really need to understand that what you did, leaving a note, that stuff is serious. And it's not just about you, you're pregnant too.'

A warmth rises in both my cheeks. My blood feels hot and my heartbeat quickens in my chest causing tremors that extend to make my fingers shake.

'I know that, Mum. I'm quite aware I'm pregnant and I know I left a note. But my husband killed himself. Unlike him I didn't actually do it though! I'm still right here and still pregnant.'

She takes a breath and calms her voice. Says firm and slow, 'That's not the point. What's to say you won't try again at some point in the future? That baby really needs you, Emma love. It needs you here. It needs you well. And so do I.'

I hold the bump protectively. I want to block my ears, to make her stop. My face is now on fire.

'But things have changed,' I say, quiet.

'What's changed? Exactly what? What's different now?'

She keeps her calm. She gets up from the table, slowly takes a mug and rests it on the worktop carefully so that it doesn't make a sound. I hug the bump a little tighter and underneath my touch a limb responds, it reaches out. I take a breath. I try to slow my heart rate down. I try to settle my own voice.

'I just don't feel like I did before. Is this about the photographs, because I've put them all away? As usual you were right. They didn't help at all.'

'This isn't about them. Although I'm glad you've finally seen some sense. It's just that sometime soon you'll be at home with a small baby. That's hard enough for anyone, without the awful thing that you've been through. You have to find some peace somehow.' She pauses, takes another breath. 'I think that you're depressed, Emma.'

'Of course I am,' I mutter.

'So, you're not actually okay?'

'Not really, no.'

'Finally,' she says and breathes as if she's been holding her breath for a long time and moves her chair so that it's next to mine. She takes her arm and wraps it round my shoulder, waits until my body, which is stiffened in defence, begins to melt into her hold. 'Sweetheart, I know you're not. Of course you're not! And no one would expect you to be otherwise.'

'I don't know what to do,' I whisper out the words. 'What exactly do I do, Mum? What am I supposed to do?'

'Well,' she says, still holding me. 'We need to find a counsellor who deals with grief, a specialist. And you need to see a midwife too.'

The thought is overwhelming. Just imagining all the talking that I'll have to do, the memories that I'll have to face. I think about the peppercorns, like dark shrapnel, spread out across the kitchen floor and the fridge containing dahlias. It feels too much.

'I don't think I have the energy,' I whisper into her soft neck. It smells of home, of childhood, of soothing timeless bedtime songs. She props me up by both my shoulders, holds me upright and looks deep into my eyes.

'But I do, Em. I have energy for both of us. It's what us mothers do.'

Reality

The quiet blooms and fills the room, enjoyable. Like everything that will end soon, the silence feels precious. The mothers are exploring, Anne keen to show my mother all the secrets of the village: the complex maze of footpaths, the bakery with baskets of fresh loaves, the small café with ground coffee that makes pizzas on a Thursday, the next bay over where we swim, the pub that serves cold golden ales.

I lie in bed and try to rest. A breeze teases at the curtains, tickles at the corners, makes the fabric gently dance. It moves around the room and catches at the edges of the many feathers on the windowsill, which fill the jar like a bunch of oxeye daisies. Small gifts from Jane. Small treasures taken from the beach. I like the sounds. The seagull calls and curtain sways, the clips of chatter and light laughter that carry on the air from the last day-trippers walking up the lane beneath my window. In this moment now the world actually feels almost bearable.

I stroke my bump. Despite the fear of motherhood and guilt that lingers in my consciousness, I can't deny that it's a thing of wonder now. A large beach ball. A giant moon. A baby actually growing in my body. I listen to the pacifying sounds which lull me gently into sleep, the whole village a lullaby.

My mother rouses me, calling from the doorframe.

'Come on now, Em. It's time to go. This will be good for you,' she briskly says.

I rub my eyes and groan out loud.

'Well, so are Brussels sprouts and I really can't stand them.'

'Just try it, Emma. You promised. Please!'

I sit and fold my arms beneath my bulging chest and rest them on my bump.

'Why can't I just stay here?' I whine. 'It's such a lovely evening. We could go and have a barbecue for dinner on the beach instead. I think we've still got sausages.'

I go to stand, intend to search the fridge for sausages and reasons not to go.

'Emma. You promised me you'd go!' my mother warns. She swings Anne's car keys on her finger. The metal makes a jangling sound. I think of prison officers and school teachers. Of iron bars and plastic desks. The urge to run away is irresistible but my bump makes running anywhere impossible and I really need to wee right now. 'You're going. That's the end of it,' she adds, her voice rigid, her words final.

Ankles

'I'm glad you made it to that group,' says Pete.

'Really? Is there anyone who doesn't know my every single move?'

'Doubt it,' Pete says and shrugs. 'That's village life for you.'

We stare down at the water for a while. The sea is lapping at my ankles, which I know are there but I can't see, my giant sweep of stomach hiding them from view. The sun is making patterns in the clear water, small ripples on the undulating seabed, bright marbled veins of moving light. The sunlight bounces back. I scrunch my eyes against the glare.

'Turns out that humour doesn't go down well in Suicide Support groups. Or maybe it's just me that doesn't go down well.'

'Sometimes humour is the only thing we have,' Pete says. He wiggles his large toes.

'I might have taken it too far. I told them that I'd murdered

Jay and made it look like suicide to avoid being arrested.' Pete laughs his low and gentle laugh. 'That wasn't the reaction from the group,' I say.

'Did it help at all?'

'Lying?' I ask. 'Not really, no. I wouldn't be surprised if the police arrive to question me again.'

'I meant the group. Being with people in the same boat.'

'I don't know,' I say. 'I guess the listening helped and seeing that I'm not the only one . . . There was this lady there whose son . . . and I . . . ' I spin my wedding ring around my finger, rotate the band with the top of my soft thumb. 'She helped explain that suicide isn't really about wanting death but needing suffering to end. I don't think Jay ever meant to hurt me.'

'Of course he didn't.'

'I just found it all so sad. And I still can't talk about what happened.'

'Then maybe you're not ready yet. Just being there's a start.'

He puts his arm around my shoulders. A little further out to sea a group of brothers are playing with a paddle board. They try to see if three of them can balance on the board at the same time. It tips, upturns, upends them all. They reappear bedraggled, laughing at the dunking that they've had and begin to try it all again, the trio clambering and splashing.

'How's Evie at the moment?' I ask, changing the subject.

'I'm not sure she has much time left now,' Pete says, his

brow crinkling, the worry lines deepening across his face like battle scars. 'Let's just say I've never painted quite so many paintings in my life. Some days the painting helps me more than swimming does. I suppose it's not too different really. Total immersion in a thing.'

Photographs

I can't draw or paint but . . .

Jay's camera is wrapped up in the chest of drawers and swaddled in his winter scarf. I unwrap it like a present that is precious. I hold it like a newborn. Soft skull. Soft bones. Unbroken skin. The camera feels far lighter than I remember it. It reminds me of some tribe I read about somewhere from the Amazon, I think, where they only have a single phrase that means 'to photograph' and 'steal a soul' as if they are the very same thing.

Jay and I were eating pizza from the box. 'Captured any souls today?' I teased. Jay gave a tired smile and took another slice of pizza. He pulled an olive off and pulled a face then carefully wiped his fingers on some kitchen roll. 'I wish,' he said. 'It's ironic that I spend my days trying to add some soul to faceless objects. Perhaps the camera captures mine instead.'

I take the well-worn strap and hang the camera round my neck. It rests easy on my baby bump, which is large enough to form a ledge. I pinch the lens cap off and place the plastic circle carefully on the chest of drawers. The camera feels good inside my hands. Like an extension of myself. I try it out. I lift it up to look through the small viewfinder.

The world has shrunk. I can only see what's offered up within the frame, a window with firm edges. The periphery has disappeared. All that's left exists within a measured space. My mother's favourite mantra plays inside my head: 'If life becomes unmanageable just break it down into small parts.' I look around the room through the tight cloister of the camera lens. Parts appear inside small rectangles, the camera only letting in a little life at once.

Perhaps this is the answer. I need to focus on far less.

August

Arrival

'Bloody hell. You're fucking huge!' squeals Jude, grinning.

She drops her heavy bag onto the platform in the August midday sun as the carriages behind her start to heave and slug away towards the lure of the far West. The heat has soaked into the concrete and it rises up in hazy waves and makes the train tracks in the distance seem to shimmer in low ripples that extend along the line. My sister throws her arms around me, bending over, her body curved into a comma just to reach me, the baby bump a solid thing between us both.

'Really? I say. 'I was going for the Kate Moss look. I think I've absolutely nailed it.'

'Just two more weeks to go,' she says and claps her hands.

I smile wide and run my hands over the bump that's truly enormous now and protrudes from out the front of me, almost far too large to comprehend. Jude's face is solace, utter balm. She looks just like the Jude I keep beside me in my mind always. The only thing that's different is her hair, which is cropped into short curls around her face, the mass of long witch locks all gone.

'What happened to your hair?'

'Don't ask,' she says. 'It's my mini-midlife crisis. I guess it could be worse . . .'

'Really?' I say. 'I'm not sure how.'

She laughs and I twirl one of her curls around my fingertip. Jude grins wider, takes a wrap of chewing gum from her pocket and offers some to me. I take a piece and slowly chew, my mouth filling with peppermint.

'Oh, it's just so good to see you. But seriously, Em, you're huge. I know the boys are only young but I can't remember ever being quite as large as that.'

'You definitely were,' I say. 'I used to tie your shoes for you. You couldn't even reach your feet.'

We laugh at the shared memory and linger for a moment in the heat. She drags her bag up off the cracked concrete and slings it back across her shoulder, takes my arm in hers so easily.

'Come on, let's go and see this village and I can't wait to meet your friends. God, it's so green here. Can you believe I'm actually child free for once?'

Her conversation jumps around and she chatters fast as we slowly climb the station ramp, cross the narrow bridge that spans the tracks and pass the platform for the trains that head the way she came, back towards the cities of increasing size: Plymouth, Bristol, London. We chat about my nephews, about Rob's new boss at work and the heat in London, which is apparently oppressive and unyielding and driving everybody mad.

'You look so tanned! I love your dress,' Jude says, her eyes drawn down towards the bump again.

'It's closer to a tent than a dress. It's been really hot here this summer, although not as hot as London.'

'How is it living next to Mum?'

She asks the question cautiously.

'It hasn't been for long and I'm not sure weekdays count as properly living here. But Dad's away so often that, staying at Anne's, it seems to stop her getting lonely.'

'I just can't believe you haven't actually killed each other yet.'

'If we lived in the same cottage it might be another story,' I say and laugh. 'But the walls are really thick and, well, she's different when she's here. She's less uptight.'

'Really?' asks Jude.

She looks suspicious, as if she doesn't think that's possible.

'Last week I swear that she and Anne were both smoking a joint. They're denying it of course. But it's not as if that smell can be much else.'

'Nooo!' says Jude, then, 'Fuck!' She laughs and shakes her head as her whole idea of who our mother is, is disassembled, rearranged. 'Wow!' she finally says after a lengthy pause.

Brian stands there waiting by the car in the small car

park. He is leaning his wide back against the heated metal side panel and chatting to some guy I do not recognize while typing something in his phone. 'Wow,' she says again, her eyes now fixed on me.

'Wow what?' I laugh.

I stop before we reach Brian and turn to face my sister.

'You just seem different too, I guess.'

'Of course I'm different. Look at me.'

We both look at the giant bulge.

'I don't just mean the baby.'

'It's the shoes. I know . . .'

'Oh God, I hadn't even noticed them! My sister wearing Birkenstocks. What has the world come to? And anyway, it's not just that. You look . . . well, less . . . you look less . . .'

She doesn't say the words I know she's thinking, thinking better than to spill them out into the world as solid sound.

'I'm getting there.' I answer all the questions that she hasn't asked, remark upon the thing she is implying. 'I have my days. Not all of them are good, and some of them are absolutely awful. But today is good. You're finally here!' I grin and grab a sprig of cow-parsley that's growing in the leafy bank and break it at the root and tuck it into her short hair. The sap sticks to my fingers and I gently suck it off. 'You're in Cornwall now!' I say.

'I can see that, Em. Just from your feet. I never thought I'd see you wearing shoes like those.'

A proper laugh escapes my mouth.

'I know. I know. It's terrible. It's just that they're so comfy.'

'Wow.' She says the word again. 'This place has really changed you!'

Normal

'Does he always talk that much?' Jude says.

'Brian?' I ask. 'Always,' I nod.

'And that thing about the car park and the butcher?'

'Who knows,' I say and laugh. 'It's like he has no filter when it comes to local gossip. Although I really hope that one's not true! I mean, it can't actually be legal.'

We cackle at the very thought.

Inside the cottage Jane has left a futon on my bedroom floor with soft pillows and a pile of fresh quilts for Jude.

'Are you sure you're happy sleeping here? Mum's changed the bedding in her room in case you want to stay at Anne's, sleep in a proper bed?'

'No, don't be silly, Em. I want to stay with you. I hardly ever see you anymore.' Jude rummages around inside her bag, which is so stuffed full of things I wonder if she plans to stay forever. Eventually she finds a swimsuit and a large beach towel and sunscreen that is waterproof and intended for small children. 'Ready?' she asks.

'You're keen,' I say. 'Hang on. I need to wee again.'

Jude follows me into the bathroom and peers out of the window as I wrestle with my underwear and sink onto the toilet seat.

'This place is truly stunning, Em,' she says with half her body hanging out the window frame.

'You should see it in the winter. It's not quite so stunning then. It can be a little bleak some days.'

But even in the winter there's a beauty in the slate-grey skies and granite sea and dogged rain that washes everything afresh, the water like a baptism. I look up from the toilet at the cottage roofs and topaz sky and sweep of hill that's lined with lush green summer trees and see what Jude is seeing now, the things that are my normal.

Colours

The village is a paint box full of colours that a city can't contain. The cottages meander in their myriad of pastels, their window boxes full of blooms and curtains hung in pretty shades with bright front doors half open letting air drift in. Leant against the cottages are body boards and kayaks, pairs of oars and little lines of upside-down beach shoes left out to dry beside collections of beach rocks and treasured driftwood that have washed up on the shore. A deluge of coloured flotsam, jetsam and long-forgotten lagan. The weekend sound of fiddles drifts from the pub and spirals up the winding lane. We head towards the noise and pass the locals and the tourists who have spilt out of the tiny pub and are scattered on the pavement in the sun.

'Hello,' I say to all the people that I know.

'Hello,' says Jude, her arm in mine.

A load of people smile back and raise a glass, say warm hellos. There are people, people everywhere, piled onto benches, perched on wooden boxes, and sitting on top of empty stainless-steel kegs of beer. They all nurse pints of cool Doom Bar and almost-pints of cheap white wine that mark the height of summertime.

The beach is like a patchwork quilt, with coloured squares of picnic blankets, sun umbrellas, pop-up tents and brightly decorated towels. I scan the cove that in a few more hours will empty of the tourists, all tired from their day, leaving the beach just for us locals once again. Pete and Claire are sat propped up in the near distance, their backs against their favourite rock, and Jane appears to be spread-eagled like a summer version of a snow angel, her body splayed out on the sand. She looks like she has melted in the heat.

'She won't lie on a towel,' sighs Pete as we reach the roasting trio.

'Sshhhh,' says Jane, her eyes tight closed. 'I'm reconnecting with the energy.'

'I think she means the radiation from the radon,' says Claire, adjusting a bikini strap and getting to her feet. 'The famous Jude!' she grins. 'Welcome to our tiny piece of paradise. You've picked a perfect day to come.'

Jane opens her eyes and starts to lumber to her feet.

'Oh, Jude is here! You should have said.'

There is sand stuck to her sticky skin that falls off her in patches as she moves herself to standing. She tries to brush the sand away, but it clings to her large limbs and leaves coarse flecks, beach glitter in her rainbow hair.

'As if that would've made the slightest bit of difference! Hello, Jude,' says Pete.

'Hey, guys,' says Jude. 'I've heard so much about you all!'

'Where's Anne?' I ask, looking about. 'Wasn't she supposed to be back yesterday? She only had one meeting with the mediator. Has anybody heard from her?'

But it seems that no one knows exactly where Anne is.

Water

Jude takes to swimming in the Cornish sea just like a natural.

'This is totally amazing!' Jude calls out across the water and spins her body round. She paddles on her back using her hands as mini-fins and lifts her feet so that her neon-painted toes appear above the crystal blue. She rotates and takes a breath and dives beneath. I roll onto my back and push my body flat, lie my head down in the lift of salt. The bump appears above the water like a rising island of its own. A small foot pushes at the side and quickly changes the topography of flesh. Jude reappears from somewhere deep, her wet hair flattened to her head, and smooths the water from her face and blinks her eyes to readjust, a grin as wide as the horizon on her face. 'It's cold but it's delicious. I can't believe you swim all year!'

'It's even better when it's colder.'

'Ha! I don't believe that for a second. Does our mother ever swim?'

I laugh at just the thought and so does Jude.

'Don't be stupid. I mean, she'll paddle if it's really hot but she says she only swims abroad. Apparently she's not designed for this cold climate.'

'Well, she's missing out,' yells Jude who takes another breath, exhales air and sweeps her arms to pull herself beneath again to swim down deeper than before. She flicks her feet before she disappears under the blue, leaving a spray of water drops which catch in the strong sunlight and sparkle in the glare before she reappears beside me.

Sister

Our hair is wrapped in mismatched towels as we sprawl in underwear and baggy T-shirts on my double bed. I shift myself, uncomfortable. A small limb pushes out beneath my solid ribs and I slowly stroke the bump. Jude rubs my tired feet. The sash window is pushed up high and evening air makes all the photos Blu-Tacked to my bedroom wall dance lightly in the summer breeze.

'Did you find more?' Jude asks, confused, getting up to look at all the photos that are fluttering and flickering like bunting. She paces up and down the room, examining each image in the fading light. 'These ones aren't Jay's,' she finally says, looking at me.

'No,' I say. 'You're right. They're not. That lot are mine. Except that one.'

I point towards the photo I can't fathom and have stuck back on the wall, hidden carefully among my own so that my mother will not notice.

A blur, a smear. A colour that's not entirely clear. A sweep of something soft maybe.

'You're kidding me? They're actually yours? They're beautiful!' Jude says.

She looks at all my shots in turn; the last remaining fisherman holding a crush of crabs and fishing nets that knit and fray, the locals stood by torrid seas and peeling buoys, the photos of the sea swimmers, their eyes alive with icy glow, their pupils huge, sea-drugged, tide-struck. The photos of a village life.

'They're not that good and I still have loads to learn but I can see why Jay . . .'

'. . . why Jay loved it?' Jude finishes my words for me. I nod my head. 'You're talking rubbish, Em. They really are that good. In fact, they're more than good,' she says.

'Hmmm.' I shrug my shoulders, stroke my bump. 'Pete's been teaching me about colours and exposure compensation. It's a whole new language. And it's helped somehow. Jay's photos didn't really show me anything at all but using his old camera, just carrying it around with me, I guess I feel more joined to him. I've even sold a few.'

'Really? That's amazing, Em.'

'Yeah, the agency are actually using those three on the left in a new ad campaign.'

'Wow, that's great. It really is.' She sits back down and takes my swollen feet again and plops them on her lap. I sigh and close my eyes as she draws deep circles on the soles with her warm thumbs. 'You haven't mentioned work in ages.'

'I'm not officially back yet and they've given me maternity leave. I know that this sounds crazy but I'm hoping I can work from here. Anne said she'll help with childcare. I could consult maybe and only travel up to London when I need to. I have Jay's life insurance and there's a gallery in Fowey that has agreed to show my photos too. Apparently the owner likes the stories that they tell. Perhaps something will come of that, you never know.'

I stare at all my photos, at the possibilities they pose.

'I'm so proud of you,' Jude says. 'I really am.'

'And there'll be money coming in from Ben. I've agreed to rent the London house to him.'

'To Ben? Have you gone mad?' she asks, her mouth open like a written 'O' that sits inside the centre of the word 'shocking'.

'He feels really awful, Jude.' She rubs my feet more firmly, which just feels good so she presses hard until I yelp. 'Which he obviously should,' I quickly add. 'And at least it keeps things easy and I know that he'll look after it until I decide what to do.'

'Well, at least he's doing something vaguely helpful,' she says finally, begrudgingly. 'And these photographs are brilliant. They really are.'

She looks impressed, properly surprised, as if she didn't know I had it in me.

'Which one do you like best?' Jay was scrolling through an endless stream of photographs of plain white bowls for some new homeware brand. I glanced over at his laptop but couldn't tell that they were different shots. 'They all just look the same to me,' I said. His face fell flat and sad and made me feel bad. 'They all look great,' I added but too late, the hurt already done.

Jude removes my feet from her lap and walks back towards Jay's photograph that is stuck up in the middle of the montage on the wall. 'So all Jay's photos . . . they really were of nothing then?'

'They weren't what I was hoping for. I'd hoped . . .'

'I know,' Jude says.

I nod my head, relieved to have my sister here, someone who knows exactly what I'm thinking and already knows the words when words elude. Jude yawns, the swimming and the sunshine and the rich sea air enticing sleep.

'Come on. Let's go and meet the others at the pub,' I say, pulling on a clean dress. 'I need to feed you soon before you fall asleep.'

She yawns again and searches for an outfit in her giant bag.

'Aren't you the one who is supposed to have no energy?' she says, now watching me intently.

'I haven't felt this good in absolutely ages.'

Chips

'Still no Anne?' Pete asks, dunking a giant wedge of granary bread into a pile of mussels that are steaming in a bowl. The whole pub smells of frying fish, of fragrant garlic, wine and cream.

'Not yet,' says Jane. 'She's not appeared next door and I've tried her mobile twice.'

Pete's forehead crinkles in a frown, the flesh forming deep peaks and troughs that look like undulating sand after the tide retreats. His lips have almost disappeared.

'We just walked past The Nook on our way here,' I say. 'No one was home.'

'I wonder where she is?' Jane pauses, shakes her head. 'If she isn't back tomorrow I'll phone Martin. See if that man knows anything.'

She nods as if affirming her decision and takes a giant swig of golden Korev, the bubbles rising in the pale lager and bursting into nothing on the surface of the glass.

'Mmm, this food is really good,' says Jude, cramming

another fork of local crab that's mixed with mayonnaise and lemon juice into her mouth, oblivious to our concerns. She swallows, licks her greasy lips and grins. 'I saw the boys at breakfast, but that feels like forever ago. Who knew a single day could be a proper holiday?'

Jane puts an arm around Jude's shoulders and hugs her like a life-long friend. Jane smiles too, my sister's happiness contagious.

'It's a shame that Claire's not here tonight. We never usually do this, and I doubt we'll get another chance before the baby comes. She'd have loved to come along,' says Jane.

'That woman works too bloody hard,' says Pete, prising a mussel shell apart.

He drops the splayed and empty husk into a metal bowl.

'Well, thanks for coming out,' says Jude to everyone. 'It's been so great to finally meet you all.'

She lifts her wine glass up and we all raise our glasses too.

'We should be thanking you!' says Jane. 'It's nice to have a good excuse. We tend to stay clear of the pub in summertime. I'd almost totally forgotten just how good the chips are here.'

'They're triple cooked,' Pete adds, wiping his fingers on a paper napkin.

Jude stretches her right arm across the pine table, being careful of the glasses, plates and bowls that clutter up the space. She grabs a large handful of chips from my plate and adds them to her own.

'Oi!' I say, mock-angry. 'Those ones are mine. You've eaten yours already.'

My sister laughs and says, 'What was that thing our mother always said to us when we were small?'

'Which one?' I ask her as she dips a chip into more mayonnaise.

'Sharing is caring.'

She muffles out the words through a mouth filled with potato. Her cheeks bulge hamster huge as she tries to swallow down the food. It's not her most attractive look. I can't stop myself from smiling.

'Oh, I thought you meant, "If the wind changes, your face will stay like that."'

And everyone around the table joins us laughing, chatting, eating chips.

Light

I try to sleep but sleep won't come. Jude gently snores beside me on the futon on the floor looking annoyingly serene, while my legs keep moving, running strides beneath the bedcovers which tangle up around my feet. I toss and sigh, entwined in sheets. I'm wide awake and damp with sweat, uncomfortable and fidgety. It's far too warm to stay in bed or be indoors.

According to my phone it's almost one o'clock. Trying to creep past sleeping Jude and sleeping Jane is challenging given my size. I sway and stumble down the stairs as silent as possible, gripping carefully to the bannister. My swollen feet slip into waiting flip-flops in the hall and I gently close the cottage door. Outside the air is clean and cool but everything is far too bright, much brighter than the full-moon light. The lane is lit up, sharp and clear, by an artificial glow.

It seems as if each single light in every room has been switched on and is now flooding out the windows of The Nook.

Dark

'Anne!' I say. 'Oh God!'

My mouth falls slack in horror but she simply turns away. I close the door and waddle down the narrow hall behind her to the kitchen where she sits herself down carefully on a kitchen chair among the too-bright lights, a whisky bottle and a china mug laid out in front of her.

'I'm all right,' Anne says, her voice almost inaudible.

'No,' I say. 'You're really not.'

Anne is shaking as she uses both her hands to pour more whisky in the mug. There are marks that look like burns running in vile tracks around her wrists and a ring of pink around her neck, the same colour as dahlias. She takes another sip and strokes her throat with her thin fingers.

'Did Martin do this to you, Anne?'

She nods a 'yes' and makes a noise that's like a murmured laugh but lacking any humour. Her eyes stay focused on the mug.

'When?' I ask. 'But how?'

I want to hold her in my arms but worry that I'll hurt her. She reminds me of a baby bird that has tumbled from its nest.

'I was stupid, stupid.'

She curls all her fingernails into the soft part of her palm.

'No,' I say, but she isn't really listening.

'Stupid, like I usually am. He was so reasonable with all the lawyers there. I never learn.'

I have to lean in hard to hear exactly what she's saying.

'It's not your fault,' I say. 'You're not the one to blame.'

'It is,' she says. 'He was being far too nice to me. I should have known. He said I could go to the house, collect some of the things I'd left behind.'

'And he did this to you there?'

She nods again and lifts a shaking hand towards her neck again, examines her dry fingers as if expecting to see blood. A loud and sudden banging at the door makes both our bodies jolt in fear. She takes a large swig from the mug and stares ahead, her eyes cloudy with alcohol and shock.

'He wouldn't . . . ?' I take a breath. 'Just stay right there. I'll go get it,' I say, sounding far braver than I actually feel.

Jude and Jane are standing in the lane, both knocking frantically with panicked arms.

'Please stop!' I say, their fists now hitting air, no longer making contact with the wooden door. 'You're scaring her. And me!'

'Oh, thank God, Emma. We thought . . .' Jane throws her arms around me. She squeezes me against her giant breasts which are just about contained inside an old Pantera T-shirt that was black and now a washed-out grey. I can hear the frenzied beating of her heart.

'I woke and you had gone. You just weren't there,' says Jude, taking my hand and squeezing hard.

She shivers barefoot in the cool that is a Cornish summer night.

'We were headed to the beach to look for you but saw the lights were all on here. We thought . . . we thought that something awful might have happened, Em,' says Jane.

I look at Jane. Look in her eyes. I search for words.

'It has,' I finally say, after a pause. 'But not to me.'

Truth

Jane takes one look at Anne and starts to cry. Great ugly cries that make her body heave and shake. Anne takes another sip of drink and stares straight at the wall ahead.

'I'm not sure this is helping, Jane?' I gently say.

'He did this to you, didn't he?' Jane says through sobs. 'Martin?'

Anne nods her head a fraction, winces in discomfort before uttering a quiet, 'Yes.'

'But this is all my fault,' Jane says.

'Not you as well,' I firmly say. 'The only one at fault is clearly Martin.'

'But if I'd spoken up about the wall when Jay was young, you might have left him years ago.'

Anne looks up from her mug of booze, refocuses, fixates on Jane.

'What wall?' Anne asks in a small whisper.

'I'm so sorry, Anne. Jay came to me when he was small

and I thought it was a story. Just a boy's imagination.' Jane wipes her streaming nose on the bottom of her T-shirt. 'It's just that Martin seemed so lovely and you always looked so happy, both together with your gorgeous son. A perfect little family.'

'I don't understand,' Anne says.

Jane sits down and Jude rummages in cupboards, finds more mugs and pours a large whisky for Jane and another for herself. I look at the whiskies longingly.

'I think that Martin hurt Jay too.' Jane says the words and bites her bottom lip.

Anne looks confused as Jane continues crying.

'Jay left a photo of a wall.' I try to find the words that Jane has lost to tears. 'It sounds as if Martin hit Jay's head against a wall and told everyone that Jay had fallen off his bike. Jay spoke to Jane but she didn't for a second think it might've all been true.'

'If I had I would have done something, done anything . . .' Jane says. 'I'm sorry, Anne. I'm so sorry.'

'But when?' Anne asks.

'When Jay was ten,' Jane says. The sobs are finally subsiding.

'That was just before Martin insisted he start boarding school,' says Anne, her words a shallow whisper still.

'Anne?' Jude says. 'Have you spoken to the police? Have you even seen a doctor yet?'

Anne shakes her head.

'I took the train and came straight here. I had to leave.'

'I could have stopped all this,' Jane says and hangs her head forlornly.

'No,' says Anne firmly, a little louder now, still shaking. She takes Jane's hand in hers. 'You couldn't have.'

'It will be our best adventure, Em. We get to choose the kind of parents that we want to be.' Jay was standing with his toothbrush at the bottom of our bed. I frowned, put down my book and broke its fragile spine. 'I need more time,' I finally said. He shook his head, as if to tell me I was wrong. 'But we could give it what I never had. We could make our baby's childhood a magical and perfect thing. And trying for a baby could be fun!'

Anne tries to lift the mug up with her right hand but the weight of it bleaches her face.

'Anne,' Jude calls, but she seems lost, far out at sea. 'Anne, we need to tell someone, report all this.'

Anne keeps hold of Jane and nods her head, agreeing to whatever needs to happen next.

'Claire will know exactly what to do,' I say to Jude.

I push myself to standing, pressing down with two flat palms against the firmness of the tabletop. The telephone is lying by the kettle near the sink. It is just steps away, just out of reach. I pause and wait.

'Are you okay?' asks Jude.

I do not move. Stay statue still. I breathe in deep.

'I might be needing Claire's help too,' I finally say.

AFTERWARDS

I turn around and look at all the women in the room. They are staring as clear liquid starts to gently trickle down the inside of my leg.

443

Oblivious

I hold onto my sister, climb the stairs inside Jane's cottage to my bedroom and my bag that is all packed and ready, waiting for this moment.

'Do you think that Jane's all right to be caring for Anne?'

'Yes,' says Jude. 'She's stopped crying and stopped drinking and it's not for very long. You said that Claire lives close to here.' She rummages inside my bag to check I have the things I'll need. 'Can we just focus on you now? You're about to have a baby!'

There are loud noises as someone treads the cottage stairs, taking two or three steps at a time. We both look up as Claire walks fast into the room.

'An ambulance is on its way. The police are coming too.' Her voice is even, doctorly and very calm.

'How's Anne?' I say.

'In shock,' she says, 'and I think her wrist is broken. But she's going to be all right. We'll all make sure of it. You know we will,' Claire firmly says. She turns to me, unzips her bag. 'Now let's see what's happening here.'

'Honestly, not much,' I say. 'You should go and wait with Anne. Contractions actually aren't so bad. Why do the movies make them look worse than they really are?'

Reality

The movies don't show half of it. They were clearly all written by men. The reality is brutal.

'Make it stop,' I plead. 'I want my mum.'

'Really?' says Jude, sounding surprised and trying not to laugh.

'Yes. I want my mum,' I say again and mean it.

I am hanging semi-upright on the back seat of the car with my head against the headrest and my hands gripping the leather, facing backwards as the village disappears behind the car before my eyes.

'Is she okay?' I hear Brian, his voice all high and nervous.

I can hear him rip a wrapper with his teeth and take a bite of something that smells cloying, sweet and sickly. The crunching sound his teeth makes is infuriating. I want to punch him in the face.

'SHE'S FUCKING NOT. JUST DRIVE THE CAR!' I holler loud.

'Yes, Ma'am,' he mutters grumpily, crumbs spilling from his mouth.

'She's fine, Brian. You're fine, Emma,' says Claire calmly.

I groan as yet another wave of cramping flesh consumes my whole.

'No, I'm not. Why aren't we in the ambulance?' I moan and groan, all miserable.

'They can only take one patient at a time,' Claire explains for the third time. 'First babies usually aren't as fast as this.'

'This isn't usual?' I ask panicked. 'Oh, not again!'

I bite into the fake leather and spittle dribbles out the corner of my mouth. Another moan escapes from some-where low as I lose myself inside myself.

'Just breathe, just breathe,' Claire's calm repeat.

Jude whispers, 'You're okay,' into the seashell of my ear and Claire rubs small circles with her palm over my bulging tailbone and presses firmly on my back.

I catch my breath as the world reappears and sounds return and I can see again. A small respite that won't last long. Another wave is waiting.

'Mum and Dad are on their way,' Jude says excitedly, checking her phone.

'Oh fuck. Oh no,' I howl as more contents of the sea pour out of me and gush down my legs over the seats and soak the foot well, wet.

'Please tell me that's not . . . '

'Shut up, Brian. Not now,' says Claire.

'Just grip my hand,' says Jude.

I fumble, find her hand to hold. I try to crunch her fingers with the same intensity that grips my whole but my body is no longer mine. It's ripping and it's stretching from the inside out. It's doing things I can't control.

'Oh God,' says Brian. 'Those seats have just been cleaned.'

All time falls down and sounds press down and voices fade and in the dark the road behind us blurs and night sky slurs.

'Just breathe,' says Jude. 'You've got this, Em.'

Another wave begins to build, tsunami large, horizon huge. I bite the leather headrest, sink my teeth into it hard and groan again, my eyes tight shut. There is silence in the car except the sounds I make as we wait for what this is to pass. The pain begins to fade, subside, and I lay my cheek against the sticky headrest, breathe in the fruity scent of Jude's shampoo and try to rest before the next.

'Brian,' says Claire, less calmly now, 'you need to turn the car around. We're never going to make it to the hospital in time.'

'Oh God,' he mutters once again.

Clarity

Pete is waiting at the door to help us back inside. I want to be upstairs but the stairs are like a mountain. They tower up ahead of me; too far to walk, too high to climb. Jude is carrying my canvas bag that was intended for the hospital, the one I packed, repacked and packed again with my mother's helping hands. I think of all the things in it that I can't imagine actually ever needing. The tiny hat, the yellow-dotted folded baby-grow, the nappies that are minuscule like folded origami squares. They look too small. Impossible.

'You sure you want to be upstairs?' says Jude.

I nod a 'yes' and think *Hell No*.

'Then you really need to move,' Claire firmly says.

Jude takes my arm and drags me up the first wooden step, while Claire stays just behind us both, her palm held flat against my back. I slowly climb the looming stairs, my nails digging little lines into the old and softened oak of the bannister rail.

'Stop,' I gasp, no time for 'please'.

The swelling pain, it rises up and turns my legs to tentacles. We stop, a huddle on the stairs as I moan and groan, supported underneath my armpits. The women flank me silently as I grip hard, then squat down low and shiver-shudder, my legs jelly and useless on dry land.

The pain reaches its perfect peak of anguish and leaves me wordless, sweating, spent, before it starts to dissipate again.

'Come on . . .' says Claire, heaving me to upright. 'They're very close and lasting for a while. We really need you up these stairs.'

'Can I help?' asks Pete, sounding out-of-depth and awkward, as if he's praying that the answer will be 'no'.

'Just listen for the door,' says Claire.

I somehow make it to my room and kneel on the floor, my body flung over the bottom of the bed. I fold my arms and turn my neck, rest my head inside the pillows of my arms and spread my knees out wide. I'm somewhere else. Beneath a sea of liquid dark. Swimming alone inside myself and all of time.

They're coming now too quickly. Fast. The time between each wave of pain is not enough to find my breath, to find some calm. I cannot gain perspective.

I am too lost.

Far out at sea.

I start to panic.

Terrified.

'I can't do this,' I say. 'I can't.'

'You're doing great. Now find something to focus on. Just find a point and keep it in your view,' says Claire.

I open my tight-shut eyes and stare around the room. In the soothing lamp-lit dim I see the photos on the wall ahead of me, most of them mine, but somewhere in the middle is the final shot of Jay's. I fixate on the paper. I make it into my whole world: the gentle curves, the subtle bend, a smudge of something soft that is ambiguous.

All sounds contract and walls fall down and pain fades in and out again and in the dark the boundaries slur, my body blurs, all edges gone.

I can't do this, I think. *I can't.*

'You can do this,' says Claire or Jude or some vague sense of Jay.

Another strong contraction fades and somewhere in the room I hear the voice of Patience, her arrival reassuring and consoling. She appears beside me, kneeling down among the women who are gathered like a coven of good witches. They whisper incantations telling me to breathe, they cast their spells to bring forth life. Patience opens up her heavy bag and starts unpacking all her things around us on the floor. There is safety in her presence here, there is magic in her midwife skills.

'So, it's time to have a baby then,' she says joyfully. 'I've got gas and air inside the car. Can someone grab the keys and get the canister? I'm parked just up the hill.'

Someone must agree to go and I hear the door creak open

and footsteps fast and fading down the stairs. I retreat inside the bubble that is filled with rushing pain, retreating pain then deep, deep rest that lasts just seconds now, a constant ebb, consistent flow. I make another sound just like the mooing of a local cow and grip the blanket on the bed. My fingers curls around the fabric, scrunch it tight inside my palms. Another one.

Another one.

I blink open my eyes as the contraction eases off and I focus on the photograph. Someone close to me is crying but I'm not sure who. Perhaps it's me? I am shuddering and shaking, cold. I retch as if I've swallowed gulps of stomach-churning sea water. My body wants to break in two.

'I can't do this,' I say again in desperation.

The witches disagree and cast their words of positivity despite the fact I know they're wrong.

And then I see the photograph, see it clearly, see just what it is.

A sort of blur, a pale smear. A sweep of something soft, I think. And in the corner of the blur, a pale smudge, a brownish dot.

The photograph.

It is of me.

Its softness is my soft of flesh, the sweep the curve of my own soft skin. I recognize the gentle arch and dip just near my collarbone. I recognize the skin as mine, the blur a birth mark near my neck. The colours of the photographs are gentle shadows, shallow light that swim across a body which is mine. I didn't know he took the shot. It must have been when I was fast asleep, oblivious and unaware that in my dreaming I was still enough. I think of Jay, his camera poised and watching me with all of his attention and his focus.

We were walking down the street in unison. 'Do you have to take it everywhere?' I asked and laughed, Jay's camera gently swung between the two of us. The restaurant door was open wide and the sweet and salty heady scent of Chinese food flooded out into the London street. He squeezed my hand. 'If I didn't bring it with me, I might miss something. I might miss a perfect moment or forget something I really love.'

I am something that he never wanted to forget.

Jay's wife.

The one he really loved.

And suddenly the all-consuming feeling changes in my body and is replaced by something different now. A strong new force that floods through me. A sensation overpowering. Omnipotent.

'It's time to push,' Patience declares. But I already know.

Words

My dearest Jay,

I don't know where to send this to but I need to write the words to tell you everything that happened afterwards.

You are a father now.

Just after dawn this morning on a perfect Cornish summer's day in the flood of early morning light I gave birth to our daughter. A perfect, perfect, tiny girl whose name is Rose.

I wish that you could see what I can see. She is small and pink with skin as soft as flower petals, her cheeks the pale flush of well-loved ballet shoes. She has your face, she has your hair. Your gorgeous hair. A perfect storm of dark straight hair. Right now she is asleep inside the curve of my left arm. Her eyes are closed but her eyelids flicker as she dreams. I hope, like me, she dreams of you. I keep dipping my head towards her head to inhale the soft scent of her. She smells of golden barley fields, of cider and of summer storms. I wish that you could smell her, Jay. I wish that you could breathe her deep. She smells of everything that's good. Of everything worth living for.

The fact that you're not here hurts me so much it forces all the air from out my lungs. You should be holding Rose now in the strong ark of your arms. You would have loved her, Jay. You would have loved her with a strength that's almost far too much to comprehend.

But you're not here. You cannot hold your newborn child. You cannot see her perfect face. Or love her with a beating heart. So, I need to let you know that I will love her for the both of us. I will love her with the same intensity that I love you, that I miss you. I need to say we'll be all right, we'll be okay, we will survive.

Your death completely silenced me. You left me with no words to say or words to write. I thought that words were lost to me when I lost you. I thought that words were empty vessels, useless scrawls of hollow space and nothing that could ever help.

But I promise I will find them, Jay; the words your daughter needs to hear. So many words to tell our child. I will find them and I'll use them all to make sure that she knows you in your absence and knows that she is loved, so loved. I will tell her all our stories, every moment I remember, so you stay alive forever in the words I'll whisper in her ears.

Afterwards was not the end I thought it was.

I love you, Jay. I always will.

Your Em. x

RESOURCES

If you're worried that your own life or someone else's life is in immediate danger, please call 999 or go directly to emergency services.

Other resources include:

CALM – Campaign Against Living Miserably
A charity offering support aimed specifically at men.
0800 58 58 58 (5 p.m. – midnight, 365 days a year)

Mind
A mental health charity offering information and support.
0300 123 3393
info@mind.org.uk

Samaritans
A charity aimed at providing emotional support to anyone in emotional distress or at risk of suicide.
116 123 (freephone 24/7)
jo@samaritans.org (response time is 24 hours)

Survivors of Bereavement by Suicide
A charity that exists to support anyone over eighteen who has been bereaved by suicide.
0300 111 5065 (9 a.m. – 9 p.m. Monday to Sunday)
email.support@uksobs.org

ACKNOWLEDGEMENTS

Thank you to:

My incredibly talented agent, Jane Finigan, to whom I will be forever grateful. I honestly can't believe how lucky I am to work with you. Not only did you use your exceptional skills to help turn *Afterwards* into an actual book, but you listened to me complain about bras for an inordinate amount of time. Thank you!

The entire team at Simon & Schuster. You're all wonderful. I'm especially grateful to my amazing and brilliant editor, Clare Hey. Thank you for your insight, honesty, wisdom and passion. Huge thanks also to the truly marvellous Louise Davies, Sabah Khan, Tamsin Shelton and Hayley McMullan.

Jonathan Heaf for encouraging me to write from the heart about things that are important, and to Tom Bromley at the Faber Academy, for being the best teacher and mentor.

The lovely Rankin for making me look as if I hadn't just been swimming in a pond, and to James Day for answering my endless questions about photography.

All my fellow winter swimmers and the inspiring community of women and lifeguards, including Jane Smith, at the Kenwood Ladies' Pond. But most of all to Janet. When we first started swimming through the winters, our friends told us we were crazy. Just look at them in their bobble hats now!

Everyone who shared their personal stories of loss with me. I feel both privileged and deeply honoured. The ways in which you have navigated grief and found the courage to move forwards have been nothing short of awe-inspiring.

My mum and dad for showing me the joy of swimming in the sea and for always, always being supportive.

Lucy, for being my sister. I couldn't ask for a better one. And to Ruth, Kana, Ginny, Anna, Louise and Eileen for being the very best of women. You have all helped in so many ways.

My sons: Jack, Finn and Noah. This book was only made possible with your support. Thank you for your patience and help when I was writing. I adore you all.

My husband, Nils. For absolutely everything.